DRAGONS ARE A GIRL'S BEST FRIEND

ISLA FROST

Published by JFP Trust
2021 First Print Edition

ISBN: 978 1 922712 02 8

www.islafrost.com

CHAPTER ONE

Most traffic jams are caused by human error. This one was no exception.

The giant, slime-covered walrus-caterpillar nightmare glared at me through the pinkish slits I'd pegged as its eyes. Three yellowing tusks as long as my forearm glistened with venom that had already eaten through several inches of tarmac. And trapped beneath the nightmare's bulging layers of fat in the cage of its many chitinous legs was a six-year-old girl.

Traffic was ground to a halt behind it, and all the pedestrians but one had fled. Some jerk in a sporty red look-at-me Mustang laid on the horn like *he* was the one with something to complain about here. And the last remaining pedestrian—a woman I guessed was the girl's mother—screamed hysterically on the sidewalk.

I blocked it all out and focused on the next ten seconds.

My gun had the best chance of taking the monster down. But I was in the middle of Cerberus Avenue, Las Vegas, and my target was an unknown entity.

I didn't know how fast this thing could move or how dense those rolling layers of flesh were. If I missed—unlikely—or the bullet plowed through the blubber and kept going, there was too much risk of a casualty. Even if the bullets did land where I intended, the little girl beneath the giant monstrosity could wind up crushed or injured.

And if I merely pissed the creature off instead of incapacitating it? The slippery nightmare might contort its gelatinous body past the dislodged grate of the storm drain and take the girl with it.

If it got into the network of sewer tunnels beneath the city, this rescue story wouldn't end well.

The little girl was quiet now, her wide-eyed attention fixed on me—mirroring the monster that towered above her. Tears had left wet tracks on her cheeks, but the sight of a glorious copper dragon swooping down to deposit me onto the road had momentarily distracted the summoned creature from its meal, and distracted the meal too.

Her mother, not so much.

The best course of action was to have my dragon partner yank the monster skyward while I dove to protect the girl. But Aurelis was busy going after the idiot who'd summoned the nightmare walrus so he wouldn't summon any more.

Technically, we were supposed to stick together to protect each other's backs, and if either of us got hurt—usually me—we'd be taken to task for it. But jobs rarely slotted so neatly into the LVMPD's play-nice regulations.

The girl was about the same age as my youngest sister, and I was trying very hard not to imagine Sage in her place. Trying very hard not to imagine Sage's dark brown eyes shining with that heart-wrenching combination of terror and trust.

A trust I might fail to live up to.

How could anyone live up to the trust of the innocent?

My hands trembled with adrenaline when I needed them to be steady, and sweat pooled beneath my body armor. High above, the late-morning sun bore relentlessly down on us, unmoved by the disaster waiting to happen.

If only I could be similarly unmoved.

I needed to focus. Think rationally.

My eyes flicked back to the asshat who'd laid on the horn. He was conceited enough to have a vanity plate advertising his personal brand of power. *TELEKIN.*

Telekinetic magic would come in awful handy right now.

But the magic revolution had demonstrated how fantastical superhero stories were. Turns out if you give a bunch of people superpowers, most of them just use it to help themselves.

I dashed to the Mustang, yanked open the door, and grabbed Jerkface's wrist.

"Hey—"

Power flooded up my arm. I flung it in the monster's direction.

Bigger isn't better when it comes to telekinetic magic. I chose the smallest and lightest targets that would get the job done.

One of the chitinous legs flew upward, and the girl shot out from under the nightmare's abdomen.

"What the hell?" Jerkface tried to yank his arm out of my grip.

I hung on and used a fraction of the magic I was drawing to slosh some of his cold-brew coffee on his shirt. That'd give him something else to worry about.

The monster roared its outrage as its meal was snatched out of reach. I concentrated on sending the girl skimming over the tarmac until she crashed into her mother's arms.

No time for relief.

I let Jerkface go. "Thanks for your cooperation, sir."

He sputtered something, but I didn't hear it, already sprinting toward the raging monster.

I shouted as I ran, needing it to focus on me instead of its stolen prey.

The walrus thing turned. I freed my magitech Taser, shoved it up to maximum voltage, and shot.

My target writhed, the slime coating its body probably making the electricity coursing through it more painful. Painful, but not paralyzing. And not painful enough to persuade the summoned nightmare to flee back to its own plane. The violent thrashing dislodged the prongs, and the creature squeezed down the sewer opening.

"Crap."

If I lost track of it in the tunnels, it could emerge anywhere in the city to wreak a fresh round of havoc. And the homeless sometimes used those tunnels for shelter.

I dove down after it.

I knew I'd erred when I was slammed against the wall of the tunnel. Without my body armor, the force of it would've splintered my ribs. As it was, I felt like I'd been bitch-slapped by a dragon.

A particularly foul-smelling dragon. The rank, musky odor of the slime coating its body and now mine as well tickled my gag reflex. But I didn't have time nor space to vomit.

It was dark, but not pitch-black, thanks to the light filtering down through the open drain hole. But with my cheek squashed against the rough concrete, my field of vision was seriously limited. Worse, my dominant arm—the one with access to the Taser and gun—was pinned behind my back.

I pushed through my body's shock and into the creature's disgusting clammy flesh at the same time. I couldn't pull a shred of magic from our undesirable contact. But with the tiny wriggle room I created, I used my sort-of-free arm to yank out my tactical knife and shove it into the smothering wall of fat and muscle.

The monster flinched away, and I whipped my gun up and fired. One. Two. Three rounds right into its center mass. Not that *that* was a difficult shot right now.

My ears protested the blasts, the din amplified by the close confines of the tunnel. But at least the bullets didn't ricochet.

The creature bellowed and reared back on its powerful tail, getting as high as the space would allow. Multiple legs grappled to secure me in place while it readied those tusks to drive deep into my skull.

The spindly legs were stronger than they looked. I slashed at the nearest of them with my knife, kicked away several more, and launched myself toward the creature's abdomen, hoping it wouldn't anticipate my trying to get closer. I slashed again, carving a big jagged wound in its bulbous gut that squirted slippery ink-colored fluid all over me.

This time its roar was one of definite pain, and it slammed its body to the ground, trying to flatten me. I dove out of the way, scraping my hands and knees against the gritty floor. Hard.

Before we could repeat that delightful experience, I rolled to shoot more bullets. This time at its head.

Another earsplitting shriek. The half-risen creature

jerked and crashed into one side of the tunnel. The whole tunnel vibrated at the force. Then the monster winked out of existence, leaving only slime, venom, inky fluid, and a foul odor behind.

CHAPTER TWO

I swore—for cathartic purposes—and pushed to my feet.

My hands were bleeding, my body ached, and I was covered in goop. But perhaps that slimy layer had protected me from the venom because nothing burned or stung except where my skin had been scraped off.

The body cam on my shoulder was cracked, which my boss was sure to be unhappy about. But there were zero casualties, so I was chalking it up as a win.

Cars thudded over the open drain above, apparently deciding their commute was more important than preserving the integrity of a crime scene. The noise made me realize what was missing.

My earpiece. A beam of sunlight obligingly bounced off the tunnel wall to reveal its location. On the ground... covered in goop.

With a sigh, I recovered it, wiped it on the *inside* of my filthy uniform, and shoved it in my ear.

"I'm fine," I reported to my partner Aurelis. Just on the off chance she cared. "The walrus thing has returned to its own plane to lick its wounds." And wouldn't be able to return unless some other idiot took it into his head to summon it into this one. "Have you got the summoner?"

"Yes. And I'm growing tired of looking at him, so kindly join us on the street at your earliest convenience."

Dragons didn't have the vocal cords for human speech, but a handy piece of magitech spoke for her. The recorded voice made her sound even snarkier than she might otherwise. But out of a hundred voices to select from, she'd chosen this one.

"Any trouble?" I asked.

"None."

I bit back a second sigh. That was usually how our partnership worked.

Being a cop these days was a lot like being a cop before the magic revolution. You still got shoved around and spat on a lot—only now it was by a greater number of species.

You'd think having a dragon for a partner would be advantageous, but even the criminally stupid tended to be smart enough to be intimidated by a dragon. Which just meant all their vitriol and bodily fluids ended up directed at me.

Yet for all Aurelis's majesty, strength, speed, and intimidation, I was still better than her at some things. Like cuffing the criminals for example.

Praise be for opposable thumbs.

I hauled myself out of the sewer and dodged the passing traffic. Aurelis was easy to spot on the extra-wide sidewalk Las Vegas had been rebuilt with. Her polished copper scales soaked up the hot sun and reflected it back in a way that made me wish for sunglasses. The guy responsible for this mess was pressed under one clawed foot.

He *could* have still used his magic until I put the special cuffs on him, but the talon by his ear seemed to be succeeding in making him think better of it. An ambulance sat on the curb a dozen yards away, and two uniformed EMTs were talking to the girl and her mother.

I limped up the sidewalk, detached my slime-covered cuffs, and slapped them on the summoner.

Aurelis did not immediately remove her talons.

I couldn't blame the perp for the wet patch at his crotch. My dragon partner may only be five feet five at the shoulder—no larger than a horse or polar bear—but add in her long sinuous neck, her even longer tail, and her twenty-foot wingspan, then package it all in the lethal predatory shape of ancient myths, and she *felt* far, far larger. I'd worked with her nearly every day for six months and still had to fight back my primordial terror every time she swung the full force of her attention my way.

Her casual comments about eating people who irritated her didn't help.

In contrast, my average human height and build—paired with blue eyes, brown hair, and a face that tended toward friendly even when I was hopping mad—was decidedly *less* intimidating.

Good for interacting with kids and victims. Not so great for facing down monsters or criminals.

"Why'd he do it?" I asked.

"His girlfriend dumped the loser. He says he summoned the monster to help get her back, but I'd bet he wanted to hurt her."

That might explain why the walrus thing had fixated on the girl. Summoned creatures were not real great at grasping more than the gist of a command. *Get my girlfriend. This is what she looks like and where she lives* might translate to *Get. Girl.*

Either that or the monster was just ignoring the feeble human that had unleashed it into a world full of delicious snacks.

I glared down at the guy. "No matter what your intention was, you endangered the lives of dozens of civilians, including that little girl over there, and racked up significant damages. This is why summonings must be conducted with a permit under the regulations set out in the *Summoner's Handbook*."

In truth, I was less concerned about the financial damages than the risk to others' lives. Not just the lives of the possible victims but the lives of those they'd leave behind as well.

I'd been thinking about the irrevocable finality of death too often these past few months. Wondering how those whose worlds were shattered by it managed to go on. How they survived, endured, and eventually outmaneuvered that impassable chasm of pain and loss that separated the grieving from the truly living.

Or was such depthless pain part of living?

The summoner evidently had other concerns. He racked his brain and came up with three suggestions for what I might do with the *Handbook* and various parts of my anatomy. I'd learned to enjoy the more creative insults hurled my way, but none of his were the least bit original. I yawned, suddenly exhausted. Worn out or worn down?

Thankfully the street patrol showed up then and escorted him into the back of their cruiser.

Which left just my partner around to disparage me. Her nostrils flared.

"You smell like a rotting walrus stewed in sewer water and set upon by a rabble of noxiously flatulent rats. You are *not* getting on my back smelling like that."

I smiled briefly in appreciation. Now *that* was how to insult someone.

"Your tender support is like a breath of fresh air," I told her. "Excuse me a minute."

Ignoring Aurelis's muttered retort about decidedly *un*fresh air, I jogged over to the ambulance and squatted down beside the girl. The girl who by some miracle had *not* become a monster's snack. It was times like these that made the grueling shifts, the frequent danger, and the isolation from my colleagues all but minor hurdles to be overcome. Times like these that made me love my job. I was learning to clutch them tight wherever I could. To shore me up for the times that were… not like this.

"Are you okay, sweetie?"

The fact she was still on the sidewalk instead of the stretcher told me a lot already. But I wanted to hear it for myself.

She nodded at me with eyes almost as wide as when I'd first spotted her beneath the monster. Then said in an adorably high-pitched voice, "You smell bad."

That's gratitude for you.

My smile cracked a little. "Yes, about that." I looked hopefully at the EMTs. "I don't suppose either of you have hydro or cleaning magic, do you?"

I *might* be in luck. Those with water-related magics sometimes gravitated toward medical fields because with human bodies being about sixty percent water, their magic could be useful for diagnostics if not healing. And a first responder who was able to magically clean and sterilize a wound could save a lot of medical complications.

But they both shook their heads.

One of them winced sympathetically at my malodorous slime-covered state and offered, "I can spare you an extra-large gauze pad?"

I tried not to let my shoulders slump as I took the proffered item. It was hotter than bad-tempered dragon's breath today, and the slimy, tacky goop would likely set before I'd get the chance to shower. Dabbing at it with a gauze pad would be as effectual as dabbing at an ocean of snot with a napkin.

"Thanks," I mumbled.

The mother looked like she was having a harder time recovering from shock than the girl, her glassy stare traveling from her daughter to her hands and back again, so I didn't get a thank-you from her either. But if I'd wanted gratitude, I would've chosen a different profession. Like prostitution for example.

I walked back to Aurelis and looked around for my hastily discarded motorcycle helmet.

I didn't own a motorcycle. But while none of the fictional dragon rider books I'd read mentioned the characters choking on bugs or being unable to see a thing because of the wind scouring their eyeballs, the reality was a different story. So I'd given up my chance of being a supercool badass leaping off the mighty dragon with my long hair tousled to windblown perfection… and taken to wearing a helmet instead. And unlike the fictional heroines who used those, when I took it off, *I* always had helmet hair.

Pfft, and people had once thought magic was a fantasy.

With a grimace, I shoved the clean helmet over my decidedly unclean hair.

Aurelis snaked her serpentine neck down to match my own meager eye level.

"What part of you're not getting near me smelling like rotten walrus didn't you understand?"

I resisted the urge to flee and regarded her majestic head coolly. Interlocking copper scales were reinforced by an array of armored ridges and wicked horns that adorned and protected her crown, neck, and eyes of liquid gold. She was magnificent, alien, and fierce, and as always evoked wonder and fear in equal measure.

I folded my arms and feigned indifference.

"The part where you've changed your stance on paperwork."

Her slitted pupils contracted, and I knew then that I'd already won.

"But I don't mind walking back if you wanna fly on ahead and get started on the backlog of incident reports…"

Aurelis huffed out a hot stream of air that would have affected me much more had I not already put my helmet on. Ha!

"You owe me a voucher to the scale spa," she grumbled.

Six hours later, Aurelis was lounging around reading, and I was slumped behind my desk being bested by an endless stack of digital paperwork. I was taking a brief break to stretch out my aching fingers and think uncharitable thoughts about my partner when the energy in the station shifted.

I raised my bleary gaze to see another creature of myth. One I'd glimpsed on a few video calls but never in the flesh.

Thin gray skin stretched taut over sharp, jutting bones. The figure was humanoid but with the familiar proportions *stretched* to near breaking point. Even with his distinctively hunched posture, he reached an easy eight feet. Overlong arms hung from narrow, rounded shoulders and ended in fingers stretched twice the normal length. He'd done us the courtesy of donning a pair of dark green shorts, but they seemed to be having a hard time clinging to his narrow hips, and beneath them, his long legs were no thicker than his arms. I could never quite tell if the skull that covered his face was a well-fitted mask or a natural exoskeleton, but it looked very much like a deer skull, antlers included, until you saw the teeth. Sharp, pointed, predatory teeth. A carnivorous deer maybe.

The figure trudged through the laneway of desks toward the captain's office as if the weight of the world sat on his bare shoulders. But then he always looked like that.

My limited understanding was that Enkoo was a wendigo. What one of the northern forest-loving creatures was doing down in the Mojave Desert, I had no idea. But everyone knew he was the LVMPD's clairvoyant consultant.

The rumor mill said he was paid in human flesh. Deceased, presumably. I'd never asked.

My fellow officers were trying and failing at pretending not to stare. I was afraid I was guilty of doing the same.

Enkoo never came here. Not in person. He was a shut-in who seemed to hate the world and everyone in it. Captain Gadson had mentioned to me once that Enkoo believed the depressive mind state was closest to enlightenment. I figured I might be depressed too if I had to keep seeing the future.

But why was he *here*?

I tried to think of a positive explanation. Maybe he'd won the lottery, fallen in love, and was handing in his resignation? Yeah, even I couldn't swallow that one.

Enkoo reached the captain's office and raised one long, long arm to knock, then pushed open the heavy doors and trudged inside. The effect of his beleaguered body language and gloomy nature was sort of like a very creepy Eeyore. An observation I kept firmly to myself.

But *why* was he here?

No matter how gifted you were, future telling remained a tricky business. Visions and impressions of what lay ahead were fluid, fluctuating, and often vague, which rendered them not all that helpful. But ignoring a foretelling was a negligence lawsuit waiting to happen, so we had to make the attempt.

Best-case scenario, the captain would be in a foul mood for the rest of the day. Not due to Enkoo's delightful company. But because *knowing* fecal matter was about to hit the fan—but not how to stop it—tended to do that to a person.

Worst case?

Well, worst case had gotten an awful lot harder to guess at since the magic revolution.

Not that it had been all bad, but giving every member of humankind a random magic gift had led to a great deal of chaos. Which was the most popular theory on why the supernatural community had done it: to deflect attention away from those who wanted to come out of hiding. The supernaturals of course claimed it was a gift—to put humankind on more even footing with themselves. And my vampire dad who'd adopted me amid those early years of upheaval mostly stuck to the supernatural script.

I stared at the extra-large, all-species-friendly doors behind which Enkoo and Captain Gadson were now conferring while my mind whirred over the possibilities.

I wasn't the only one speculating. The buzz of conversation was growing louder and more energetic now that there was no one to pretend for. A growing huddle around Lieutenant Castro's desk made me suspect a betting pool was in the making. But no one asked me.

Unfortunately, I couldn't blame it on the lingering fragrance of slimy walrus gunk. I'd showered and changed my uniform—and all right, the dried slime had proven painfully *disinclined* to be washed out of my hair —but this was business as usual with my colleagues.

The Rapid Response unit attracted competitive, driven types, and being paired with Aurelis meant I got some of the most critical assignments, even though I'd only been doing it for six months. Neither my peers nor the more experienced officers were happy about it. And I couldn't even blame them.

The only person who tended to talk to me was David Pinkerton. And *he* had the sort of personality that made me wish he wouldn't.

Speak of the devil. He oozed up to my desk and made himself comfortable by sitting on a corner of it.

I made a mental note to purchase some spiky table ornaments.

"Lyra the lizard lover." He sneered. "Think you're better than the rest of us, don't you? But you're nothing without your lizard. Everyone knows it."

"Are you calling Aurelis a lizard?" I inquired in a much louder voice than the one he'd used.

Pinkerton flinched.

I smiled.

One of the reasons I'd wanted to become a cop was to stop bullies like him. People who judged themselves superior and figured the rules didn't apply to them. People who believed power could only be acquired by taking it from others.

It had been disappointing to find some of them among my peers.

Pinkerton's face turned red—or pink rather—with fury. "You have to hide behind your partner, don't you, lizard lover?" he hissed, lizard-like. "Because your piece-of-crap magic makes you a walking liability to this department." He leaned in, still flushed, but smiling now, almost excited. "And a little birdie told me I'm not the only one who thinks so."

I hid my own reaction and stared him down. "Funny. *I* recall wiping the floor with you in shooting, hand-to-hand, and just about everything else at the academy."

In actual fact, I'd fought him hand-to-hand only once. And while I'd managed to win, I'd never be able to pull it off a second time. Once his magic sheathed his entire body in liquid metal armor, I couldn't reach his skin to siphon any of it. And even Pinkerton wasn't arrogant enough to underestimate how fast I could lunge twice.

As if thinking along the same lines, his magic slid over his arms and hands, forming into spiked metal gauntlets.

I tensed, uncertain if things were about to get ugly. Pinkerton might be an idiot, but so far as I knew, he was decent at his job. He liked playing hero. Liked a valid reason to throw his weight around maybe. I didn't know what would happen if the job stopped being something he cared about, but…

Well, perhaps if he *did* break my face, I'd be doing Las Vegas a favor by getting him off the streets.

Before I could decide whether to prod him again and see what happened, the oversized doors I'd been staring at earlier swung open. And Captain Gadson strode out of his office.

Pinkerton slid off my desk and tucked his arms behind him as they transmuted back to pale flesh.

Judging by the captain's face, whatever Enkoo had come here for, it wasn't good.

"Attention please." The bullpen fell silent with a swiftness powered by curiosity. "As of this moment, each and every one of you is either on duty or on call tonight, so cancel any plans you had to enjoy the festival. I want you sober, attached to your comms units, and ready to go. Is that clear?"

Groans, complaints, and questions erupted across the room, then cut off again when Gadson held up a hand for silence.

"I'll be sending out a memo shortly with all the details, including compensation. If you still have questions after that, ask them then."

Dread wrapped its tentacles tenderly around my torso and squeezed.

I'd never heard of every single officer being on call for a single rotation before. What had Enkoo seen?

That was when Gadson's gaze zeroed in on me.

"Officer Ridley, see me in my office."

CHAPTER THREE

What could the captain want with me? Surely *I* didn't have anything to do with whatever Enkoo had foreseen?

Pinkerton smirked, like he knew something I didn't. He was probably bluffing.

I squared my shoulders, straightened my uniform, and made my own walk through the laneway of desks.

Enkoo trudged past me on his way out, his cheerless gaze landing on me for an unsettling second too long. Or maybe I was just unnerved and imagining things.

Captain Gadson was already seated and waved at me to take the other chair. Everything from his well-ordered desk to his neatly pressed uniform and tidy steel-gray buzz cut reflected a precise and organized mind needed to herd his large, diverse force of interspecies personnel in roughly the same direction.

I shut the doors behind me and tried to tell what was coming by his expression.

This confirmed I was definitely *not* clairvoyant.

"Officer Ridley, well done on saving the child this afternoon."

I released a breath but didn't relax just yet. No one responds to looming trouble with the sudden desire to praise the rookie.

"Thank you, sir. But it wouldn't have happened without Aurelis. We barely got there in time as it was."

For some reason, my statement made his jaw tighten. "Yes, I've seen the report. And you're the only one she'll agree to fly anywhere."

"It's because I do the paperwork, sir," I explained helpfully.

Aurelis was the biggest bookworm I'd ever met (in the literal and figurative senses), but she loathed paperwork with the fiery passion of... well, a dragon. So we'd struck a deal. She'd get *both* of us on-site faster than anyone else could travel, and I'd do the reports. Sometimes I thought Aurelis had gotten the better end of that bargain, but it was a huge concession for a dragon to deign to carry a human, and our intervention before a fatality rate was better than any other duo in the unit.

Hence, all those important assignments that so frustrated my colleagues.

"It's not *just* because you do the paperwork. Last time you took sick leave, Perez offered her the same deal and Aurelis insisted he take a ground vehicle. She arrived six minutes ahead of him, and the perp fled into a pre-revolution building where she couldn't follow without causing property damage. The perp had a gun and plenty of time to find a good vantage point, so we had to send in a team of six to get him out again."

Unable to help myself, I asked in morbid fascination, "Did Aurelis actually *do* the paperwork afterward?"

Surely she'd gotten out of it somehow…

"Yes, it was the best report I'd read in a year, and she delivered it in a much more timely manner than you."

My tired fingers clenched. *Unbelievable.*

Captain Gadson rubbed his temples like he was getting a migraine.

"I have, however, received another complaint."

My stomach twisted.

My magic was an unusual case. Stranded alone on a desert island, I was the only human in the post-magic-revolution world who could draw no magic to my aid. But if I touched someone—anyone—I could use their magic as my own until the contact was broken.

Unfortunately, because no one else's magic necessitated siphoning it from others, people didn't always react well when I helped myself. Even if it didn't harm them in the slightest.

"About my borrowing someone's magic?" I asked, already knowing the answer.

"That was not the word the *victim* used. That's what he called himself. Claimed you assaulted him and stole his magic."

"Assault?" I scoffed.

"Did you or did you not use his own magic to spill coffee on him?"

I flushed. "That was a distraction to enable me to do what was needed."

And because he'd pissed me off with his self-absorbed honking. What if that loud noise had caused the summoned monster to spook or go berserk?

Even so, I'd been stupid.

Gadson rubbed his temples some more. "Did you identify yourself as a police officer and request his aid?"

"There wasn't time."

The captain met my eyes. "I believe you. Regrettably, that will be difficult to prove in a court of law. Especially when the person you allegedly *assaulted* happens to be the Clark County commissioner's son."

I swallowed sour bile.

We'd had variations of this conversation multiple times. I wanted to believe my magic usage came under the *posse comitatus* law that allowed a police officer to appropriate a citizen's private property to aid in a case of immediate and impending public danger. The one they loved to exploit in movies—with badass cops yanking people out of their cars while yelling something about commandeering the vehicle.

That rarely happened in real life, but if you could prove the public danger was immediate, imminent, and extreme, you'd probably get away with it. Nevada law even still permitted officers to summon and deputize private citizens to come to their aid—but that would be more like my directing a citizen to use their magic to aid me.

Unfortunately, because my magic was so unusual, there were no precedents of police officers seizing someone's magic for the public good. Never mind that multiple governments around the world had forcefully conscripted the most powerful magic users into their service. The law was still scrambling to catch up to the vast magical implications that stretched across every industry. And the bottom line was, I was on shaky ground at best.

"I'm afraid I have no choice but to suspend you, Lyra. Starting immediately."

"What?" The question came out sharper than I intended.

"This isn't your first complaint—"

"I know, but—"

"This is *not* a negotiation!" he growled. I shut my mouth. "The complainant agreed that two weeks' suspension without pay would be sufficient action on my part that he would not feel the need to press charges."

Charges? Seriously? What a jerk.

But then I'd known that already.

I just hadn't known what a *powerful* jerk he was. Not that it would've changed anything.

"Think about it," Gadson ordered. "Regardless of who won, the damage to the LVMPD's public perception would be unacceptable."

I made myself say the words even as my heart sank down to my boots. "Yes, sir."

Two weeks' suspension. A black mark on my record. And no pay.

Worse, no way to stop it from happening again. Because the next time I could use my magic to save a life, I'd do it.

Captain Gadson looked no happier about it than I did.

"This is very inconvenient timing. Enkoo has foreseen a citywide disaster tonight right in the middle of the Revolution Day festivities. And by suspending you, I'll be handicapping Aurelis."

His words were a reminder that there were far bigger things at stake. *A citywide disaster?* Enkoo might be gloomy by nature, but he wasn't prone to exaggeration.

Sick fear nestled in the space my heart had vacated, nudging up against my breastbone and kneading the cavity with needle-like claws.

"Sorry, sir." Wait. Why was I apologizing for getting suspended? "Any details of what the threat is or where it's coming from?"

He hesitated. Then his eyes met mine. "That's no longer your concern."

I winced.

Gadson massaged his temples again. Definitely a migraine.

"I know you're just trying to save lives out there, and I'm not about to fire you. But if you can't make this work without pissing off the public, I'm going to have to transfer you to a desk job and assign Aurelis a new partner."

The sour bile forced its way back up my throat with a vengeance.

Being benched might be worse than the firing. I hadn't put myself through years of fitness, combat, and weapons training and then endured all the danger and psychological strain of the job to become a paper pusher. Hell, if I could've found fulfillment in being a desk jockey, I would've chosen a more lucrative career path.

The captain shook his head, and I thought I saw a flash of pity in his steely gaze. "In any case, you've got two weeks to figure it out."

CHAPTER FOUR

Suspended. Benched. Disaster. The words circled around my brain like a macabre merry-go-round as I walked woodenly out of Gadson's office.

By the time I was done going through processing (yeah, even suspended I was stuck doing paperwork) and handing over my weapons, badge, and ID, it was past the end of my original shift.

I cursed at the clock on the wall and jogged to Aurelis's reading nook to relay the news of my suspension and the events, or the *person*, that had led to it. Dragons might not show humans much courtesy, but I tried not to let her manners rub off on me.

She eyed me languidly over her copy of *Computing with Quantum Cats: From Colossus to Qubits.*

"Want me to turn his car into a lump of coal?"

"No," I said automatically. Even though I sort of did.

"Want me to slowly dismember him and eat the pieces before he loses consciousness?"

"No!"

I didn't know *how* she passed the psychometric testing to get in.

"Pity." She returned to her book.

Momentarily distracted, I narrowed my eyes at her. "The captain said you turned in the best incident report he'd ever read when I was last on leave."

She dragged her attention back to me.

"Just because I can do something better than you doesn't mean I should have to do it. By that logic, you'd be out of a job." She blinked pointedly—a power move only a few species can pull off. "I can't help it if I'm superior at everything I turn my talons to."

I decided not to yank the book out of those talons and bonk her over the nose with it. But only because she was right.

Well, that and I didn't feel like finishing up my crappy afternoon by getting eaten by a dragon.

The special-made rubber thimblettes she wore over her page-turning claws really *ought* to have made her less intimidating, but somehow didn't.

I headed for the elevator instead, unable to stop thinking about the clairvoyant's visit. About Gadson's words.

Citywide disaster.

Some people classify a disaster as something like the

caterer failing to show up. Or maybe missing out on a promotion they'd been pursuing for months.

But working for the LVMPD adjusted the scope of the word. A disaster, in my books, usually involved fatalities. And a *citywide* disaster? The tentacles were back and squeezing my chest so tight I found it hard to breathe.

What was going to happen?

That burning question was overshadowing the implications of my suspension right now. The fact my unusual magic had bitten me in the ass yet again—I could deal with later. When my family and the city were safe from whatever was threatening them.

Would I end up grateful that my elder siblings couldn't make it to Dad's party tonight? Even knowing the terrible secret he'd asked me to keep?

No. Surely if it was *that* level of disaster, Gadson wouldn't have left me to be blindsided. Would he?

He could've suggested I take the family on a road trip or get out of town for a few days. And as far as I knew, he hadn't called in military backup.

Then again, what *did* I know? Nothing. That was the problem.

I punched the elevator button with more force than necessary, then changed my mind and took the stairs.

This speculation was getting me nowhere. With considerable effort, I yanked up the hand brake on my runaway brain.

I hadn't been a cop long, but I'd already realized that

some days you got to hold back calamity, and other days… well, other days you left the horrors of work at work and went home to your family to remember there was still love and light and laughter in the world.

Today hadn't been all bad. Just the second half of it. But according to Enkoo, that second half was far from over. And suddenly there was nothing more I wanted than to be surrounded by family.

So I wasted money on a cab instead of jogging like I normally would, rolled down the windows to dilute the lingering walrus odor, and spent the short trip plotting how to repeatedly wash my hair with industrial-strength shampoo while somehow still making it to the party on time.

Whatever was coming tonight, I wanted to be there to protect my family from it.

Someone had been in my apartment.

I knew because my door wasn't locked, and I always locked my door. Being a cop meant most people left me alone, but for a select few, it made me a target instead.

Yet there were no signs of forced entry, and the intruder could be long gone. Or not. I reached for my Taser as a precaution and came up empty. Screw the inventory clerk's thoroughness anyway.

Chances were I'd already given myself away by jingling the keys, but I slipped through the door, left it open for a possible retreat, and made my steps soft and silent against the vinyl plank floor.

Four paces in, I relaxed my coiled readiness. "Hey, little one."

My sister, in all the ways that counted if not by blood, was sitting in my living room, dwarfed by the cheerful but sturdy teal couch.

I'd given her a key to my apartment to use whenever she wanted some space or a different kind of company, but she usually locked the door behind her. She might only be six years old, but she was smart and studious, and our family took safety very seriously.

The fact she'd forgotten suggested something was wrong.

Her black corkscrew curls framed her face but didn't entirely hide her curved horns that were growing more noticeable as she got older, nor the dark furry ears that resembled that of a deer or goat.

Those ears were a little droopier than usual.

Not good.

She looked me over with serious dark eyes, taking in my gluey, disheveled hair, the sheen of sweat coating my skin from my jog down the LVMPD's un-air-conditioned stairwell, and the rotting walrus odor my nose still hadn't gotten used to. But instead of wrinkling her petite nose like the kid I'd rescued, her face lit in a smile like every sticky, smelly inch of me was a gift.

I swallowed a sudden lump in my throat and resigned myself to going to the party with goopy hair.

"Did something happen?" I asked.

She nodded, ears drooping again and smile falling away.

"At school?"

She nodded a second time.

"Want to tell me about it?"

She gathered her skinny legs and grazed knees up to her chest and stared at her toes. As half human and half faun, she'd missed out on the hooves. But the soles of her feet were tougher than most shoes, and her toenails were the color of tree bark.

I sat down on the couch beside her and said in my best cop voice, "I need a police report, ma'am."

Her lips tilted upward a fraction. I glanced at the dried slime still clinging to my arm hairs, then decided if she didn't care, I didn't either and put my arm around her.

She hesitated for half a second, then wriggled more snugly into my side. Her magic brushed up against me, gentle and soothing, but I didn't draw on it.

Face buried, she felt secure enough to share. "Brayden said I was a demon and I should go back to hell and die."

I hissed in a breath, then forced my body to unwind. Twenty-three years was too soon to expect humankind to adjust to the greatest upheaval since the industrial revolution. Too soon and yet not nearly soon enough.

It was one of the ugliest sides of my beloved city. Although other cities were even worse, I reminded myself. Vegas had been rebuilt to accommodate all species, and in general, the people who chose to live here reflected that. This was schoolyard bullying—a particularly toxic variety, yes—but at least better than the string of brutal attacks that was happening in Phoenix.

Better did not mean acceptable.

"That was very wrong and ignorant of him," I stated firmly. "How did you react?"

"I didn't," she whispered like it was something shameful. "I just tried to walk past, but then he pushed me."

I recalled the fresh grazes on her knees in an abruptly different light, and familiar fury rushed through me. The little twerp must've pushed her from behind to leave grazes like that.

I kept my voice calm to keep from upsetting her. "Did you use one of the moves we practiced after that?"

Sage shook her head, her ringlets bouncing.

It wasn't for lack of ability. Miles made sure all his kids could defend themselves. Some of us enjoyed it, some of us didn't, but everyone achieved a level of competency. And Sage was supernaturally fast and wiry and could headbutt with the best of them.

But it didn't matter how capable she was at self-defense techniques if she didn't have the will to use them. And Sage was an incredibly gentle soul.

My heart ached with love and anguish for her. It was a tough way to grow up.

We were making progress, I reminded myself

36

forcibly. Not nearly freaking fast enough, but at least we were moving in the right direction most days. I had to find some solace in that.

I hugged Sage even tighter. "You are far too good and gentle and beautiful for the likes of Brayden. If I had my way, I'd keep you all to myself, except that would be selfish of me." I shut my eyes, wishing for a second that I could do it anyway. To shelter her and protect her in a life where she would know only love. But… "The world needs beautiful souls like you, my darling. Remember that."

Sage's curls nodded under my arm, and I resisted squeezing her even tighter.

"Have you told Dad yet?"

There was a pregnant pause. "No."

He didn't take attacks upon his family well, and he'd be upset both that it happened and that she hadn't stood up for herself.

Then Sage, sensitive soul that she was, would pick up on his emotional state and blame herself for it. Even though Miles never would.

"Want to keep it to ourselves, just this once?"

Sage nodded again.

"It's a deal then. Now, how about you wrap Dad's present for me while I"—I glanced at the clock, so much for my plan to shower, let alone wash my hair six times —"get ready."

The present was more than I could afford, particularly with my unanticipated suspension. But finding the perfect gift for a vampire who's been around for almost three centuries is no mean feat, and for once, I thought I might've nailed it.

There was no way I was taking it back.

Especially since... No. I couldn't think about that now. Not if I wanted to hold it together. Tonight was supposed to be a celebration.

Miles's birthday and the Revolution Day festival both.

I left Sage with the wrapping paper and raced to the bathroom. I scraped the gluey gunky strands of my hair into an updo that utterly failed to hide its gross state, wiped the worst of the sweat off with a damp facecloth, then dashed to the bedroom where I threw on jeans, a dressy, loose-fitting top, and a pair of dangly earrings I could never get away with on duty.

Another glance at the clock made me grateful all over again that I'd decided to rent an apartment in the same building as my family. Miles felt being late was a sign of disrespect, and it had saved my neck more than once.

"Ready?" I asked Sage.

"Ready," she said.

And my heart swelled to see her ears canted at what I privately thought of as their "happy height."

CHAPTER FIVE

Vampires aren't nearly the scariest thing out there. I should know. I was raised by one.

They share enough in common with humans that we could understand each other on a lot of basic levels— facial expressions, body language, and intrinsic desires. Plus Miles always claimed that when the supernaturals revealed themselves, the vampires were more scared of the teeming, screaming *Twilight* fans than the other way around.

Okay, the ability to wipe the past few minutes from your memory was a little unsettling, but there were plenty of people out there with more alarming powers. And of course many found the human-blood-drinking thing disturbing. But as Dad pointed out, any vampire that constrained themselves to drinking 350ml at a time —the size of a blood donation—took zero lives in the process. Which was more than any meat-eating human could say. After all, human blood is one of the most sustainable foods around.

Besides, actions speak louder than appetites. And Miles *cared* about the world and the peoples in it. He took in kids who had nowhere else to go and stood by them no matter what trouble they got into.

And yet as a queer redheaded vampire who'd lived on this earth for 284 years, the world had so rarely shown him even an ounce of that same consideration.

I loved him so much it made my chest ache. I didn't want to imagine what my life would have been like without him. Didn't want to imagine what it would be like when—

No. I focused on the present.

Sage and I walked hand in hand across the two dozen yards that separated our apartments. I'd wanted to live close to family, but with at least one apartment between us so I didn't have to worry about vampiric superhearing every time I brought company home.

My sister was barefoot and still wearing her school dress, but I was afraid she looked a helluva lot more presentable than I did. Oh well. I squeezed her hand in encouragement, braced myself against my wayward thoughts, and led us inside.

The fresh and spicy scents of my favorite Mexican takeout washed over us, and my stomach growled in appreciation. Thank goodness Miles had decided to order in for the occasion. He was an atrocious cook. Something about only drinking blood did not lend itself to skills worthy of *MasterChef.* Or the spinoff series of *MonsterChef* for that matter.

I never faulted Dad for it. I just tried to bring food over a lot so that my siblings could eat something that *wasn't* bland, oversalted, burned, soggy, or undercooked.

In many other ways, vampires were peculiarly suited to single parenthood. They required very little sleep, could juggle multiple kids, prams, and nappy bags without twinging their backs, and they had lightning-fast reactions.

We never got to play the universal toddler game of chucking our eating utensils onto the ground and watching our parent pick them up—because Miles always caught our projectiles. Even if he was in the middle of vacuuming up shifter fur or ruining another recipe. Unfortunately for him, watching our parent miraculously catch our flying objects turned out to be just as entertaining to our toddler brains. But his heightened senses *did* mean it was difficult to cook up mischief in another room without being overheard. A challenge we tackled with relish.

Miles beamed when we walked in, not bothering to hide his pointed fangs. Despite his nearly three hundred years, he had an attractive, almost boyish face with laughing blue eyes, liberally freckled cheeks, and a mop of dark red hair. His tall and slender frame was outlined by a contemporary black tee and close-fitting sand-colored chinos, and if you saw him on the street, you'd guess mid-thirties.

"My darling daughters! I'm so pleased you could join us."

Even knowing him as well as I did, I couldn't *quite* tell if that was a dig at my not-quite-punctual arrival.

I kissed him on the cheek. "Wouldn't miss it for the world, you old coot. You're the best father in it after all."

Sage wrapped herself around Miles's waist. "What's a coot? Daddy, Lyra got you a present!"

"Did she now? Even though the invitation explicitly said no presents?"

"Did it?" I asked innocently. "I must have missed that."

Archer, who'd been putting away food as only a growing shifter can, dashed over and climbed Miles like a tree to hug him around the neck. He used to do that to me, but at nine years old, he was getting too big.

"Did someone say present? Do I get a present?"

Archer was a fox shifter and almost the entire reason I'd offered Sage my apartment as a quiet escape. That and the boys outnumbered her three to one. He had two speeds. Full throttle and fast asleep.

"It's not *your* birthday," Sage informed him importantly.

"But I bet I could use some help unwrapping it," Miles promised.

I glanced around for the missing twin. "Where's Blake?"

Archer rolled his eyes. *"Reading."*

He said it like it was a filthy word.

The "twins" weren't actual twins. Archer was a fox shifter and Blake was a black jaguar shifter, but biologically correct labels never meant much in our family. They'd been so close in age that Miles had started calling them the trouble twins as a shorthand. It was an identity they'd both embraced and one that still forged a bond between them even as their interests grew farther apart.

"I'll take him a plate, shall I?" I offered.

Miles eyed me suspiciously. "Sure. But then you'd better come back and tell me what happened to your hair."

He lifted Sage into his arms. "And you, young lady, had better get something to eat before you fade away into nothing more than a ray of sunlight in a dappled glen. And while we're doing that, you can tell me about your school day."

Sage's panicked gaze sought mine.

"Tell him about your science project," I suggested. And relief crossed her face.

Miles's expression didn't change, so I didn't know if he'd missed our exchange or was just pretending to. The day his degenerative brain disease progressed far enough that we truly got something past him would be a hollow victory indeed.

My eyes stung with suppressed tears. Ugh. So much for staying in the present.

When I'd accidentally caught him at the hospital and learned the truth, he'd pleaded with me to keep it secret. And this right here was exactly why. The rare disease would slowly erode the neurons in his brain in a process that would take a decade but render him unable to remember who he was or the family he'd worked so hard to build, unable to remember how to speak, how to move, and eventually how to breathe. It was cruel and unstoppable, but it typically advanced slowly until the final year or two. Chances were good that he'd retain most of his mental and physical faculties for eight or more years yet, and he didn't want grief and anxiety coloring all the precious time we had left. Not until it progressed to the point of being unavoidable.

Archer leaped from Dad's back to mine, and my legs almost buckled. "Piggyback! Giddy-up! But when are we opening presents? Eww, your hair smells bad."

I was grateful for the distraction.

"Oh, don't you like my new walrus-slime perfume?" I asked, plonking him down on the floor after a few tottering steps.

"Gross," he said in a tone that anyone else would use for *cool!* "Why would you want to smell like a slimy walrus?"

"To attract other walruses I suppose." I slapped my hands together like flippers and made barking noises probably more appropriate for a seal. Archer giggled and joined in.

Extricated temporarily from my painful thoughts, I remembered I was supposed to be bringing a plate to Blake.

I nodded at Mrs. Zucker, our neighbor from across

the hall who occasionally babysat in a pinch, and waved at Janis who was an *old* friend of Dad's, but we managed to avoid being diverted by anyone.

Did Janis know? Or had Dad withheld the news of his diagnosis from his closest friends as well?

Neither of the two siblings closer to my age had made it. My brother Dimitri, younger than me by all of two weeks to his eternal annoyance, was an arctic selkie working in Antarctica. Flights were both ludicrously expensive and rare to boot, and he always claimed he'd had enough of the Vegas climate for one lifetime—no matter how many family trips we took to nearby saltwater pools.

My older sister, Kaida, was as human as I was and lived only as far away as New York. But she rarely bothered to call, let alone visit. She'd been through hell in the foster system before she'd fallen into Miles's care, and while she'd eventually grown to appreciate what Miles had done for her, that appreciation worked better from a distance.

But both of them would've made the effort to be here if they knew.

Except that was the other reason Miles was keeping quiet. He'd never taken on parenthood so he'd have someone to look after him in his old age. After all, until his diagnosis a few months ago, he'd expected to outlive us. And he was an unwavering advocate of each of us getting on with our lives in whatever way made us most fulfilled. The diagnosis hadn't changed that.

Archer and I loaded a plate and found Blake in the room he shared with his brother, reading a tome of a book titled *Ancient Funerary Practices Around the World.*

His interest in end-of-life practices reading material had nothing to do with Dad's disease. So I chided myself to act normally.

Blake was smart. Almost painfully smart. And despite his excellent shifter senses, he was so absorbed in the pages that he didn't look up until the mattress sank beneath my weight.

"Hey, kiddo," I said. "Figured out how you want to be laid to rest yet?"

"Hmm. I wouldn't mind a sky burial so I get to be torn apart by vultures. But there's a people group in the Philippines who bury their dead upright in the hollowed-out trunks of living trees, and you get to pick your own tree, which is cool." As a black jaguar shifter, Blake did *love* climbing trees. "Or"—he watched me out of the corner of his eye and scrunched up his mouth like he was trying not to grin—"maybe I'll make you follow Kribati tradition and have you dig up my skull after a few months and carry it around with you wherever you go."

I suppressed my own smile. "That might get me into trouble at work."

He broke into a grin and took the plate I offered. But only after he'd set the heavy book carefully aside.

"There's a party happening in the living room. Are you going to come out?"

He wrinkled his nose. "Mrs. Zucker always tells me off for being depressing, and Mr. Petrovis smells funny."

"That is all undoubtedly true," I agreed seriously, "but I think Dad would like it if you came out and wished him a happy birthday."

Blake sighed and slumped back against the pillows, but I knew his love for Miles would win out now.

My phone rang as I was leaving him to wrestle with his conscience. Unknown caller. I ducked into the bathroom to answer it.

"Boss, is that you?"

Only one person called me boss. My sometimes homeless, always paranoid, accidental criminal informant. "Yep, it's me."

"Prove it. Why did the dragon cross the road?"

"Because she wanted to eat some chicken. But Stewie, I've told you before, it's really not appropriate to make jokes like—"

"Ha, you always say that, boss. That's how I know it's you."

I rolled my eyes upward and studied the ceiling. "Why are you calling?"

"'Cause these people are acting reeeeally freaking weird."

"What sort of weird?"

Stewie was paranoid, which actually made him a good CI so long as he wasn't in the middle of one of his more extreme episodes. Once he'd called me down for

47

people doing "some suspicious shit" in the park to find a family playing Jenga.

Since then, I'd learned to ask for clarification.

"They look like utility workers with high vis vests and hard hats and all that, but, boss, they have guns. Every one of 'em."

Guns were common enough in Nevada. But they were a long way from standard equipment for a utility worker.

"Are you *sure* they're guns?"

"What else would it be?"

Good question. "I don't know. A radio or something?"

He grunted. "I know what a gun looks like, boss. I've seen 'em up close and personal."

"What are they doing?"

"Going up and down manholes. And lugging something heavy. Except get this, two go down, one comes up. And the rest are about to move on to do it all over again somewhere else."

I frowned, remembering the storm grate that had been left open on Cerberus Avenue.

Coincidence?

"Have you taken any special substances lately, Stewie?"

"Nah, boss, I'm clean. I swear. Stewie don't do that stuff no more. Not this week anyway." He giggled.

Well, *that* was reassuring. Still, what he was saying didn't quite add up. What were they carrying into the sewers? I'd feel like an idiot if it turned out to be preparation for the festival or just ordinary maintenance. But what if it wasn't? What if it was something sinister?

Enkoo had foreseen something disaster-level bad happening tonight.

Under any other circumstances, I'd get the details and call in a nearby patrol to check it out. The problem was, Stewie's paranoia extended to all cops except me.

Officers in the Rapid Response unit weren't even supposed to have criminal informants, but ever since I'd saved Stewie's dog from a hungry meth-addled sprite, he'd decided I was "good people" and refused to cooperate with anyone else.

But hells, I wanted to be with my family right now, not to mention I was *suspended* from duty. So I gave it a shot.

"I'm not working tonight. Would you mind if I send a patrol around to—"

"That's not the deal, boss. Anyone but you, I vanish."

I closed my eyes, considering. The sounds of conversation and laughter between most of my favorite people drifted through the door.

I could trick Stewie into telling me where it was and then send a patrol anyway, but he'd never trust me again. And while he could be a pain in the backside, his timely intel had stopped something bad from happening more than once.

Besides, I kinda liked the guy.

But what if going out there meant I was away from my family when the disaster hit?

On the other hand, what if *not* going out there meant I'd be ignoring a chance to prevent that disaster altogether?

I wasn't on duty. But it wasn't my badge that made me care about this city and the people in it. No. That was the doing of the huge-hearted vampire in the next room. He who had protected me and shaped me, loved me and inspired me... and was possibly listening in on this conversation.

I blew out a breath. If I borrowed Miles's car and left now, I could make sure whatever was happening in the tunnels wasn't a threat or hand it over to the authorities if it was, then either way do my damnedest to race back here before things went sideways.

It was no choice at all really.

"Fair enough. I'll come take a look. Tell me where to meet you."

"Corner of Smoke Ranch Road and Rainbow Boulevard. I'll find you."

CHAPTER SIX

The corner of Smoke Ranch Road and Rainbow Boulevard was in the northwest suburbs—on the other side of the city to the walrus monster incident and the open storm grate.

Vegas was usually pretty good for traffic, but tonight the streets were clogged with people out for the Revolution Day festivities. The holiday memorialized the day magic forever changed the world, and while for some it was a day of mourning rather than celebration, Vegas did what Vegas does best and threw a huge party every year. I rolled down the windows and tried to let some of the festivalgoers' enthusiasm rub off on me.

It was the perfect evening for it, warm and windless, with nothing to dampen the cheery excitement. The plan was for my family's little gathering to migrate down here later for the parade and magically augmented fireworks parts. I still hadn't decided whether to beg everyone to stay home instead.

What had Enkoo seen?

Fortunately for my drive time, I was traveling in the opposite direction to most of the traffic. Of course, I wouldn't be so lucky on the return journey, and I was already stressing about how long this was going to take.

Even with the windows open, the scent of walrus goop was inescapable. But I was far more discomfited by the lack of the police equipment I usually carried. The utility belt was bulky and uncomfortable, but I'd trade it in a heartbeat for the single weapon I was carrying now. Tucked into the slimline holster beneath my loose-fitting top was my trusty personal handgun—the 10mm Rock Ultra MS I'd learned to shoot with. And while I knew it intimately, it was still an older-style gun with no magic upgrades or enhancements. If the need arose, I'd hit my target. But if the situation called for a nonlethal weapon or my target was too powerful for 10mm rounds to take down, I'd be screwed.

My route took me through one of the city's bustling retail districts, which was extra busy with so many people out tonight. A few streets farther to the east were the colloquially coined "magic markets" where vendors sold the newest magitech, potions, and gadgets promising—but not guaranteeing—to solve any and all of life's problems. Sometimes they even worked. And a few miles beyond that was the hallmark of Vegas: the infamous Strip.

I usually appreciated the glittering shops and market stalls that stood as a testament to humankind's ability to adapt—and turn absolutely any turn of events into a money-making opportunity. But today they reminded me just how much money I didn't have. There was no doubt in my mind that Dad's present was worth being short on cash for a while though.

I left the retail district behind and skirted around Nevada's highest security prison. It might've seemed an odd decision to house some of America's most dangerous criminals between a busy commercial quarter and a middle-class residential zone, but the magic revolution had transformed the prison systems too.

The safest way to keep a bunch of ridiculously powerful magical criminals under lock and key was to keep them fast asleep. All you needed was a sleeping beauty—the term we'd given those whose magic could keep people asleep indefinitely—and some clever tech innovations that kept the sleeping prisoners in good shape despite their long-term inactivity, and *ta-da*. Safe and economical containment of the world's scariest offenders.

And given sleeping beauties needed to stay within a few miles of their "patients," putting maximum-security blackout prisons in the middle of desirable city districts made it easier to attract candidates to the position.

This particular facility was tucked away inside a large but innocuous-looking brick wall covered in pretty murals that were designed to proclaim *Nothing dangerous here, folks.*

Of course, the rest of the magic revolution changes couldn't be so neatly tucked away.

During the fifty years leading up to it, as tech advanced and the human population doubled from four to eight billion, supernaturals were becoming more and more restricted in their mandate to stay hidden. At some point along the line, they grew fed up with those limitations and decided enough was enough.

Twenty-three years ago, the year before I was born, they'd come together in an unprecedented display of cooperation and inflicted—or gifted depending who you listened to—humankind with magic.

As an opening move, arming your potential adversary with new power is a counterintuitive way to go. But it worked. Sort of.

Making everyone magical leveled the playing field somewhat. And arming every idiot in the world with magical powers gave humankind something more immediate to fear than the seemingly well-behaved supernaturals. Especially with all the positive press about the heroic soldiers, doctors, firefighters, and social workers who'd been living among us all along.

It came out later that they'd carefully bought up key media outlets before pulling the trigger on their plan so they could massage the reactions of the masses. They spun the magic revolution as their gift to the world. Some conspiracy theorists even claimed they'd orchestrated the Harry Potter phenomenon to ensure humankind would accept it as such.

Even so, for the governments those early days were like an impossible game of Whac-A-Mole. But most of the world survived.

Las Vegas was one of a few cities to be razed to the ground during the transition period. Turns out the people that frequent Sin City are not the safest people to give magical powers to.

Miraculously, or more specifically, thanks to the hard work of the gold-loving goblins who'd had their sights on the casinos for decades, only a few people died. And a new Las Vegas was built in its place.

Except now that the chimera was out of the bag (so to speak), the city was built to suit *all* species. Establishing Las Vegas as one of the most diverse and integrated cities in the world.

(Well, the aquatic kinds like Dimitri were less well catered for, but that had more to do with our location in the middle of a desert than for want of trying.)

But as the schoolyard incident with Sage made painfully clear, it would take more than twenty-three years for humankind to embrace the changes.

Never mind that the magical revolution was far from all bad. The melding of magic and tech allowed huge advances in environmental protection, food supply, and health care. New industries had arisen, old powers had toppled, and new ones had emerged. For those who got lucky with their magic, the world was full of opportunities. And if it wasn't for the kindness of one vampire, I would have grown up in the not-so-tender care of the human foster system.

None of those things stopped factions of the populace believing all magic and magical creatures were inherently evil. There were large communities where any magic use, magic-derived food, and so on was strictly prohibited. Some entire cities lived within anti-magic fields, preventing anyone within them from being able to use magic. And this in turn prevented supernaturals from lingering.

Ironically the devices that formed those anti-magic fields were magic in nature, but everyone just ignored that.

I huffed out a breath, trying to let go of the frustration causing me to throttle the steering wheel.

It wasn't like humankind had a monopoly on ignorance or idiocy. Respective population numbers just meant our idiots vastly outnumbered those of other species.

And *progress takes time*, I reminded myself. Miles had been reminding me of that for years… and given he had about three centuries of experience, I made a point of trying to listen to him.

There were limits to what I could accomplish.

Although Miles was *also* fond of quoting "the people who are crazy enough to think they can change the world, are the ones who do."

Right now what *I* needed to do was to check out this

probable false alarm and hotfoot it back to my family. *Before* whatever disaster was brewing tonight struck.

I parked just off the designated street corner, got out my car, and murmured, "Stewie, I'm here."

A couple walking past gave me an odd look. Fair enough since I was standing in the middle of the sidewalk, talking to myself.

But thirty seconds later, two familiar figures popped out from beneath a shadowed hedge.

Stewie squinted at me. "You do something different with your hair, boss?"

He was eye to eye with my own five feet seven and built with a compact sturdiness that held stamina and strength. His round, honest face was deeply lined by fifty-odd years, some of them lived rough, and his dark blond hair was salted with white. Accompanying him, as always—come rain, sun, or more sun—was an overlarge lavender rain shell jacket, a midsized army-green rucksack, and a small, scruffy black dog.

I sighed at the question, then bent down to pet the dog. "It's a long story, and I'm not sure we have the time."

Zeus was some sort of terrier-poodle cross with wiry fur and intelligent dark eyes. He accepted an ear rub and the proffered jerky treat, then trotted back to his master's ankles to eat.

"Righto. Follow me then and keep quiet."

The last was an impossibility with Stewie's magically augmented hearing, but I did my best.

He led me to someone's unkempt and unlit yard to a tall wooden fence with gaps just wide enough to peer through. I felt a twinge of guilt for trespassing, but there might not be time to find a different vantage point, and I figured Stewie's superhearing and paranoia would've made sure the place was vacant.

The view through the fence was that of an average suburban street in Las Vegas Valley—houses in muted earthy tones, eclectic low-water gardens, and a palm tree or three on every other lot.

A crew of three utility workers, all human as far as I could tell, stood around an open manhole while several temporary road signs diverted traffic around them.

According to Stewie, two more "workers" were in the storm drain below and had taken a large tool bag with them. One of the remaining men was holding a matching tool bag, and yet a third tool bag had stayed at the first location Stewie had spotted them, about three miles to the northeast.

With some luck and my talented informant over-hearing where they were going next, we'd managed to arrive shortly after they'd finished setting up. (Stewie didn't say *how* he and Zeus had kept up with them over that several-mile stretch. But Stewie was like that.)

My CI was right. They were not your usual utility workers. At least, I didn't think so.

For a start, every one of them was a good six feet tall and muscle-bound. Second, they all carried SIG Sauer M17s with aftermarket magitech modules beneath their high vis gear. And third, one of them was wearing their hard hat backward.

In isolation, none of these things might've warranted attention, but the statistical probability of *all* of them randomly sharing that level of homogeny seemed slim.

However, the thing that really set off my bullshit radar was the way they held themselves.

They were too focused. Too vigilant. No one was staring idly off into the distance, dreaming about the freezer meal and video game waiting for them at home. No one was subconsciously shifting their weight off feet that ached from a long day's work or scratching their noses or butts. No one was bored.

The effect was nearer to that of a special-ops team than a group of utility workers.

But just because they weren't your garden-variety workers didn't mean they were up to no good. I needed to know what they were saying.

I hovered my hand over my companion's arm. "May I, Stewie?"

He shrugged and rolled up his jacket sleeve. "Go for it. It's nice to be touched sometimes."

Sound rushed in like a tidal wave, swift and furious and engulfing. Raucous laughter, the thunderous growl of car engines, the thwack of rubber on tarmac, pounding footsteps, doors slamming, a guy hawking magically enhanced fireworks at the traffic lights. I winced in pain and fought to control the magic. To narrow in on that group of high vis vests and the two suspects Stewie assured me were below.

Slowly I wrangled the onslaught into submission, the other sounds fading to non-painful levels.

This was another problem with my own magic. Borrowing other people's powers for a few minutes here and there was not enough to master them.

"You got the right GPS coordinates?" One of the men I had eyes on asked.

GPS coordinates? My brain tried and failed to come up with an explanation for why they might need them.

A reply came back through the radio and the tunnel below. A younger voice. "Yes, sir."

I hunted for the owner of that voice, pushing my borrowed magic farther along the tunnel than I would've guessed. Doing so stretched my capacity to its limits, and my "grip" on the sound felt shaky.

"Double check them," ordered the first speaker, the one aboveground. "Then have Jones check too."

"Yes, sir," said the same young voice from the tunnel, and I heard him clearer this time as if he were standing right next to me.

I also heard the clink of metal on metal and someone tapping a device with the keyboard sounds turned on.

Then a third voice that must belong to the second guy in the tunnel. Jones maybe. "Yeah, that's right. Now hold it down while I secure it."

Secure *what* dammit?

DRAGONS ARE A GIRL'S BEST FRIEND

Something clicked. Stewie jerked out from under my arm just as the overloud whir of a drill erupted inside my skull. Too late. The rapidly fading residue of his magic was still enough that the screech of the drill hitting concrete brought me to my knees.

I whispered a curse.

"Sorry, boss." The look he gave me was infinitely empathetic.

It was lucky his magic hearing somehow circumvented his actual ears or I wouldn't be able to hear anything after that assault.

"Not your fault. Thanks. For pulling away, I mean. Well, for all of it."

He shrugged. "Sure."

While I was already on my knees, I gave Zeus another ear scratch. He squirmed in ecstasy and licked my fingers.

I continued around to chin rubs while I attempted to gather my wits through my burgeoning headache.

I was almost certain by now these guys weren't just utility workers doing ordinary tunnel maintenance. But GPS coordinates didn't sound like any bombing scheme I'd heard of. It might make sense if you were targeting something very specific from below, but we were in the outer suburbs. There wasn't much out here besides roads, houses, and swimming pools. Except the aforementioned palm trees anyway. And right now most of those homes were in the process of being vacated as everyone headed downtown for the festival.

My cheeks felt hot even imagining calling the already-harassed cops out to investigate what turned out to be a local geocaching team or something.

The local geocaching team who were all built like Ken dolls and carried guns, mind you. But still.

I had to get closer and work out what they were installing in the tunnels. To figure out what we were really dealing with here.

A fourth figure emerged from the manhole with a drill in one hand and an empty tool bag slung over his shoulder. Apparently, the drilling was finished.

This guy looked like the others. Same apparel, same physique, same gun.

Which left one below, exactly as Stewie had said.

Why?

Was the fifth guy remaining behind to continue work on whatever they'd lugged down there? Was he standing guard?

Wincing, I reached for Stewie's magic again. If they'd just say something *useful,* it would save me a lot of time and effort.

"All right, last one, boys. We'll rendezvous at the meet point in an hour."

An hour. That was good, right? That meant there was still time to figure out what was going on. Unless their rendezvous point was far away.

The speaker inched the radio even closer to his mouth. "And if anyone forgets which side to stand on"

—a few chuckles here—"you'll deserve what's coming to you."

Yikes. *That* sounded less good.

I hoped I was wrong.

The four aboveground left the road signs on the street, strode to a white utility truck, and got in.

I absently jotted down the license number.

Should I stay or should I follow? If I went after the four moving members of the Ken Doll crew, they'd presumably repeat the process I'd just witnessed with the final tool bag. Which meant the only way I'd learn anything new was if they happened to say something I could overhear.

On the other hand, if I could find a way to deal with the guy in the tunnel, I could learn exactly what they were keeping down there.

Stay then.

That final comment about standing on the right side kept looping around my brain.

Stewie picked up Zeus. "You thinking of going in, boss?"

I grimaced. "Yeah, I guess I am."

He nodded sagely. "Stewie knows these tunnels." Still holding Zeus, he rummaged through his rucksack, carefully withdrew a pencil stub and an old pet store receipt, and started sketching. "This is the manhole over there, and they took twenty-six paces this way before stopping. There's a junction up a ways. You can get into one of the adjoining tunnels through a loose grate over here and reach the junction in about fifty paces. It'll be as dark as the inside of a cow though."

The phrase tickled something in my brain. I quirked an eyebrow. "You a Mark Twain fan, Stewie?" I only knew the phrase and its author because Aurelis had quoted it to me once.

"Sure, he's all right."

Forcing my brain back to the business at hand rather than Stewie's mysterious past, I studied the crudely drawn map and wished I had Aurelis here for backup.

As useful as Stewie had been, it was time to get him and Zeus out of here in case things got out of hand. Suspended or not, my duty was to serve and protect, and those guys had been wearing their guns like they were prepared to use them.

"Thanks, Stewie. You did great. Is there anything you need right now? Cash? A place to sleep? A hot meal?"

He grinned at me. "Nah, boss. I got everything I need right here." He gestured at his filthy rucksack and the little dog at his feet. "You've got responsibilities, I got freedom."

"What about Zeus? Does Zeus need anything?"

I swear the dog ate better than Stewie did. And now that our paths had crossed, I'd committed to making sure Zeus got to the vet once a year for his annual checkup. Even if convincing Stewie to part with Zeus and trust a vet to look at him was like pulling teeth.

Stewie looked at Zeus. "Do you need anything, buddy?"

Zeus yipped.

"Nah, he doesn't need anything either."

"Then I'd better go, but you stay safe, all right?"

He gave me a sloppy salute—"Yes, boss"—and disappeared into the shadows between streetlamps faster than should've been possible.

I turned back to the map. Looks like I was going to end my day the same way I'd started it. In the damn sewer tunnels.

CHAPTER SEVEN

I jogged over to the man still hawking fireworks to take to the festival tonight. "I'll take two. Oh, and matches please."

I made sure my hand brushed his as he passed them to me. The fireworks were magically enhanced, and if he was the maker as well as the seller, borrowing a little of his magic might come in handy.

Of course, as soon as I dropped contact, I would lose most of the power. But the residue lingered for thirty seconds, sometimes an entire minute depending on the magic, allowing me to continue using it on a much weaker level.

Power sparked up my arm. The vendor's magical affinity with fireworks allowed him to precisely control the ignition timing, vibrancy, duration, and arc of every speck of salt, metal, and gunpowder. It was an oddly specific gift, but he was making good use of it. These fireworks would be something to see.

I turned away and used his gift in a feeble imitation to slow down one fuse and speed up the other. The first would buy me some extra time to run. The second I had only vague ideas for as a last-ditch distraction I hoped I wouldn't need. I shoved the latter into the holster beside my gun.

The loose grate Stewie had marked on the map was about half a block away and would be a tight fit for the average human. That was okay. I wasn't planning on going down there today.

I made a lot of noise removing the grate. It was freaking heavy, and I'd have to remember to put it back afterward, but I wanted my target to wonder at why it was open. I swung my phone light around to make sure there was no one down there, struck a match, and tossed down the firework with the slower fuse.

Then I sprinted for the manhole.

The bang and crackle of the firework was muffled aboveground but was probably uncomfortably loud where my target was standing. It went off just about when I hoped it would. I ducked my head through the open manhole in time to see a figure silhouetted by a flashlight, stalking in the direction of the disturbance.

Good.

I used only the dim light of my phone screen to illuminate my way as I hurry-crept down the ladder and up the twenty-six paces Stewie had counted. It took me twenty-nine actually and placed me uncomfortably close to the junction. I'd have to hope the guy's use of the flashlight would mean I'd spot him before he could spot me.

It wasn't hard to find the new addition to the tunnel. The device was about the size of a small generator and bolted into the middle of the floor. But it took me a minute to identify it.

Because it made no sense.

An anti-magic device.

A big one.

Would it even work in Vegas? Their reliability was very hit-and-miss, depending on location, like the world's spottiest cell coverage. No one knew why they worked in some geographic areas and not others, although conjecture abounded. Some claimed it had to do with ley lines, others, the mineral composition of the soil or bedrock. Weirder concepts included its efficacy being influenced by mysterious intangible residues from historic events, and pretty much every conspiracy theory ever that could be twisted to suit.

Add to the fact that prices for the larger devices were set prohibitively high by the supernaturals who were the only ones who could make them, and it was even stranger.

But if the Ken Doll crew had gone to so much trouble to first acquire and then install this one with precise GPS coordinates, then I had to assume it would work.

But why? Could it be some sort of magic protest designed to go off at the peak of the festival? I couldn't imagine it being part of some sanctioned special effect.

Regardless, it was better than a bomb.

So why didn't I feel more relieved?

A swinging beam of light snapped me out of my thoughts. Crap. The light was too close. I wouldn't make it all the way back to the manhole in time. Most of the way maybe, but—

I had a split second to make a decision and then a few more to act on it.

I ripped off one of my shoes and braced a hand against the wall as if to steady myself just as Ken Doll #5 emerged from the junction. He was definitely part of the matched set.

"Hello?" I called out in my best inebriated-party-girl impression.

At least I was wearing casual clothes instead of my uniform.

The man's face—what little I could see of it—crinkled in confusion.

I hobbled toward him and kept babbling, hoping to keep that confusion going as long as possible.

"Oh, thank goodness I found someone. I fell down this freaking giant hole and hurt my ankle and I don't think I can get up and it's dark and—"

I was two yards away when the man went for his gun. His expression was still uncertain, but he was well trained enough that he'd been carrying the flashlight in his nondominant hand, so he didn't have to fumble.

I feigned a drunken stumble and lunged forward. He mustn't have a hundred percent decided I was a shoot-to-kill threat level because instead of snatching up the gun and pulling the trigger, he hesitated. Just long enough for me to snatch it instead, bounce off his hard abdominal muscles to open up some space between us, and aim the barrel at his center of mass.

Which was just as well, because the magic I'd managed to steal from him was useless. Unless I wanted to teach a goldfish tricks, that is.

No wonder he'd focused on physical prowess.

"Hands up where I can see them," I demanded. "That's right. Good. Now I'd recommend you don't make any sudden moves. I've been shooting since I was eight."

If I had backup, I'd risk getting close to pat him down and retrieve my discarded shoe while I was at it. But he had about eighty pounds of muscled weight on me, and I couldn't take the chance.

Instead, I backed up, putting enough distance between us that he couldn't lunge for the gun.

"I'm going to make a phone call," I informed him. "You just stay nice and still, and no one needs to get hurt."

Keeping the gun trained on his torso, I fumbled for my phone and went to dial 911 but stopped.

This would take some explaining.

I called a different number instead.

"I'm not changing my mind," Captain Gadson growled.

"Yes, sir. That's not what this is about. I have a situation here, and I need backup." Except I was suspended. "I mean, a unit…" I filled him in.

My suspect turned his head a fraction, and I readied myself for sudden moves. But he was only checking his watch.

The increased tension in his stance after seeing his watch, however, was *not* reassuring.

The captain didn't sound any happier than the guy I was holding at gunpoint, but by the time I finished my explanation, three units were already on their way. One to rescue me, the other to the first location Stewie had told me about, and a third to track down the utility truck.

As soon as I hung up, Ken Doll #5 started talking. "Look, I'm cooperating. Just let me stand over there"— he gestured to the tunnel behind me with his chin— "and I'll *keep* cooperating."

I resisted glancing back.

"How about you share first, and then I'll think about it. Tell me what's happening."

He shook his head. "You're too late. It's impossible to stop now." His escalating tension suggested he believed it. "But trust me, we both want to be on *that* side of the device when it happens."

My stomach twisted. Why? What was I missing? And how many would die because I was missing it?

Not having his fish-persuasion magic shouldn't be making him so edgy. So what in the world was happening here?

"Have you tampered with the device somehow?"

Had I been wrong about what it was? But a bomb wasn't about to explode in only one direction… Was it?

Regardless, I backed up an extra couple of steps so that *I* was over the line.

He shook his head again, the movement jerky with strain. "There isn't time to explain everything first." He glanced at his watch again, and a note of pleading entered his tone. "C'mon, lady."

My heart thudded in my ears as I tried to figure out what the heck was going on and what on earth I could do about it. I wanted to study the device at my feet, but I couldn't take my attention off the man in front of me. Hell, maybe all this was just an act and that was exactly what he was hoping for. Besides, I had zero experience with anti-magic devices.

I wished again for Aurelis, who seemed to know something about everything.

The faint sound of police sirens drifted down to us in the tunnel, and Ken Doll #5 shifted his weight.

I made my voice as hard as I could make it and raised the gun a fraction. "I wouldn't do that if I were you."

But whatever the guy was afraid of, it wasn't me.

His watch began to beep.

Behind me, a familiar voice asked, "Aren't you supposed to be at your dad's party right now?"

I glanced back instinctively, and Ken Doll used my moment of distraction to start running.

Not toward me and the alleged line—likely thanks to the formidable dragon who'd just thrust her head through the manhole—but away. Toward the junction.

I hesitated for half a second, then leaped into pursuit.

Just as something magical burst into existence and knocked me on my ass.

CHAPTER EIGHT

The tunnel had grown very dark without Ken Doll's flashlight. I groped for my phone and turned on its light function.

My head was throbbing, and the salty tang of blood called for my attention. I'd bitten my tongue when I'd collided with... whatever that was. It had felt like running into a wall.

Some sort of commotion was starting on the street above. And weirdly, the sirens I'd assumed was my backup had faded. Had Gadson just sent Aurelis then? I could hear voices raised in anger or protest, and more than one car horn honked, but no one sounded terrified, so I decided they could wait a minute.

I held up my phone. Its light reflected off the surface of something that hadn't existed thirty seconds ago. Something that, as I pushed to my feet to explore its parameters, blocked the entire tunnel. Had Goldfish

Guy had a second magic ability I hadn't noticed? It wasn't impossible if one of his parents or grandparents was supernatural. Or was this barrier some sort of defensive magic gadget he'd had in one of those pockets I hadn't searched?

Warily, I prodded it. The clear, transparent surface was hard and warm like glass in the sun. But pinpricks of bright orange light sparked out in a radial pattern beneath my fingertips.

A decoration or a warning?

"Are you seeing this?" I asked Aurelis. Just in case I'd hit my head harder than I thought.

She didn't answer.

I glanced behind me and saw the circle of streetlight from the open manhole but no dragon. Maybe she'd gone to deal with the commotion above. Or to apprehend Ken Doll if he was foolish enough to surface nearby. Good.

I angled my light at the device that had lured me into the sewers in the first place. It *was* an anti-magic device. A big one. I was almost certain of it…

And it was splat bang in the middle of the two-foot-wide magic wall force field thing.

More concerningly, a blinking white light and soft humming noise indicated the device was now active.

I swallowed. Ken Doll had been right. I'd been too late to stop it. But I still wasn't sure what *it* was.

Could the barrier's purpose be to protect the device rather than block Ken Doll's escape? Because anti-magic devices were, ironically, magic by nature, the null area they projected began a few inches inward so they didn't incapacitate themselves. Which meant this magic wall thing *could* have been intended to work in sync. By design the devices were difficult to tamper with, but the magical barrier would make that harder still.

Aurelis's voice broke into my thoughts. "Um, Lyra? You might want to come up here."

I'd never heard the dragon sound uncertain before. My own anxiety spiked.

I forced myself to do a quick self-appraisal before scrambling up to the street. I had a nasty headache, two firearms, one firework, and a single shoe.

Great.

I listened in vain for the nearby wail of sirens promising backup and climbed up through the manhole.

Which was when I learned the barrier didn't end in the tunnel.

The two-foot-deep transparent wall extended as far as I could see to the east and west, soaring upward and curving in on itself like the world's largest dome. From the outside, it was barely visible in the moon and street-light. But evidence of the chaos it had caused was all around.

The force field had gone straight through buildings, palm trees, and even roads, causing who knows what level of structural damage. None, because magic? Or would everything need to be rebuilt from the sewers up? At least I couldn't see any people trapped inside.

A car traveling east along Smoke Ranch Road had smashed into it with enough force to crumple the hood. I dimly recalled the screech of metal at about the same time I'd run into the wall—but in the pain and confusion, my mind had just lumped it together with all the other things that didn't make sense.

The driver seemed okay though. People didn't tend to curse that continuously when they were dying. If only because they didn't have the breath for it.

A small crowd was milling around—more fortunate drivers who'd pulled over to gawk, pedestrians who'd stopped to do the same, and people from nearby homes, coming out to see what all the fuss was about. They were checking their phones for explanation or holding them up to capture the unexplainable. A person on the other side—the inside—was pounding the wall with his fists, and I realized he'd been separated from his partner and their two crying children. Separated from his family.

Like me.

Distantly, I noted that the force field had a dampening effect on sounds from the other side. Which was why it took me long seconds to realize what was going on over there. The magic was gone. Magitech decorations that had been put out for the festival were dim and stationary. As was every single thing that ran on a magitech engine, including most modern vehicles.

Holy craps table. How big was this thing? I remembered that dislodged storm drain on the other side of the city and swore in disbelief. Had there been an anti-magic device bolted to the floor somewhere nearby? It wasn't like I'd gone looking. I cursed again and found fresh sympathy for the guy who'd crashed his car.

I was so transfixed by the barrier and its corresponding chaos that I didn't even notice Aurelis step up beside me.

"I see you still haven't washed that walrus goop out of your hair."

I stared at her. "*That's* what you want to comment on right now?"

She huffed. "I thought it was preferable to pointing out that Gadson isn't going to be pleased you let the guy responsible get away."

I winced. Even though I was convinced Goldfish Guy *wasn't* responsible, he still would've had valuable intel. "Right."

My phone rang.

"Ridley," the captain barked. "Tell me what's happening with that anti-magic device of yours. *Succinctly.* Because Enkoo wasn't kidding about that citywide shitstorm, and we're so inundated with phone calls we can't even answer them all, let alone send units out."

He sounded like he was wound as tight as a bowstring and just as liable to cause harm if triggered.

I filled him in. Succinctly. And it spoke to just how chaotic it must be at the precinct because he didn't even comment on my failure. Instead, he asked, "Aurelis? What's she doing there?"

"Um, I thought you sent her, sir?"

"I did not."

"Oh, I can ask——"

"Doesn't matter. Since she's outside the damnable barrier, tell her to fly overhead and search for any potential openings or weak points."

Aurelis launched herself skyward. Apparently, dragon hearing rivaled vampires'.

"Hang on a minute, Ridley."

Through the phone, I heard a second voice. Sergeant Lange.

"Sir. A brief update as requested."

I strained to catch the words.

"The barrier caused multiple simultaneous vehicle collisions when it emerged, and any vehicle with a magitech engine has stopped running, so traffic is stalled all over the city. We've given emergency services the go-ahead to drive on the sidewalks as necessary.

"All magitech in this building is dead. Backup systems are functioning okay. But the situation is presumably the same everywhere and not everywhere has backups.

"We have huge numbers of people out on the streets for the festival who are liable to panic when they figure out the roads are unusable and they can't get home. Uniforms are being deployed to the most congested areas to try to prevent hysteria.

"There are many reports of families being separated, including parents who can't reach their children. We're passing those on to other departments at the moment.

"Finally, our tech department has used satellites to figure out that the dome extends over a twelve-mile diameter, centering right over the Spaghetti Bowl. In other words, exclude Henderson and it's affecting the majority of the population in Las Vegas Valley, especially with so many downtown for the festival. Whoever's behind it went for maximum impact."

Gadson grunted like it hurt. "Thank you, Sergeant. Dismissed."

I assumed Lange departed then. So when the captain didn't say anything after a few seconds, I offered, "Sir, given the force field is magic in nature, the person responsible has to be on my side of the barrier. What do you want me to do?"

"Do?" he repeated. "Did I or did I not suspend you three hours ago? Go home and get some rest."

"But, sir, I can't go home—"

He growled low in his throat in a way that confirmed my suspicion he wasn't a hundred percent human. "You're still suspended, Ridley. Stand down! And let the rest of us do our jobs."

CHAPTER NINE

I paced the stained beige carpet in my tiny motel room and tried not to punch a hole through the paper-thin walls.

It was several hours before dawn, and I was supposed to be trying to sleep. But I couldn't. No more than anyone trapped inside the massive dome caging the population of Vegas could. Anyone who *was* managing to get some shut-eye would be waking up to an entirely different world.

Aurelis had confirmed there was no way in or out from above and had returned even snarkier than usual. Meanwhile, a segment of the special task force that had been assembled was apparently checking subterranean options. But the bastard behind this, whoever it was, had shown too much precision for me to hold out much hope for that.

People were strung out with anxiety over questions

no one had answers to. Reactions so far ranged from terror to outrage. Personally, I'd opted for switching back and forth between both in exhausting rhythm.

It had taken a while for the penny to drop about just how serious a trap had been sprung. The repercussions were bad enough on the mundane level—nothing in or out meant no food or medical supplies, no exports, and no people movement. Truckers who'd crossed the Mojave Desert expecting to drop off their consignments in Las Vegas had nowhere to deliver to. Incoming flights had been redirected to other airports. Outgoing flights were grounded. And it wasn't like there were alternative transportation options either. We were facing no in or outbound travel in a city that lived and breathed tourism. Visitors who'd come for a weekend to chance their luck on the machines were now trapped indefinitely. And locals from both sides of the barrier had been dislocated from their homes.

The casinos were making the most of it, putting people up for cheap and making a killing on gambling. But other businesses that relied on any of those systems to function were left hanging.

The magic-related repercussions were far worse.

As I'd feared, there were eleven other anti-magic devices spread around the dome's perimeter, unable to be deactivated without first taking down the barrier. Which meant magitech was out across the entire 113 square miles of imprisoned city.

The most critical systems had backups in place—

hospitals, government, law enforcement, and prisons. But those backups weren't designed for long-term use. And sometimes those systems just didn't work as well. There were people in hospitals who would die for want of magically aided medical advancements.

Meanwhile, systems of less importance, including many of those relied on by the average private citizen, didn't have backups at all. And with most post-revolution vehicles having been built with magitech engines, nearly two-thirds of the cars being driven at the moment the anti-magic devices went active were now clogging the roads. Which meant even those with working vehicles couldn't get anywhere.

But these frustrations, fears, financial losses, and inconveniences paled in comparison to what the supernaturals trapped inside the anti-magic zone were facing.

For humans, magic was something added. Supplemental.

It was useful, it was an integral part of our daily lives, and losing it was an inconvenience, but it was not essential.

For the supernaturals, magic was woven into their blood, their bones, their very essence.

And cut off from it, they would die a slow, painful death as the magic leeched from them. Like a human deprived of water.

I'd called my family last night, and they'd been doing well all things considered. They and the rest of the supernaturals would be uncomfortable but safe—for now. But after two or three days, the casualties would start trickling in, and after four or five, that trickle would turn into a flood. A deluge of death I didn't want to begin to comprehend.

If the army of task force personnel had figured out who was responsible, they weren't sharing the news with the rest of us.

Was it by design or unhappy coincidence the perpetrator had selected Vegas—a city with such a large supernatural population—to spring their anti-magic trap?

What was their agenda? Why would someone want to hold an entire city hostage?

And more pressingly—how long would it go on?

The terrifying unknown was preying on everyone's sanity. No one knew what was coming, which left fear and wild speculation to run rampant.

I knew this because the TV and internet still worked both in and outside the anti-magic zone. I wasn't sure whether that would prove a blessing or a curse.

And I couldn't help thinking that if the task force *was* withholding information, it must be bad if those in charge had decided to keep it to themselves.

Turned out I couldn't help thinking about a lot of things.

Three steps, reach the paper-thin wall, turn, three steps, reach the barely used bed, turn, three steps, contemplate banging my head against the wall because the pain would be preferable to the fear gnawing my belly, turn.

Gah. I had to get out of this motel room.

Aurelis. I'd bet money she was awake and listening to the police scanner. And she wasn't suspended either. Which meant she might know something I didn't.

Thus inspired, I shed my crappy motel room like a too-small skin and jogged the six blocks to her far more upscale hotel. Dad's car was stuck on the *other* side of the freaking barrier, naturally. So I'd braved the chaos of the shops earlier to acquire a pair of shoes, and I was glad for it now. Any action, any new information, any progress, even if it left me just as powerless to act as before, was better than climbing the walls of my room.

The difference between Aurelis's hotel and mine was like night and day. But I didn't care about any of that. I navigated my way to her door and knocked.

As soon as it opened, the muted voices of both the police scanner and TV news confirmed my guess about what my partner had been up to. Good.

Aurelis looked down her majestic nostrils at me.

"Nice shoes."

All right, there hadn't been a lot of options when I'd gone shoe shopping. Especially once I narrowed them down to a pair of within-budget trainers I could run in. I'd had a choice of vomit green, boring black, or all-over sparkles. Maybe I'd already been going crazy because I'd chosen the sparkles thinking they might cheer me up.

They hadn't.

But perhaps they'd provide my dragon partner some amusement. The situation wasn't any easier on her.

"Jealous?" I asked, prepared to stretch this moment of levity out for all it was worth. For both of us maybe. "All the stories say dragons like shiny things."

She huffed. "Material wealth is easy to obtain. Especially for one with a dragon's advantages. Knowledge is a far superior challenge."

There. She looked cheerier already.

"That sounds noble and all, but we both know you just want an excuse to spend all your spare time with your snout in a book."

Her reptilian copper head acquired a hoity-toity air. "As your Mark Twain once wrote, 'The man who does not read has no advantage over the man who cannot read.' He may have been ignorant enough to exclude other species and genders in his musings, but he wasn't wrong."

I bowed my head to hide a smirk. "Ah. Well, as it happens, your wealth of knowledge is sort of why I'm here."

I looked up hopefully, and she stepped back, allowing me to enter.

"Any inside news?"

"No," she said curtly. Her tail lashed, and I feared I'd undone all the good of our conversation. But the movement must've been performed with great restraint. Otherwise, she'd cause far more damage to her room's very nice solid walls than I could have to my flimsy, inadequate ones. "There are too many lesser incidents clogging up the lines. How am I supposed to learn if someone's broken into my home?"

"Um…?"

"My book collection, koala brain!" she snapped.

I knew this as an insult only from her tone and past explanation. Apparently, koalas have one of the smallest brain-to-body ratios of any animal and their brains are smooth to boot, which means that they're so dumb they can't even recognize their sole food source if you put it on a plate and hand it to them. Literally.

"My *hoard*. Its protection relies on the threat of my presence and a series of magical defenses. Now would be an ideal time for a thief to breach my stronghold."

I bit my tongue on the first three responses that popped into my head and said carefully, "I'm not sure stealing books is on the top of everyone's minds right now…"

Despite my care, my comment went down like a six-hundred-pound pig denied the gift of flight.

Her head snaked to my level, and hot, smoky breath curled over my skin. "It doesn't *need* to be on everyone's mind. Only one underhanded scumbag's!"

I squirmed and swallowed back the usual primordial fear.

When someone's downright terrifying, it's sometimes hard to remember that they still share more things in common with you as not. Pain. Fear. Vulnerability. Unmet need. These things are universal, and in my experience, most intimidating behavior comes from those places.

Aurelis was upset.

I reminded myself that to a dragon, their hoard was as close as they came to family. There was less known about dragons than I'd like, but one thing we did know was their social structures left a lot to be desired. Like turtles, their eggs were laid and then left to fend for themselves. Connections were so unimportant that family names didn't exist in dragon society. There was a reason Aurelis had few social graces.

Unlike turtle hatchlings though, baby dragons came into the world knowing more than some humans learned in a lifetime and were perfectly capable of defending themselves.

"I'm sorry. That must be... hard."

"If someone takes so much as *one* page of *one* book from my collection, I will hunt them down, burn the flesh from their bones, and use their femurs as toothpicks."

I didn't know why Aurelis became a cop. I just knew it wasn't to help people. The hell of it was, she was still a better cop than I was.

I opened my mouth to remind her that that'd be going against the oath she swore as an honored member of the LVMPD, but shut it again as something caught my attention on the flat-screen.

The recurring grim-faced reporters and seemingly endless footage of the upheaval cut away to a man I'd never seen before sitting against a plain white background. The text at the bottom of the screen announced:

Las Vegas Hostage Taker Makes Demands

I scrambled to turn up the volume as my information-starved brain sought out every detail.

The man's manner was calm and confident as he faced down the soon-to-be millions of viewers whose lives had been thrust into turmoil by his hand. Calm and confident—from a safe distance of course.

He was clean-shaven with light brown hair in a professional side part, and he wore a dark navy suit jacket paired with a pale blue shirt. A color that, according to various academic studies, was perceived as trustworthy. The camera frame was perhaps intentionally similar to that of the news anchors we'd just been watching—showing a sliver of the desk he was seated behind and stretching to a few inches above his head. He looked about the same age as some of the more senior news anchors too, in his early fifties maybe. But there was a stiffness to his face that suggested more than one round of cosmetic surgery, making his true age hard to peg.

Anti-aging treatments aside, he was making no attempt to conceal his appearance. But the video setup had been carefully arranged to give us nothing that might point to his location. Artificial lighting. A featureless off-white wall with nothing on it except a hole where a screw had been removed. And that sliver of stained-oak desk.

"My good people of Las Vegas," he began. "No doubt many of you are wondering why you find your-selves in this predicament." His face shifted in and out of a smile so practiced it had been drained of all mean-ing. "Bear with me as I try to explain."

Then he clasped his hands together on the desk in front of him and deadpanned into the camera like a wannabe David Attenborough.

"Twenty-three years ago, the supernatural commu-nity banded together and inflicted magic on humankind. They did it without consulting us, and even now, decades later, they refuse to share how such a feat was done. It is clear that despite their lip service, they do not trust or respect us as equals."

I groaned. I'd heard this rhetoric before. As far as I was concerned, not telling us how they'd done it was about as mysterious as why the government didn't grant everyone access to the nuke codes.

I knew not everyone saw it that way—and that everyone was entitled to their opinion. But it was this sort of conspiracy garbage that propagated negative sentiment toward the supernaturals and empowered kids like Brayden—no doubt emulating his parents—to tell my six-year-old sister to go back to hell and die.

Those sentiments turned even more dangerous when the little Braydens of the world grew up.

"Well, now that I have the country's attention"—this

time the smile that flickered across his face was unstudied and self-satisfied—"I, for one, am uncomfortable with this power imbalance. What's to stop them deciding to tear magic from us as forcefully and thoughtlessly as they bestowed it? Humankind *must* overcome this power imbalance and achieve magical independence—or live forever at their mercy."

I'd encountered this one before too. They were simultaneously angry at being given magic and angry they hadn't been given more.

Blah blah blah. But what on earth did that have to do with the Las Vegas hostage situation? Who the hell was this guy?

Whoever he was, he leaned into the camera.

"So let me tell you a little secret that the supernaturals don't want you to know…"

During the long dramatic pause that followed, I checked off a few of the wilder conspiracy theories on my fingers.

The world is flat, but the fae glamoured it to look round to hide the existence of Faerie. A werewolf pack killed J. F. Kennedy for having an affair with the alpha's daughter. And the Easter Bunny was fabricated to give the horned, carnivorous rabbit-like Almiraj easy access to its favorite snack: human children.

What the man actually said was, "If they truly wanted to offer humankind equal footing, all they'd need to do was gift us with a single powerful artifact. An artifact they used to bring about the magic revolution.

An artifact without which they would not have the ability to reverse what has been done. *The iron key.*" His voice caressed the three words.

I chafed, caught between grudging curiosity and wishing he'd get to the damn point. The part where any of this mattered to the people of Las Vegas.

He picked up something from the desk and held it up for his audience. A printed photo of a teenage girl with the same light brown hair, only hers was long and dyed blue at the ends. She was hugging her knees, and her eyes were overshadowed by dark makeup, but the smile she gave to whoever was behind the camera was genuine.

"This is my darling daughter, my Madison. She's turning eighteen next month. And for the past several years, she has worked tirelessly to identify and locate this artifact on behalf of humankind. Recently she made a huge breakthrough and discovered that the iron key has been jealously hoarded in Faerie all this time. Doing nothing. Benefiting no one. It is little wonder the fae are so standoffish, so rarely seen outside their beloved land. Little wonder they grant visas to an exclusive few. They don't trust us, yet they expect us to trust them."

The daughter looked vaguely familiar, and the name Madison rang a bell too. I chewed my lip. Why?

"Well, after learning this, Madison jumped through all the right hoops and was granted a visa to enter Faerie. A few days later, she rang me to say she'd *found* the key. That it exists. That she couldn't wait to share with the world what they had kept for themselves. And then the fae arrested her on trumped-up charges."

For the first time since beginning his spiel, the man in blue didn't look quite so relaxed.

"For three weeks, I have pleaded with the fae to provide evidence of her alleged crimes and allow her to stand trial in her own country. But they refuse to hear me. Refuse to negotiate. Refuse to grant me a visa to visit my own precious daughter. They won't even let me talk to her on the phone!" Perhaps noticing his hands were beginning to clench, he clasped them again in front of him. "They've left me with no other choice but to *force* them to negotiate." His tone had turned brittle with what I suspected was real emotion.

But going to Faerie was like traveling anywhere else: you agreed to be bound by the laws of that country.

And I suddenly remembered why her name and face seemed familiar. Madison Hale had tried to *steal* the artifact.

Which meant the fae were well within their rights to imprison her for it.

"So, this is my message to the fae." Another studied pause as he composed himself, one that would have the viewers leaning in to listen. "Return my daughter to me with her mind intact. Let her speak the truth of what she has seen, and as an added measure of good faith, send the iron key with her. Or"—he belabored the word, making the single syllable grow in size and volume—"thousands will die for your selfishness. Not humans, since I doubt you'd lift a finger for us, but thousands of your fellow supernaturals. And the world will learn the truth about your nature and treat you with the contempt you deserve."

Fury and terror punched through me as my worst fears were realized. The anti-magic trap was exactly that. This jackass was purposefully threatening my family and every other supernatural inside the dome.

He cut in before I could even begin to process that.

"And to the good people of Las Vegas, I apologize for the inconvenience. But this is just a taste of why we need to control our own magic. Of what we'd be left with if the supernaturals changed their minds. No one *needs* to die. The decision lies in the hands and hearts of the fae."

He was silent for three painful heartbeats.

"Let us hope they aren't so callous as their treatment of my daughter has made them seem."

The broadcast ended.

Blood beat a hot angry rhythm in my skull, and I distantly noticed my ears were ringing.

No one needs to die? At least three people had already lost their lives from colliding with the barrier, and those numbers were doubtless climbing as the sick and injured were denied magically assisted medical treatment. Meanwhile, he was threatening to massacre thousands of innocents for his own agenda. *Hundreds* of thousands if something didn't give. Was he seriously

DRAGONS ARE A GIRL'S BEST FRIEND

trying to paint himself as the victim—the good guy—in all this?

Yet many would buy it, I realized. The people who already demonized those different from them. They would use this propaganda to shore up their own beliefs.

They would even celebrate when supernaturals suffered and died.

When my family suffered and died.

No.

No, dammit. That wouldn't happen. Couldn't happen.

I was so worked up I'd forgotten whose hotel room I was standing in, or even that I was standing in a hotel room. Until a surprise lungful of smoke launched me into a coughing fit.

"Where is he?" Aurelis demanded. Smoke escaped from between her teeth, and her powerful body was coiled with tension, tail lashing at dangerous speed. In contrast, her voice was soft with menace. "I'm going to bite off his stupid, smug head."

I stared at her for a moment, stomping down the familiar urge to flee, and tried to rally my usual lecture on upholding the values of the LVMPD.

But all I could think of was how I wanted to punch him in his stupid, smug face first.

CHAPTER TEN

There was no way I was going to sit on my hands while this power-hungry parasite threatened my family, community, and twenty-three years of integration progress. If Gadson wouldn't give me a job to do, I'd make one for myself.

I was suspended, not stuck in a cell. How I chose to spend my free time was up to me.

Aurelis still had access to the magic registry and police databases, so we looked him up. Knowing what we did about his daughter, he wasn't hard to find.

Jason Hale.

But for a man ready to massacre hundreds of thousands of people to get what he wanted, his records were bland and unenlightening.

He had no criminal charges. He'd grown up in Nevada and had moved to Los Angeles to study and practice law. But he'd let his license lapse just six months after the magic revolution, possibly to pursue a magic-based career. Today he had residences and driver's licenses listed in both California and Nevada, although his most recent vehicle was one of the self-driven variety. A marriage certificate said he'd walked down the aisle twenty-five years ago, and a death certificate told us he'd been widowed twelve years later when Madison would've been about five years old. Probably not recent enough to have triggered the current course of events.

It appeared he'd raised Madison single-handedly after that and sent her to one of the most expensive private schools. All indicators from police records and their social media accounts pointed to the idea that he'd led a relatively ordinary life of privilege and that he was in no way hurting for money.

Good for him.

About the only *useful* information we found was the magic registry's confirmation that Mr. Hale had been whacked with the lucky end of the magic stick. Unlike me or poor Goldfish Guy. He could create force fields. Really freaking big ones. And apparently, he was the only known thing that could pass through them.

But that was all his listing in the magic registry said, which wasn't unusual. Trying to track over ten billion humans' individual magic gifts was a logistics nightmare. You either relied on self-reporting, which made it all but useless as a tool in fighting crime, or you expended far too many resources trying to identify and catalog every-thing. Even if you *had* the resources, you frequently had to take a person's word on the details and limits of their magic unless you had magical means of confirming it. And even if you somehow had all the information with guaranteed accuracy, recording and categorizing billions of powers all with their own quirks and variations was a cataloging challenge for far smarter minds than mine.

We looked up Madison anyway. And discovered her gift had been recorded as "the ability to disappear from living creatures' sight."

Interesting. It didn't go into her limitations or anything helpful like that, but it shed some light on why Mr. Hale might have allowed his daughter to travel into Faerie in the hopes of illegally acquiring the artifact.

I wanted more information on Jason Hale's magic though, since *his* was the one keeping Las Vegas imprisoned. I chewed my nail for a few seconds and then googled *Jason Hale force field*.

Sure enough, there was a website advertising his services, which he either hadn't thought or hadn't bothered to take down.

Halesecuritysolutions.com (he'd gotten real creative there) informed us he worked as a freelance security specialist for a number of private, corporate, and government entities across Nevada, California, Utah, and Arizona. The high-end security business was a lucrative game, and Jason Hale had done well for himself. His client list included everything from private collectors, museums, banks, and even a few casino vaults in Las Vegas.

DRAGONS ARE A GIRL'S BEST FRIEND

"A thief and a security specialist," Aurelis mused. "I wonder if they ever combined forces to pull one over on Hale's clients."

I jerked my head around, decided I didn't care right now, and jotted down the four states on my notepad. That they all adjoined suggested there was a limit to his magic. Probably relating to distance. Which meant wherever he was holed up, he had to be sort of close to Vegas. Unfortunately, a four-state limit was still a *lot* of ground to cover. Nearly five hundred thousand square miles, in fact.

According to the unsubstantiated claims on his website, his force fields were impossible to break, pierce, puncture, blow up, unlock, drill through, or otherwise physically compromise. Even more notably, they reflected any magical attacks or manipulation from the outside and "reacted violently" to attempts at anti-magic disablement. No wonder his business had taken off.

Unless that last detail was a fabrication that had been added to his website specifically for this hostage situation? I trusted the task force would test the validity of those claims.

Of course, the weakest link in his security service was Hale himself. Kill him, and robbing Aunt Bertha of her collection of Fabergé cockatrice eggs suddenly became a lot easier. Or if you weren't the murderous type, you could threaten Hale into lowering the barrier for you.

But Mr. Hale would've been all too aware of that

vulnerability. Throughout his career, he must have invested a great deal of his wealth into personal protection. Even more so now. He'd known releasing that video would bring the full force of law enforcement down on him.

Known—and felt secure enough to do it anyway.

Which meant getting to him would take more luck than a winning streak at a casino. And while I was feeling *slightly* more optimistic after finally managing to wash most of the walrus gunk out of my hair in the hours I'd failed to sleep, lucky seemed like a stretch.

I looked over the notes I'd jotted down and then back to Hale's client list. The public version anyway.

The massive force field over Las Vegas had to be pushing his limits, right?

I googled one of the names at random and dialed the number that came up.

"Hello, is this the Art Preservation Society? Good, yes, I'm calling because I just saw on the news that your security specialist Jason Hale has turned rogue. You might want to check the protection you hired him for is still in place…"

The man at the other end sounded flustered. "Oh, um, let me have a look. Oh my goodness. I don't believe it—"

"The force field's down then?"

Suspicion replaced confusion. "Who did you say was calling?"

"Just a concerned citizen," I chirped. "Have a nice day."

I called the next client just to make sure the first one wasn't an anomaly.

The woman who answered was shrewder than the first. She thanked me for the information, promised she'd have someone by the name of Valentino check it out, and hung up so I couldn't overhear the results.

I tried another one at random and went through my opening spiel.

"Is this some sort of joke?" demanded the voice on the other end.

"Um?"

"The entire residence has just been taken over by law enforcement saying they'll be conducting testing on the force fields *with* the valuables inside! I swear if they damage my boss's irreplaceable one-of-a-kind—"

I scrunched some of my notepaper against the phone. "I'm... sorry... cutting out."

Aurelis snorted at the childish ruse. But I was itching to act on our information, and this way the poor personal assistant was less likely to call me back.

I tapped my pen against my now screwed-up notepaper. "So the task force must be experimenting on smaller versions of Hale's force fields—ones without over a million people trapped inside. That's good."

Mr. Hale had probably never had the entire might of law enforcement putting his force field to the test. Maybe they'd find a way to break through.

Then again, maybe they wouldn't.

"And it sounds like he's stretching himself pretty thin if he's letting some of his customers down. That's bad business 101 right there."

Aurelis gave me her you're-an-idiot look. Dragon facial expressions aren't easy to read, but I'd seen this one often enough to recognize it.

"Since he released his identity to the media, he can't be betting on his life ever being the same again. Why would he bother keeping his clients happy?"

"You're right. Geez."

We both knew what that meant. Jason Hale had jumped in without a life jacket. All or nothing. He wasn't planning on returning.

Which meant he'd do anything to win.

I ducked Aurelis's lashing tail.

"All the more reason to bite off his stupid, smug head," she growled. "Let's go check out his closest known address."

I made one last effort to do this through the proper channels. I called the task force's general line to offer our assistance. Not that I was certain Aurelis would even agree to offering hers.

The guy who answered—Special Agent Someone-Or-Other—asked in an efficiently bored tone, "Can I help you?"

"I was hoping my partner and I could help *you*," I clarified. "We're LVMPD officers outside the anti-magic zone"—no need to mention I was suspended—"and—"

"What division?"

"Rapid Response unit."

His tone didn't seem to change and yet somehow gave me the sense of him looking down a long aquiline nose and doodling *loser* on his notepad. Some considered the Rapid Response unit only one step above beat cops, and I suspected Special Agent Whatshisname was one of them.

"Thank you for your willingness, Officer. But the people assembled here are the best of the best, and we have the situation in hand."

The clear implication being that I was *not* one of the best and should stop wasting his time.

He was probably sour about being placed on phone duty.

"But my unusual magic might help," I persisted, explaining how if I could just touch Jason Hale, I could use his magic to safely lower the force field.

That got a shift in tone. Just not the one I was hoping for.

"If we've got hands on him, Officer," he said in grim exasperation, "we won't *need* your magic."

He hung up without giving me a chance to respond.

Aurelis shifted impatiently throughout the short exchange. She looked like she was ready to fly out of this hotel room—without the delay of using a preexisting exit first.

I hastily entered Jason Hale's Nevadan address into my phone's GPS and realized I had a transportation problem. The residence was a two-hour drive away. Decidedly too far to jog. And the limited roads through the Mojave Desert meant the distance by car was far greater than as the crow—or dragon—flies. Not to mention the given address didn't seem to connect to any of those roads.

And if I took too long to get there, I was afraid Aurelis might burn the place to the ground before I could lay eyes on it. I'd never seen her this agitated.

The TV news was running a piece on opportunistic thieves taking advantage of empty residences, and Aurelis hissed.

Why hadn't I parked Dad's car just a few extra yards down the road?

"Aurelis? Partner?"

Her head swiveled toward me with unsettling intensity.

I forced myself to sound casual. "We're doing this together like usual, right? Or else I suppose you could have a nap while I find a car hire place and drive the longer route along the roadways and then meet me there in a few hours. But if you're anxious about leaving your hoard unattended, taking me with you would be faster."

She snarled. And trust me when I say that when a dragon snarls, it's freaking terrifying.

"Get on!"

My stomach flipped, and I was abruptly aware of the need to pee. My campaign to convince her to carry me didn't seem so clever anymore.

"Um, are you su—"

Her tail whipped toward me, wrapped around my waist, and plonked me unceremoniously on her neck. She burst through the double doors to the balcony and was taking off before I'd had a chance to find a handhold.

Fantastic. No helmet.

The wind groped my hair and skin with greedy, grasping fingers as we plummeted downward. Then she snapped her wings up.

I clung to her spikes. "Aurelis," I squeaked. "Remember I'm not made to soar the skies like you."

I was just realizing how carefully she usually flew to accommodate that fact.

She snorted. "Like it would be possible to forget."

Without my helmet or comm, it was hard to hear her over the rushing wind and the thrashing fabric of my decidedly inappropriate party top. At least my dangly earrings were still on my motel's nightstand. "Speak up please," I shouted. Then coughed and choked on a bug that lodged itself in my tonsils.

Aurelis did as I asked, but reminded me, "I can hear *you* just fine."

Gritting my teeth to prevent my throat accumulating any more unwanted guests, I muttered, "Sorry."

Her flight leveled out as we reached her desired altitude, but her speed was still increasing. I took the opportunity to tear off some of the excess flapping fabric and tie it over my face like a biker's bandanna. But the rushing wind still left me a little breathless.

Or maybe that was the wonder of flying dragonback that never truly went away. I squinted my eyes against the wind and peered down past the huge powerful wings that corralled the air itself to her will.

The fiery orange glow of dawn edged the eastern mountain ranges, transforming the inky night sky into a deep, dark blue. Throughout the basin, streetlamps and the lights of early risers glimmered in their final farewells before being rendered unnecessary by the coming sunrise. And the dome, transparent but visible, hunkered over the city like a predator over its kill.

I squeezed my eyes shut. Against the wind and menace both.

Who would die first? Those with the most powerful magic because they'd sooner notice its loss? The old and the ill, like my father? Or the small and the weak who possessed less magic to begin with but were just as reliant on it to survive? Like Sage.

I wrenched my mind away from that line of thinking. We or the task force would save them. Or the fae would give in to the bastard's demands. There was no other option I could accept.

The sun came up as we flew. I was lying low over Aurelis's scales, trying to find what shelter and warmth I could from the bone-chilling wind. And soon I'd have to worry about heatstroke and sunburn.

I so wasn't dressed for this.

Taking a risk, I levered my phone out of my pocket with frozen fingers and checked the news. Had the fae responded? I knew it was probably too soon, but... nothing.

My GPS showed we were close now. I peered over Aurelis's shoulder, searching for signs of our destination.

The desert we were flying over was rocky, mountainous, and largely barren but for low-lying shrubs that were probably creosote, burrobush, or blackbrush. I couldn't see anything that resembled a house. Or even a road. But something glinted in the sunlight. Was that a dark window or a shiny section of rock?

Aurelis dipped closer.

No way. Hale had built a freaking mountain fortress. *Inside* the mountain.

Except if we were in the right place, where were the task force personnel? As Special Agent Whatshisname had so kindly pointed out, they had the best of the best working for them, and they should've been way ahead of us.

That was when a magitech drone appeared out of nowhere and opened fire.

I bent even lower over Aurelis's neck as a hail of bullets pelted her scales. The thing about dragons is that they're *very* hard to kill.

Me? Not so much.

Yanking my gun from its concealed-carry holster and ordering myself sternly not to drop it, I returned fire. Out here, I wasn't too worried about hitting a bystander by accident. I was more worried about running out of bullets.

Especially because firing at a moving target while erm, being carried by a fast-flying dragon—Aurelis would chargrill me if she so much as heard me *think* the word ride—was harder than the movies made it seem.

Lucky I'd been practicing for most of my life.

I hit the drone on the second shot, right in the vulnerable power source, and it dropped, swiftly losing altitude.

Aurelis—far from being grateful—exhaled a cloud of smoke so that it would blow back in my face. "*I* was going to swat that annoying gnat. Do you have any idea how long it takes to buff out bullet scratches from my scales?"

I swiped at my already moistureless and now stinging eyes, wishing again I'd somehow had the foresight to bring my helmet with me when going to meet Stewie. Then blinked rapidly to clear my vision. "Um, looks like you'll have plenty more playthings to work out your irritation on."

Six more drones had launched from an opening in the mountain fortress and were heading our way fast.

Then as one, they winked out of sight.

Crap. Camouflage drones.

They weren't completely invisible, but their magitech

plating was fast and smart enough to make them very hard to see, especially against the undemanding homogenous background of bright blue sky.

Damn. I didn't have enough bullets to fire when I wasn't sure to hit something. Maybe I shouldn't have handed Ken Doll's firearm in as evidence.

I squinted, gun ready, trying to get a clear sight on one of the sneaky machines. Were they sticking together or maneuvering to attack from all sides? A faint blur in my peripheral vision made me snap my head to the left just as Aurelis dropped away beneath me. I didn't have time to shriek before she'd completed the maneuver—a complete barrel roll—and taken the volley of bullets on her chest.

She'd protected me, I realized.

And somehow used her magic to keep me on her back at the same time. I'd felt the pressure of it on my shoulders and thighs. The cushion of it supporting my neck. And for a breathless moment, I hadn't even felt the relentless wind.

I didn't know she could do that.

Dragons' natural magic resistance meant that using my power to draw on Aurelis's magic was like drawing water from a stone. Difficult and freaking exhausting, with only a meager supply of magic to show for it. Now I knew she'd been holding out on me. Her powers over the sky extended well beyond her ability to fly. Hell, any time she'd carried me over the past months, she could've stopped the wind from endeavoring to tear out my hair and turn my eyes into dried, shriveled husks. I needn't have even bought a helmet.

But she *had* just protected me.

Another staccato of gunfire rang out, and I shoved away my shock to raise my Rock Ultra MS again. The drones were fast and agile and apparently smart enough not to get within dragon teeth, talon, or tail range. And Aurelis was hindered in trying to protect me. Which meant I needed to shoot some more of these machines out of the sky.

Aurelis dove suddenly and crumpled a drone that had been foolish enough to fly beneath her. Again I felt her magic pressing me to her back and cushioning me from the rapid g-force my own body wasn't designed for.

But the maneuver caused me to remember the hard object digging into my ribs was the leftover firework from my sewer adventures.

Hoping it was an impressive one, I ditched it in the direction of more gunfire. "Would you mind lighting that?"

Aurelis obliged, and the firework went off, shooting light in every direction. We retreated to force the drones to fly through it, and the camouflage technology couldn't quite keep up. I picked three more drones out of the sky while the light lasted.

One bullet left.

Two drones to go.

Aurelis swerved and released another torrent of

flame. Parts of her target simultaneously melted and caught fire, and it fell, trailing smoke like a funeral pyre.

One.

Was that a blur? I raised my gun again, shielding my body behind Aurelis's neck.

"Mine," my partner snapped.

She snaked her head toward the indistinct haze and exhaled a stream of fire. The drone dodged. But Aurelis's magic took command of the wind so that her flame changed course with it, and a second later it exploded in a light show almost as impressive as the firework.

CHAPTER ELEVEN

When we set foot on the hot dry earth, it was littered with drone parts. Some of which were still smoking.

It was hard to tell, but I got the impression there was more debris than could possibly belong to the seven we'd taken down.

Had someone else arrived ahead of us?

I supposed we'd find out.

Aurelis was glowering at the scuff marks on her scales, and I was pretty sure she hadn't caught on that I was using her considerable bulk as a source of shade. The heat of the early-morning sun promised that today would be a scorcher.

"Thank you," I said. "For lugging me all the way out here and shielding me from a bucketload of bullets."

Even apart from the bullets, people died out here in extreme temperatures, and I was feeling extra glad to have an almost indestructible dragon as my partner.

Never mind however many other murderous surprises waited for us around this fortress.

"Sure. You're one of the least annoying humans at the precinct, so it's in my interest to keep you around." One liquid gold eye rolled toward me. "You're still annoying though. And your ridiculous shiny shoes are hurting my eyes."

I hid a smirk. Being around Aurelis as well as little kids who blurted out what everyone else was thinking made one pretty hard to offend. And I was starting to think Gadson was right. My dragon partner might actually *like* me.

"Only your scales could shine more brightly," I agreed cheerfully. Then I turned to face the fortress.

The question was, was Hale inside? Or something else he didn't want us to get our hands on? Or were the drones and who-knows-how-many other defenses intended to keep law enforcement busy while the supernaturals wasted away inside his death trap?

Fear and anger surged, but I stomped them down again. Later. I would allow myself to feel things *later* when they were safe.

But the enormity of that ambition as I stood outside the imposing fortress surrounded by the vast, lethal stillness of the desert left me feeling foolish. What was I going to do, walk up and ring the doorbell? I hadn't even brought *sunscreen*. How could I pretend I was prepared for this?

Aurelis finished her scale inspection and followed the direction of my gaze. Unimpressed.

My resolve hardened. My family was relying on me. I would do whatever I had to.

As soon as I figured out what that was.

Maybe even simple surveillance would be useful. The task force was doubtless stretched thin covering every possible avenue of investigation. If they were waiting on a search warrant or they'd deemed this a low priority, they might miss something. Maybe Hale's housemaid would come by and deliver some gem of information into my hands. Maybe Mr. Hale himself would sneak back in to check he hadn't left the stove on.

Or maybe I'd sit in the desert heat until my brain turned to mush and learn absolutely nothing.

We could spend days sitting outside his mountain home. And we didn't have days.

Alternatively, we could break in.

Which was highly illegal.

In the state of Nevada, citizens—and therefore suspended cops—were allowed to make a citizen's arrest. But breaking in to do so was another matter.

Then again, so were shoot-on-sight drones and holding an entire city hostage.

"Do you think there's more than one entrance?" I asked Aurelis. Not that I'd decided to break in, exactly. I was merely scoping out our options. "Or maybe you could see if there's a better vantage point anywhere? We need to get eyes inside."

DRAGONS ARE A GIRL'S BEST FRIEND

"I have some ideas on how to achieve that," she threatened. But she flew around the mountain rather than through it.

I was doing some of my own reconnaissance around the base of the rocky mountain—waiting for Aurelis to return, keeping an eye on the front door, and willing my brain to remain uncooked—when he stepped soundlessly up beside me.

At first I thought the figure was a mirage. Or that my brain had turned to mush after all.

Helluva surveillance job I was doing.

A stranger, probably in his late twenties, was watching me with eyes that were dark and deep and held mine. His black hair was mid-length and tousled except where it cut away at the sides, and his lips were full and inviting. But there was nothing effeminate about the hard planes of his face. And while the clothes that hugged his lithe, muscular form were perfectly modern, there was something about the way he held himself that put me in mind of the heroic knights of old. Tall, resolute, and deadly.

By my evaluation, he was as hot as the desert he'd slunk out of. And likely more dangerous.

But my tongue was only stuck to the roof of my mouth because I was dehydrated. Definitely.

"Hale isn't inside," the stranger informed me.

I'd pretty much figured as much since the task force hadn't shown up en masse. Still. "Oh? How do you know?"

He asked his own question instead of answering mine. "Are you part of the task force? I thought they'd decided it wasn't worth surveilling."

I studied him again but didn't see any sign of a badge or gun or anything else that might identify him as law enforcement. Not that he couldn't be plainclothes.

"Are *you* part of the task force?"

"Are you going to respond to everything I say with a question?"

Whether he was feeling amused, irritated, or indifferent, there was no sign of it on his striking face.

I flashed him a smile. "Are you?"

Hey, I was off duty. No need to be on my best behavior. Besides, for all I knew, he might be working for the other side.

But when even that failed to get a rise out of him, I relented. I was no trained interrogator, but I'd heard establishing rapport was the first step to weaseling information out of someone.

"I'm here for personal reasons."

I gestured vaguely as if to suggest *personal reasons* were perfectly valid for being out in the middle of nowhere. And that the explanation meant more than it did.

In reality, I was attempting to casually brush against him so I might learn what his magic was.

To my annoyance, he just as casually—but far more gracefully—maneuvered out of reach.

I gave up and waited. Maybe I hadn't done a very

good job of the rapport thing, but silence was another way to draw someone into speaking.

He considered me while I pretended to stare at the front door. "I saw you and your dragon ally fight the drones."

I figured there was a point to this admission, but he didn't immediately share it with me.

I glanced askance at him. "Hope you enjoyed the show."

One corner of those full lips quirked. "How could I not when it included actual fireworks?" He hesitated. "How is it that you convinced a dragon to carry you?"

There was genuine wonder behind that question, so I decided to give him an honest answer rather than one of my more flippant set.

"Paperwork," I told him. "Lots and *lots* of paperwork."

He looked startled, then shrugged it off, uncertain whether I was joking.

Ah well. I'd tried.

"Let me start again. I'm Ronan Nightwing, the designated representative of the Faerie Governing Council in the matter of the Hale family and the artifact."

It was my turn to look startled.

"You're a fae?" I blurted, belatedly noticing the slight point to his ears.

All right, not the most pertinent question, but I'd never met a fae until this moment. It was almost unheard of for them to venture outside of Faerie. Their symbiotic relationship with their land wasn't well understood in human circles, but in simple terms, their magic was deeply rooted in Faerie, and Faerie was deeply rooted in the fae. Which meant international travel was reportedly like going around missing two of your limbs. You'd live, but no one chose it for long.

Ronan inclined his head, his expression one of polite forbearance.

"I am. And I underestimated this place's defenses as well as my own... limitations."

Limitations outside of Faerie, he must've meant. Inside their infamous land I'd heard they could do damn near anything, but anywhere else they were greatly weakened. Vulnerable.

Except he didn't *seem* vulnerable.

"So I would appreciate you and your dragon friend's assistance to get inside and search," he finished.

Someone who *wanted* to work with me? What a novelty.

I was immediately suspicious.

To buy myself time to think, I asked, "What court are you from?"

I didn't know much about fae since I hadn't dealt with them as either criminals or victims on the streets of Las Vegas, but all the old lore mentioned how they were divided into seasonal courts.

Ronan sighed as if he'd been asked this question a thousand times. "My ancestry is that of Autumn and

Summer if you trace it back far enough. But the fae have evolved over the centuries, if not as rapidly as humankind, and the courts were long ago consolidated into one. In fact, I believe around that time some of your ancestors were still convinced vulture remains would protect them from harm, while others worshipped rocks and cats."

This part of his story at least must be genuine. Exasperation like that was hard to fake.

I thought of the internet.

"I guess we still kind of worship cats."

Humor flashed in his dark eyes. "Well, we no longer organize ourselves within seasonal courts and wage war among ourselves. The kind with swords anyway." He paused, then added, "Stars, one day we might even make it to democracy and stop the political war games too."

Something about the way he said it made me think it was a much longed-for wish.

"But if it's all the same to you, I'll give you a history lesson later. We need to get this matter settled as quickly and quietly as possible before people begin to wonder just what makes this artifact so special."

"And save the hundreds of thousands of supernaturals stuck in Vegas," I pointed out.

"That too."

The order of his priorities unsettled me. But the first tactical steps of either goal were aligned… for now.

What I'd do when they diverged could be figured out then.

I looked back to Hale's mountain fortress. "Do you have jurisdiction to break in and search the premises?"

"Sort of."

I considered that for a moment. I didn't want to break the law because cops who started on that path found it a slippery slope. And I'd been around criminals enough to know they always believed their cause was justified. But skirting around a harmless gray area to save lives?

"Good enough for me. I'm Lyra, by the way."

CHAPTER TWELVE

Breaking in would be easier said than done. It took a devious mind to turn defensive magic like Hale's into a weapon of mass murder.

"You don't happen to have any 10mm rounds, do you? Because I only have one left."

Ronan frowned. "No, but I might be able to reconstitute the ones you've used." He knelt—gracefully of course—and pressed his fingertips into the dirt. Bullet casings skittered toward us from amid the fallen drone parts, reshaping themselves as they flew across the desert floor. A moment later, five bullets lay in a neat row at my feet. Two less than I'd started with.

My sparkly feet. I winced.

"I had to give them a magical propellant since the gunpowder was used up, but they should work as normal."

I was impressed but didn't want to reveal how much. "Should?"

Ronan stood, a fraction too slow, and a second frown flickered then vanished from his face so fast it was like another magic trick. How much of his limited power had that just cost him?

"There are no guns in Faerie," he explained, "so that was a first for me. But they'll do you less damage than anything that warrants shooting at."

I accepted this and reloaded.

Aurelis descended from the sky and landed close enough to send a gust of wind and dirt into both our faces. Rather than waste my breath complaining, I sneezed and proceeded to make introductions.

"Aurelis, this is Ronan Nightwing, Faerie's designated representative in the Vegas debacle. He wants our help in searching Mr. Hale's premises and apparently has jurisdiction to do it. Ronan, Aurelis, my esteemed partner and officer in the Rapid Response unit of the LVMPD."

Ronan made a courtly half bow he hadn't bothered with for me. "Pleased to make your acquaintance."

Aurelis eyed him unfavorably like a book-eating insect she was about to barbecue. "You know I was just reading *A History of Faeriecraft* about the many special-made dragon-slaying weapons crafted by fae and fae-kin over the centuries…"

I hid a wince.

Ronan's muscles shifted in readiness, but his expression remained perfectly neutral. "Oh? And did you find it interesting?"

"*Fascinating*," she breathed menacingly.

I somehow doubted Ronan had forged any dragon-slaying swords lately, and fae-kin was an umbrella term for all the other native species of Faerie, so their actions could hardly be his responsibility. Still. I cleared my throat. "Don't worry. Aurelis doesn't like anyone."

The tension didn't break, but my comment set Aurelis up for one of her favorite rants.

"It's hard for lesser beings to live up to my own majestic company." She arched her serpentine neck to show off some of that majesty. "At least books offer more interesting things to talk about than the petty trials and tribulations of humdrum lives or, fires forbid, the *weather*." She shuddered.

"There's not a lot of civilian interaction in the Rapid Response unit," I explained to Ronan's raised eyebrow. "And when there is, I tend to do most of the talking."

Aurelis flicked her tail. "Indeed. A little too much of it sometimes. Let's storm this place already."

I turned to the man who must've had at least *some* cooperation with the task force and presumably had the resources of Faerie behind him as well. "How do we do this? What's your intel?"

"Most of Hale's defenses are concentrated on keeping people out. All the entries, even the hidden ones, are heavily warded with a wide range of both magic and tech. But if you make it inside, there are additional traps for the unwary scattered about."

"I don't suppose he forgot to ward the windows?"

"Unfortunately not."

Hmm. Dragons were hard to kill, but Hale had already proven himself capable of imperiling thousands of hard-to-kill beings, so I didn't want to risk Aurelis forcing her way past. And if Ronan was capable of disabling all those wards, he wouldn't have needed to ask for help. How were we going to—

Aurelis lifted her head. "Is that another drone?"

Trusting her superior senses, I dove for cover.

But it wasn't drone fire I needed cover from. Aurelis slammed her tail into the mountainside, a dozen feet from the nearest window. Chunks of rock and dirt pelted down around us as a fissure opened up in the fortress "wall."

"Oops, false alarm," she said in satisfaction. "But look at that, a new entrance that isn't heavily warded has just opened up. Shall we?"

I shook a second smaller rockfall out of my hair and top. The grit that had gone down my jeans was going to be harder to get rid of in front of an audience. "Aurelis!" I hissed. "You're an officer of the law; you can't just—"

"He's threatening my *hoard* and *your* family, and this fae rep here is the only one with the power to give him what he wants."

I clicked my jaw shut. It was done now.

Aurelis took my silence as assent because she

widened the crevice until she could squeeze through it. Then—since she was the most indestructible of the three of us—went through first.

Nothing happened.

No screeching alarms or explosions of magic or salivating swarms of summoned monsters.

I climbed through after her and learned why.

Someone had already searched the place.

In addition to the rocks and plaster dust, more drone parts and other unidentifiable rubble littered the floor of the grand hall we stood within. The vast space was somewhere between ballroom and grandiose boardroom with a retro checkered floor and ornate furnishings against crisp white walls in a merging of modern and old. The high arched ceiling and its ostentatious chandelier comfortably accommodated a dragon, although I couldn't imagine that had been Hale's intention. Tall narrow windows offered natural light and pretty glimpses of the desert beyond. And every piece of furniture had been moved, opened, emptied, or overturned by whoever had come before us.

The acrid scent of smoke and chemicals permeated the air, and Aurelis was inspecting scorch marks around an archway leading to the front door.

She shook her head. "That couldn't have been more than two thousand degrees Fahrenheit. Hardly impressive."

But I was only half listening as I surveyed the interior with a sinking stomach.

The task force had come here after all. Or another party had. Either way, our chances of finding something useful had just dropped to almost nil.

My trainers squeaked against the tiles as I picked my way across the mess they'd left. I headed for a doorway on the opposite side of the windows. This room was for entertainment. I suspected Hale's private quarters—or at least anything he wanted hidden—would be deeper inside the mountain.

Maybe whoever had gotten here first hadn't searched the whole place? Maybe they'd found what they'd wanted here and left the rest of the dwelling intact.

"Wait," Ronan ordered.

He strode through the rubble as if it didn't exist—and once again it was impossible not to notice the fluid grace with which he moved. Impossible not to wonder whether that grace translated to the bedroom.

Not that it mattered. Right now I'd settle for taking my own pants off just so I could shake out the grit.

Ronan halted beside me in front of the door I'd been about to go through. "There's an active ward on it."

I looked for whatever had clued him in but saw nothing.

"How do you know?"

"Because fae can see magic. And it's glowing brighter than a tempest of lightning sprites drunk on maple syrup."

I took a moment to absorb that. To imagine a world where magic was a visible, tangible thing. Even dragons couldn't sense anything but the most powerful of magic, probably because they were about as magic-proof as it was possible to get anyway.

Then I got to the more pertinent implication. "Does that mean whoever got here first didn't search every room?"

Ronan shook his head, but I got the impression he was barely paying attention. He extended his palm toward the doorway without making contact. "It was the task force. But it appears Mr. Hale's security system had some sort of built-in reset."

"If they've already searched the place, why are we here?"

He replied without an ounce of self-consciousness. "Because they didn't have me with them."

I narrowed my eyes. "All right. So why weren't you with them? Why aren't you working directly with the task force instead of relying on strangers you met in the desert?"

"Why aren't you?" he countered, still more focused on the door than our conversation.

I grimaced. I would've liked to tell him it was none of his business, but that would only invite him to say the same. So I settled on the truth. Some of it anyway. "I offered. They turned me down."

He nodded without apparent judgment, and I liked him a little better for it. "In my experience, whenever a bunch of bureaucrats from different divisions converge, they can't cooperate to save themselves.

Let alone an entire city. I prefer to work independently."

I could hardly disagree after getting hung up on before I could finish stating my case. And "saving the city" was an encouraging sentiment.

But I wondered if there was any more to it. Even if he didn't want to team up with the task force, why leave Faerie and come here without backup? Okay, his people skills weren't great, but if Aurelis could find a partner willing to work with her, so could Ronan.

He withdrew his hand from the door, and those dark brown eyes held mine again. "It makes sense for me to take lead since I can spot magical traps, but if you'd guard my back against other threats while I'm distracted, I'd appreciate it."

"I can do that."

His assumption of my competence rather than incompetence was... refreshing. And I realized, as I agreed to do as he'd asked, that it made me want to try my damnedest to prove him right.

Interesting. Was that calculated or unintentional? Maybe I was underestimating his people skills. Maybe he had me right where he wanted me: uncertain yet following him into the unknown.

Ronan opened the door and slipped into the passageway beyond.

Aurelis eyed the space with a displeased expression. It would be a tight fit.

"Please don't break any more walls."

"I wasn't breaking walls. I was merely adding doorways."

I snorted and hurried to catch up to Ronan.

The hallway was just large enough for Aurelis to walk through. I was less sure it'd be large enough for her to turn around in, but she plunged in behind me before I'd thought of a polite way to ask.

Well, so much for the option of retreat.

The first doorway opened to a dining room. There were no windows, but automated magitech lights did an excellent imitation of daylight. Ronan announced it clear of magic defenses but was moving on before I had a chance to do more than digest that this room had been searched too.

I hesitated, torn between my agreement to guard his back and wanting to search the room myself. "Wait. What are we looking for?"

"You keep an eye out for things trying to kill us. I'll do the searching."

I frowned. I thought we'd gotten past the not-telling-each-other-anything stage. But he didn't wait, so I went after him.

The next door concealed a bathroom, and once again Ronan moved on after only a glance. Interesting method of searching he had. I wanted to linger to try a more traditional method, but I supposed I could come back after Ronan was done. Besides, it was clear the task force had searched here too. Even the claw-foot bathtub had been overturned.

We passed an office with an empty desk, only a dust-free rectangle and dangling cords indicating it had once held a laptop. Drawers had been left hanging open and were likewise empty but for a few pens. The task force must have seized anything even remotely useful.

Well, at least they were being thorough.

A large circular patch of disintegrated threads in the otherwise pristine Moroccan rug suggested another trap had been sprung here.

There was something eerie about these empty, ransacked rooms. Or perhaps it was the idea of venturing deeper and deeper into Hale's lair. Surely someone with the precision, power, and planning needed to erect that force field around Vegas would have anticipated our search. Anticipated and prepared for it.

Either way, my unease continued to build as we traveled deeper into the mountain. Instinct? Or plain old nerves? Since the alternative was walking myself out and back to square one, I pressed on.

By the time we passed the approximately zillionth room, I was starting to appreciate Ronan's efficiency.

But the next one made me insist we linger. The decor was jarringly different from the rest—fitted out in a dark industrial style with charcoal walls and a stark steel bed frame, softened by a gentle clutter of miscellaneous items including a dartboard, a few posters, a stack of books, an acoustic guitar, and a string of fairy lights. I guessed this belonged to Madison, the probable thief and absent daughter. More dangling cords told me her computer had been seized too. Ronan took a few steps inside, and I followed, scanning the photos that had been left on the timber dresser.

All but a few featured Madison and her dad. A younger Madison holding up a trophy with Jason beaming down at her. The pair of them posing in front of various famous tourist attractions, including the Grand Canyon, Disneyland, the Golden Gate Bridge, and Zion National Park. They seemed genuinely close.

Interesting. But it was hardly going to help us track Mr. Hale down and force him to remove the dome.

I realized Ronan might have dealt with Madison face-to-face. Given the fae had her in custody, they probably knew more than we could dig up in this pre-searched room. I turned around to ask and found him back in the hallway, waiting impatiently.

Aurelis was nowhere to be seen.

How could a dragon disappear from a hallway she couldn't turn around in? I knew she was very nearly magic-proof, but what if—

Ronan nodded toward the double doors up ahead. *Those* she would fit through.

He skipped the next few rooms altogether and pushed through the larger doors into a room as large as the first one we'd entered. Except instead of lots of open space, this one was covered in floor-to-ceiling shelves overflowing with books.

A library.

No wonder Aurelis had gone on ahead. She was

ISLA FROST

peering at the titles, her wingtips brushing lovingly along the spines. I let out a breath I hadn't known I'd been holding.

Ronan, however, ignored the books to trace his fingers over a section of wall that wasn't covered in shelves.

"What are you looking for?" I asked again.

"I think there's a passageway hidden beneath the statue. I'm trying to find the mechanism that opens it."

Statue? I turned and spotted the giant bronze sculpture of a warrior astride a horse splat bang in the middle of the room. Heaven knows how I'd missed it before. Aurelis was rubbing off on me.

She must have been capable of both drooling and eavesdropping at the same time because she walked over to the statue while Ronan continued to study the wall. Then, with all the enjoyment of a cat knocking a glass off a table, Aurelis reached out one taloned foreleg and shoved.

The heavy statue crashed against the polished concrete floor with a reverberation I felt through my feet, and I made a mental note to never get between a dragon and her hoard.

Beside me, Ronan whirled. Hundreds of crossbow bolts shot from the ceiling with a deafening crack. They pelted down around Aurelis, bouncing off her scales and littering the floor. One of them hit with enough force and just the right angle to deflect off her and smack me in the cheek.

132

I pressed a hand to my stinging face, and it came away bloody. I grimaced.

On the bright side, perhaps the task force hadn't found everything after all.

Ronan rubbed his jaw and exhaled slowly. "That was why I was looking for the mechanism."

Aurelis—who had, of course, survived the assault unscathed—was peering down at where the statue had stood. "This way's faster. But the hidden tunnel isn't sized for dragons." She riffled her wings. "Very inconsiderate."

I wasn't sure why she'd expect consideration from a man happy to murder hundreds of thousands of supernaturals to get his way, but I didn't bring it up. Ronan and I crossed the room to see the secret passage for ourselves. It was dark and creepy and definitely not dragon-sized.

I could tell by the stiffness in the way Aurelis held herself that she was upset. Not because she'd made me bleed but because she was about to be left behind. I looked around for inspiration.

"Do you think there might be a first edition of *Ulysses* in here?" I asked. She'd been looking for a copy for ages.

Her golden eyes brightened. "It's possible. I'll search for it… and, um, any references to the iron key so we can learn what Hale thinks it does."

"Good thinking."

But Aurelis had already tuned me out.

Ronan was watching our exchange with amused curiosity. "Ready?"

I looked down the dark hole again. No automated magitech lights down there. "Yep."

"Keep your gun ready and stay close. Please."

I nodded, even though I'd been doing both those things ever since we'd entered the first hallway, and I was starting to feel a little useless.

I should've known to enjoy the experience while it lasted.

CHAPTER THIRTEEN

Ronan created a ball of light out of thin air and started down the rickety stairs. I trailed after him, gun ready, feeling shortchanged. His magic was so versatile. What would it be like to *see* magic, to re-form bullets from their spent casings, to unravel complex defenses with a touch, to casually light your way? Sure, I could achieve the last with the flashlight on my phone, but my fingers itched to brush across his skin. To experience that world of possibilities. Just once.

Unfortunately, he was careful to maintain a cushion of space around him at all times. Courtesy? Or did he suspect the nature of my oddball magic?

"Hey, fae boy," Aurelis called down from above.

Ronan paused. "Yes?"

"Bring her back or I'll chargrill you. I've heard crispy fae wings are better than lobster."

"Noted," he murmured wryly, not lowering himself to point out he didn't *have* wings.

I bit back a smirk. All right. He had fae magic. I had a dragon friend. You win some you lose some.

Unlike the rest of the mountain dwelling, the surfaces of the tunnel were all rough-hewn rock. The walls were narrower than an average human passageway, but the ceiling was at least high enough not to render it super claustrophobic. So long as you didn't think about the weight of the mountain above you.

Oops.

Ronan halted several times along the way to dismantle additional magic traps and once to point out a trip wire that would have been all too easy to miss without his bright light.

What the heck was Hale keeping down here?

The passageway curved continually down and to the left. Just enough so that you couldn't see farther than a few yards ahead. The restricted visuals kept me on edge. Well, that and the eclectic mix of defenses we'd encountered so far—ranging from the latest in magitech to weirdly medieval. I felt like I was on a freaking Indiana Jones expedition, only the stakes were far higher than some ancient, forgotten treasure.

So many hostages.

So many lives on the line.

And yet if I lost even one... I imagined never again coming home to Sage's adorable self being dwarfed by my couch, and my heart squeezed.

I stayed on high alert four paces behind Ronan. The gap allowed me to see what little I could past his broad shoulders and maintained enough distance that any trap we sprang would hopefully leave one of us still standing to save the other.

I knew almost nothing about the person I was following down into the darkness. Not even necessarily what he looked like since glamour came as easily to the fae as breathing. I knew he was quiet. Not that he didn't talk, but that when he did, his words were chosen with care and revealed little. I'd yet to determine whether it was the reserved, introspective kind of quiet, the brooding or reticent type with something to hide, or the sort of quiet that came from being overly accustomed to one's own company.

My dad had taught me to pay attention to the quiet ones. The loud, the brash, the showy? They wore their hearts and falsehoods on their sleeves. Even if they were unaware of it.

The quiet ones surprised you.

There were so many questions I wanted to ask. What was Ronan hoping to find down here? Was the iron key as powerful as Hale seemed to think? What did Faerie intend to do if we couldn't find a way around Hale's demands before people started dying?

But we both needed to concentrate. And if there *was* anyone left in the residence, it would be better not to alert them to our presence.

Then again, the smashing of that statue and the

crossbow bolt trap it triggered hadn't exactly been discreet.

Perhaps it was the being underground thing, but my unease was rising with every cautious footfall.

Screw it. I needed a distraction.

"So, have you traveled outside Faerie much before this?"

"Once." A pause. "I didn't like it."

Ah. "Then how was it you ended up as the designated representative?"

"Some would consider it family privilege."

"Oh. What do you consider it?"

"Funny," he mused. "No one else has asked me that."

I waited. But whatever answers came to mind, he didn't divulge them with me.

"Maybe more people would ask for your thoughts if you deigned to share them," I grumbled.

"Perhaps," he conceded. "But then you haven't witnessed fae politicking in progress."

I swallowed my follow-up question. Because the wall Ronan had just passed began to move.

No. Not the wall.

A large, thickset figure with skin the same color and rough-hewn texture of the tunnel extricated himself soundlessly from the rock.

I froze in my tracks, heart pounding as I took in the details. The lower canines that jutted upward like crooked scissor blades on a blunt, craggy face. The hulking arms that resembled twin rock pillars, equally able to pulverize lesser flesh with minimal effort. And the red, narrow-set eyes that tracked Ronan.

"Uh, hi there," I said brightly.

Ahead, the sliver of Ronan I could still see halted and turned. More slowly, the hulking figure that was blocking so much of the tunnel and hence Ronan's light, even with his back still against the wall, turned too.

"Is this your um, lovely home?" I queried. "We mean no harm to you or yours. May the moon shine her gentle light on all your endeavors."

I was *pretty* sure the being was some type of rock troll. Trolls were rare in the city since they tended to be shy and largely solitary creatures that disliked the hustle and never-ending lights of metro living. But there was a forest troll that sold her wares in the magic market some evenings, and she'd taught me this traditional greeting of the nocturnal beings.

Yet the beady eyes that latched onto me were glazed, like someone at the end of a very long pub crawl, and strangely feral. The troll *roared*. The force of its lungs blew my hair back and rained spittle over my face.

By the pungent smell of its breath—like damp moldering soil instead of fresh earth—and the dullness of the lichen growing over its limbs and torso, it didn't seem very well.

"Uh, I didn't catch that, sorry. Do you speak English?"

In answer, the troll's arm—which as previously

noted was as thick as a rock pillar and perfect for pulverizing human flesh—swung at my skull.

I ducked. The blow whooshed over my head and struck the wall instead. The impact drove the clawed club of a hand into the hardened earth and rock deep enough to catch.

"I'll take that as a no."

Ronan did something, I guessed to keep its claws stuck in the wall a bit longer. "I don't think his language skills are the problem. See that collar around his neck? I'm pretty sure his mind's being controlled by it."

I gaped at the rusty metal band I'd assumed was crude jewelry, the glazed feral look in the troll's eyes taking on a whole new meaning.

Mind control that overpowered someone's faculties or will was—thankfully—rare and strictly regulated. The only person I knew of who'd weaponized it on a large scale in recent history was safely ensconced in Vegas's maximum-security blackout prison.

How on earth would Hale have gotten his hands on something as illegal and powerful as this?

The troll tore free of the wall with another roar, and I decided the mystery could wait.

"So what do we do?" I asked.

Ronan flickered his light to draw the troll's attention, and the creature lurched toward him with fists raised. Ronan threw up some sort of magic shield, and the first blow landed with the screech of stone on metal.

"I don't know," he said. "This was the sort of thing I was hoping you'd help with. But try not to kill him."

Aurelis could have simplified the situation a great deal by sitting on our attacker. Unfortunately, I didn't think that would work for me.

The troll bellowed in frustration, both fists beating against the invisible shield. Ronan retreated a step, and I saw his brow was furrowed in pain or concentration or maybe both.

He'd expended who knew how much of his limited magic getting this far and was too diminished to keep this up.

I rushed forward without much of a plan and kicked the troll as hard as I could in the back of the knee.

His leg buckled and he went down hard. Which was when I spotted the clasp mechanism on one side of that mind-control collar. But he recovered fast for a creature the size and build of a lumpy boulder. Too fast.

He launched himself back to his feet, pivoting as he rose to come after me.

He bellowed again, even louder this time. Or maybe it only seemed that way now that his attention was turned in my direction.

I scrambled backward, wishing for my magitech Taser that might've had a chance at neutralizing him without causing serious harm.

The troll charged after me, its height surpassing mine by several feet.

I bought myself a few moments to think by bolting

backward up the passageway—which was probably ill-advised given the trip wire—then backed myself against a wall and waited until he was close enough I could see the plaque on his protruding canines.

"Do you have healing magic?" I shouted at Ronan.

The troll's oversized hand curled into a fist.

"Yes."

"Good." I shot the troll in the foot.

The creature howled and doubled over in pain. I lunged for the clasp on the corroded metal band, praying the mechanism was as simple as it appeared and not magically locked or rusted shut. My shaking fingers struggled for the necessary precision.

The troll's huge shoulders shifted—no doubt noticing his tormentor was now within reach.

"C'mon," I muttered, willing my nails to slip under the catch before it was too late.

The metal abruptly gave way, freeing the thickset neck from its clunky collar.

And the troll slammed me into the wall.

CHAPTER FOURTEEN

"I... I'm sorry," a gravelly voice proclaimed. "I have no idea who you are... but my foot feels like it's been shot or something, and I overreacted. Sorry."

His words made me wince. I gritted my teeth to stop them rattling and picked my smarting body off the floor. At least I'd managed to protect my head.

"Um, I'm sorry too. We believe you were under some form of mind control. And I'm afraid your foot *has* been shot."

By me. But I didn't mention that part.

"Oh." The troll peered at his foot again, and a tear rolled down his lumpy cheek. "I haven't been shot in half a century. I'd forgotten how much it hurts."

Ronan cleared his throat. "I am Ronan Nightwing, and I may be able to help with that. Although"—he shot me a look I couldn't read—"we're far from Faerie, so I'll only be able to remove the bullet and offer some relief from the pain for now."

The troll's forehead corrugated. "Do you... Do either of you know who I am?"

I slumped. And here I'd hoped he'd be a fount of information. That's how it worked in the stories, wasn't it? I mean, sure, I'd saved a troll rather than a pretty maiden or wise old crone, but weren't they supposed to give you just the thing you needed for the rest of your adventure?

"No. Sorry," Ronan said. "What can you remember?"

The troll rubbed his temples in a way that made me think of Captain Gadson. "Nothing really. Well, except that I got shot once. I guess that's twice now. And I have a terrible headache. I mean, not as bad as the bullet in my foot, but quite uncomfortable."

Ronan reached up and patted his shoulder. "The memories may come back in time or with more comprehensive healing. For now, may I ease the pain?"

"Please."

I kept an eye out for trouble while Ronan tended our new friend. The troll's hulking body loosened as the pain subsided.

By the time it was done, Ronan looked worn. I felt a tad guilty for giving him more magic to cast, but it'd worked, hadn't it?

"You don't happen to remember what's at the end of this tunnel, do you?" he asked.

The troll shook his head.

Ronan released a long breath. "Figured it was worth a try. Ready to keep going, Lyra?"

"I'll come too," the troll said. "I… I don't want to be left alone right now."

So the three of us continued down the tunnel, Ronan leading the way, me four paces behind, and the troll bringing up the rear.

Lucky I'd had plenty of practice at having large hulking creatures looming behind me.

The path continued to curve disconcertingly, always to the left. Always stopping you from seeing quite far enough ahead. Like driving through dense fog. We walked in silence, which left me time to wonder how Aurelis was getting on. And whether she'd heard the troll's bellows or my gunshot through however many feet of mountain now separated us.

We'd only traveled a short distance from where we'd encountered the troll when the tunnel changed. The size of the passage shrank to about six feet high and three feet across, and the rough-hewn rock turned into smooth, polished stone. Lights blinked on at our approach as if welcoming us in. But our eight-foot forgetful new friend wasn't going to fit.

Ronan paused, doubtless searching for signs of magic or mundane traps, but after a moment ducked his head and stepped through. My creep-o-meter was at an all-time high, but I followed. We'd come too far not to find out what Hale had hidden at the end of this eerie tunnel guarded by an illegally enslaved troll.

"I'm sure we won't be long," I reassured that troll now. Even though I was anything but certain.

"Lyra's right. The tunnel ends just ahead," Ronan called back to us.

"And?" I prompted, hastening to see for myself.

"There's a storage crate."

I rounded the final curve. The tunnel dead-ended in a neat rectangle of more polished stone, and sitting almost carelessly on the floor was an ordinary black plastic storage crate.

"Want to do the honors?" Ronan asked.

I eyed him suspiciously. "Why? Is it rigged to explode or something?"

"Not magically. I can't vouch for more mundane methods though."

I stepped back a few feet and indicated my gun. "You go ahead. I'll wait at a safe distance so I can rush in and rescue you if there's trouble."

His eyes crinkled in knowing appreciation. "Thank you."

Then he bent down and lifted the lid.

The storage crate was empty.

For a moment, nothing happened.

Then something scraped behind us. I whirled in

time to see a metal door slam down from above like a guillotine, blocking our only way out.

Ronan was at my side before my brain had finished processing. "Pure iron," he breathed. "Which means this trap was meant for fae."

That didn't sound good.

"But… how?"

"No magic. Just a damn trip wire set off by opening the lid of the crate."

Not that it mattered how it had been done. It mattered how we were going to get out.

We were both still staring at the solid iron door when the ceiling before it split and swung inward, and water exploded into the tunnel. The onslaught struck the floor with punishing force and surged toward us.

I was really starting to dislike tunnels.

We were shin-deep in water in seconds, the liquid almost icy cold as it climbed our legs. The small space would fill fast.

I figured if Ronan could've done anything about stopping the water, he would've done it already. It hadn't escaped my attention that the inch-thick bars spanning the hole in the ceiling looked like solid iron too. So I searched around for some kind of hidden drain or mechanism. Maybe Hale had installed an emergency override in case he set off the trap himself? Even if he hadn't, there had to be *some* kind of drainage system.

I tried to keep my gun above the rising water as I felt

along the featureless polished stone of our prison, just in case Hale had any more nasty surprises coming for us.

If only I could shoot my way out of this one.

Ronan passed me awkwardly holding the gun aloft while I checked the lower section, figuring I needed to search there first—while I could still reach and breathe at the same time.

"Don't worry about keeping it dry. The magical propellant I put in those bullets should be waterproof."

"Oh."

The water had reached our waists, and my toes were going numb. From cold or verging panic, I wasn't sure which. I shoved the gun into my holster and belatedly remembered my phone. Sure, the seller had claimed it was waterproof, but that claim was about to be tested big time. I wasted precious seconds fishing it out. No signal.

Not that a signal would've done us any good. Aurelis was the only one who might get to us in time, and I was pretty sure a rescue attempt from above would only kill us faster.

I returned to my search, cold fingers frantically feeling for hidden imperfections in the surface of the walls. Nothing, nothing, and more nothing. I braved the gushing water to try the overhead grate, almost drowning myself in the process. But it was welded in place and wouldn't budge.

The water reached my chest.

Okay, I officially despised tunnels.

Two feet to go before the surging water hit the ceiling and I was a drowned rat.

I tried not to think about it. Tried to keep moving. Keep searching. But I couldn't bring myself to submerge my head in that icy murk and risk missing my last chance to take a breath.

As much good as that'd do me.

My fingers left bloody smears above the waterline. I must have cut them on the grating.

Maybe there *was* no override. No drain. Maybe Hale had never come here except to set up the trap in the first place.

The water reached my chin.

Shit, shit, shit. Miles was going to be so upset with me if I got myself killed trying to save him.

Ronan must have noticed my increasing panic, because he came toward me, his face tight with concern.

Probably concern over the death trap. But maybe some for me too.

"It's okay," he said, his calm tone betraying none of the tension I could read in his body. "I can create a pocket of air for us to breathe in and keep drawing oxygen from the water until we figure a way out of here."

"You can?"

I was almost too relieved to be mad at him for failing to mention that earlier.

Almost.

"Yes. So we have time. I just need to stay away from the iron door, or it'll drain my strength in seconds."

I nodded, and even on tippy-toes the motion was now enough to get water up my nose. I spluttered and Ronan crossed the last two feet between us.

"A single pocket of air will be easier to maintain, so we'll have to stick close." One of his hands found mine under the water. "Ready?"

And then I *could* nod without getting water up my nose because a bubble of air had pushed the water back.

Ronan's magic felt... incredible. I'd always thought Sage's magic felt so lovely because of her gentle soul. But perhaps it was something to do with her being half fae-kin. Because Ronan's magic was like that, only ramped up to near euphoria.

I didn't draw from him, no matter how tempting it might be. I was trying not to think about the pressure that air bubble would soon be under, but the fragility of our situation was plenty clear. Ronan needed every drop of his remaining magic. Probably more than he had. And he didn't need me breaking his concentration either.

The water had risen over my head now and must be nearly at the ceiling. Yet Ronan and I stood with our faces inches apart, breathing easily.

I willed the hand gripping his to stop trembling, hoping he'd think it was due to the cold rather than fear.

And then I realized it was true.

With the soothing feel of his magic humming

between our hands, and my lungs able to draw the air they needed, I felt something akin to all right.

It was less dark than I'd feared too. The artificial lights still blazed brightly, illuminating the water around us.

I drew in another blessed lungful of air. "Okay. What do we try first?"

Before Ronan could answer, the water clouded with millions of swirling gray particles.

The world turned dark with them.

And our precious pocket of air caved in.

CHAPTER FIFTEEN

Water rushed to fill the space, flooding up my nose and into my ears. But my attention was on Ronan. His grip on my hand had turned rigid, and through that connection, I could feel his magic bleeding out of him.

Iron filings, I realized. They'd filled our death trap with iron filings.

Iron which was poison to the fae but harmless to humans.

Half on instinct, I drew some of his magic into me before it slipped completely from reach.

It felt wrong—nothing like the wonderful, warm soothing hum I'd sensed earlier. A million tiny fiery needles flowed through our contact and spread through my body, bringing pain along with power. But the power was what mattered.

Ronan's grip went slack. Exhausted? Unconscious? Dead? I didn't have time to find out.

I shoved off the wall toward the bastard iron door, moving as fast as I could in the turbulent gritty water.

The paltry amount of his magic I'd managed to siphon was draining fast. Too fast. Not because of the iron surrounding me. But because I'd let go, and he'd had so little left to give.

I had maybe twenty seconds before it was gone.

My half breath of air wouldn't last much longer.

I swam, pushing my body as hard as I could through the murky water. But my progress felt painfully slow, stealing too many precious seconds before my fingertips brushed the slab of iron blocking us in.

Fae magic probably didn't work on iron. I fought the instinct to swim upward to a surface that wasn't there and dove down instead. At the bottom, I tried to dig my fingertips into the mountain floor the way I'd seen Ronan do in the desert, but the rocky surface was unyielding. I ground my fingers against it and used the dregs of Ronan's magic to reach out to the earth and stone below.

Please, I begged. *Please shift and rearrange yourselves to receive this slab of iron.*

Either my fingers or the earth trembled.

Please.

And then the iron door scraped against my shoulder as it dropped deeper into the mountain. Half a foot. Then another.

The magic was gone.

But the water above me stirred as it found a new

outlet, rushing through the gap that had opened between the roof of the tunnel and the top of the iron slab.

My lungs burned. I waited painstaking seconds for enough of the water to escape, then pushed myself up to stand on shaky legs. My head breached the surface, and I sucked down a lungful of air, trying to clear my eyes of stinging grit so I could search for Ronan.

He was ashen-faced and leaning heavily against the wall. But alive, conscious. Chest heaving as he dragged in oxygen. And rising up past the waterline were a pair of bedraggled black wings.

Ronan's eyes opened and found mine. "Interesting magic you've got there," he rasped.

Something shifted behind me, and I whirled, heart pounding. But it was only our troll friend.

He knocked on what remained of the iron slab. "Uh, hello? Why'd you shut the door?" He leaned down to peer through the gap.

The gap that was level with my head and would be difficult but not impossible for me to squeeze through. I was less sure about Ronan and his black wings. Not to mention how close he would need to get to that mass of iron.

"We didn't, and it's kind of a long story," I told the

troll. "Is there any way you can make that gap bigger so we can get out?"

The troll's head disappeared from view, and then his huge fist hammered into the slab. Once. Twice. Three times.

More water spilled over the slab as the iron door was driven deeper into the earth.

"Thank you. That's perfect." I turned back to Ronan. His skin was taking on more and more of the ashen hue of the iron. "Can you walk?"

He heaved himself off the wall and swayed alarmingly, his wings flaring for balance.

I rushed forward and inserted myself under his arm. "Nice wings."

He grunted. I could feel the effort it took him to accept the help, and then some of his weight settled on my shoulders. Together, we took a shaky step forward through the chest-high water.

"Why did you expend magic to hide them?"

Even weak and dripping wet as he was, the wings completed him somehow. Making sense of the particular way he held himself—when he wasn't on the brink of collapse anyway. Why he'd been so careful to maintain a distance around him.

My understanding was that the fae could *look* like anything they chose, but they couldn't change form like a shifter. And I grudgingly had to admit Ronan really was as attractive as he'd first appeared.

Maybe more so with those wings. I had a peculiar

longing to see what they looked like in all their glory—with the feathers dry and glossy and free of poisonous iron particles.

Ronan pushed himself onward. "They attract too much attention. And glamour costs us very little, even away from Faerie."

Which meant for him to be stripped of glamour now implied he must be half-dead.

"Hmm."

We reached the door, Ronan leaning more heavily on my shoulders in the presence of the iron. How was he going to heave himself through and then travel all the way up the tunnel afterward?

"Uh, troll, sir? Would you mind carrying Ronan?"

"I'd be happy to."

"I do *not* need carrying," Ronan protested.

"Really? Stand on your own two feet without me or the wall then."

He failed to comply.

"You climb through first," I ordered, channeling Miles's no-nonsense voice when one of us kids required help but was feeling stubborn. "You can use my hands as a step." I laced them together and braced myself.

But Ronan eschewed them and dragged himself through the gap with none of his usual grace.

"Stubborn ass," I muttered.

"Iron doesn't impair my hearing."

"Just your good sense?" I inquired sweetly.

The troll picked Ronan up while he was busy

scowling at me and slung him over his shoulder. Ronan's wings were tucked against his back, but even so, they nearly brushed the roof. It said something about how unwell he was that he didn't raise further objection.

I scrambled through the gap with a lot more ease—if no more grace—than he had.

Out here the water was ankle-deep. But it wasn't like my shoes could get any wetter. It *would* get awful dark ahead without Ronan's light though.

I fished my phone out of my pocket. Dead. Of course. I'd have to put it in a tub of rice later and hope for the best. It wasn't like I could take it back to the seller with the freaking force field over Las Vegas. My stomach twisted. What if my family tried to call—what if they needed me—and I didn't answer? I swallowed the sudden thickness in my throat and jutted out my chin. One obstacle at a time. I couldn't do anything about my dead phone. But getting out of the tunnel and making sure neither I nor my companions wound up dead along with it would be a step in the right direction.

"You can see fine in complete darkness, right?" I asked our nocturnal friend.

"Yep."

"Great. You go first then, and warn me when we get to that trip wire."

Long, black, and sodden minutes later, we climbed up the stairs into the light and spacious library.

"I found something!" Aurelis greeted us. "Wait, who are you?"

The troll plonked Ronan down to drip on the polished concrete.

"I'm not sure."

Aurelis gave us all a second look-over. "What happened?"

"It was a death trap. Specifically designed for fae, and Ronan has iron poisoning and…" I trailed off. "Wait, why *would* Hale go to so much trouble to kill you? What did he have to gain?"

Ronan grimaced, and I didn't know if it was from physical pain or the question. "Perhaps not me specifically. But he could've guessed someone would be sent to investigate."

"But what's the point? He's already holding an entire city hostage. Doesn't killing you kind of go against the whole negotiating thing?"

Aurelis tilted her head. "Intel maybe. If you hire the right professional, a dead fae is easier to get information from than a live one."

Necromancy she meant.

Necromancers really could raise the dead, just not for very long. The reanimated retained their memories but generally ceded their will over to the one who raised them. It wasn't quite as grisly as it sounded—some homicide detectives employed necromancers to help solve cases. So long as the body was mostly intact and only recently deceased anyway.

Realization clicked. "Wait. Does that mean Hale

would know when the trap was triggered so he could send someone to fetch the body?"

Aurelis flicked her wings in a dragon version of a shrug. "Probably."

Vague notions of concealing ourselves and then trailing whomever Hale sent stirred in my head. Except the drones and all his other defensive systems would have warned him exactly who and how many of us were here. And Ronan was poisoned and could go into shock or die for all I knew if we didn't get him help. Plus the troll's limp had grown undeniably worse on the short journey up the tunnel.

Besides, Hale had been steps ahead of us the entire time. If Ronan had entered the underground passage alone, he'd be dead. And if we stuck around, we might all still end up that way.

Time to quit while we were ahead. Or alive at least.

"I need to get to Faerie so I can heal," Ronan said tiredly. He gestured at the troll. "You should come with me so we can finish healing your bullet wound and see if we can do anything about restoring your memory."

"We'll come too," I said.

Aurelis eyeballed me. "We will?"

I flashed a smile at Ronan and the rock troll. "Excuse us a moment."

Aurelis and I found a quiet corner of the library where we could bicker without being overheard. Possibly.

"They might need our protection," I whispered, "and

I'm hoping the troll will be able to remember something useful."

Aurelis huffed. "You're not on the clock, Lyra. You're suspended, remember? It's not your duty to protect every Tom, Dick, and Harry right now. And I don't appreciate you volunteering my services without consulting me."

Ah, so that's what this was about.

"Sorry. I just assumed you'd want to pursue this as far as it goes... But I suppose you can go back to your hotel and—"

"*Pfft*. And how would you get home without me, genius?"

"Um." How to answer *without* undermining the incredibly useful boon she granted by carrying me but also without changing my stance?

"With great pain and difficulty?" I hazarded.

She snorted. "Fine. We'll go. But you'd better hope that uppity fae twit digs something useful out of the troll's head."

CHAPTER SIXTEEN

Aurelis refused to carry Ronan. Or the troll. Or me. So Ronan and I used one of the bathrooms we'd passed to rinse off the bulk of the iron filings, and then the troll carried Ronan. Even after the bullet wound in his foot reopened and began to ooze blood.

I walked beside them, keeping an eye out for threats. The dragon flew lazy circles above our heads, unable to fly slow enough to match our pace but sick of being bound to the earth.

The sun was high in the sky and glared down at us with a ferocity that made me glad for my involuntary soaking. Even if it did mean my shoes squelched and underwear chafed with every step. Our nocturnal friend was fine with the heat but had to shut his secondary eyelids, which were made of something like smoky but translucent quartz, to protect his eyes from the excessive brightness.

Thankfully, the nearest gateway to Faerie proved not to be far. Either that or Ronan let us walk aimlessly until he recovered enough to open one and pretended it had been there all along. I didn't know how the gateways worked.

But as we approached the unremarkable patch of dirt and rock, my pulse sped up. I'd never been to Faerie. To humans, it was a highly exclusive holiday destination for the rich. Which had counted me out. But if tales of its splendor had lasted through the centuries, I figured it must be pretty extraordinary.

The method of getting there turned out to be less splendid.

I stepped onto the patch of earth Ronan indicated. Except I didn't. I experienced the brief panicky sensation of not finding the ground where you expect it to be just before you fall, and then it felt like hundreds of tiny, none-too-gentle hands were yanking me downward, then sideways, upward, and backward while the cold, hard claws of something ancient raked across my brain.

Then my foot landed on solid ground and all the sensations stopped.

I opened my eyes, even though I couldn't remember shutting them, expecting to see a world of soaring trees and summer meadows—postcard-perfect wherever you looked.

Instead, everything was pure white. The floor. The walls and ceiling if either even existed. Light did not work the same way here to allow me to perceive shadows or dimensions or edges. Everything was unbroken, unending, cheerfully confounding white. Besides the people who looked normal but for the lack of shadows.

Groups of affluent travelers like you might see at an airport stood waiting, glued to their phones, or walked around followed by the new automated suitcases that trailed obediently after their owners. Why not if you had the money? And if you were holidaying in Faerie, you had the money.

Several of them were turning to stare, probably at Aurelis.

Alongside the rich tourists, there were various fae-kin striding, flying, or slithering about with matching uniforms and an officious air. Some of these were checking over the baggage of incoming visitors with spheres of glittering light. Others were guiding them from one indiscernible white spot to another.

I took it all in, trying to overlook the fact that I was dripping on the pristine white floor and would no doubt leave mud prints if I dared to walk anywhere.

"Welcome to Faerie border security," Ronan said. "They won't let you in without visas, and they won't even let me in while I'm speckled with iron fragments. But this is close enough for our purposes."

A small flying pixie approached with one of the glitterballs and a worried expression on his sharp, narrow face. "Lord Ronan, we must ask you to decontaminate you and your companions of iron—"

"Of course, Oswell. Immediately."

163

Lord Ronan?

I pivoted to look at him, and my jaw dropped. I'd been wrong before—thinking I wanted to see his wings in all their glory.

Here in the strangeness of Faerie, his magic radiated from him so powerfully I could almost grasp it just by proximity. He was perfectly dry now, and the glossy velvet black of his wing feathers begged to be touched. It didn't help that those wings were held aloft and partly outstretched—like an angel bestowing some benediction on whomever he faced. And his skin, eyes, and feathers were so bright it was as if the light itself loved him so much it converged around him just to celebrate his existence.

Turned out that "all his glory" made me gape like an idiot—for a mercifully brief moment.

He waved a hand in my direction, and a warm breeze riffled over me, caressing my clothes, hair, and skin in a way that felt unintentionally intimate—and then I was dry too. A scattering of iron fragments landed by my feet, eating away at the whiteness to reveal gold-veined marble underneath, before being vacuumed up by the pixie.

My eyes strayed back to Ronan, and I sought for something to say that wouldn't give away how off-balance I felt. "Thanks." I cleared my throat. "Um, so how does your whole relationship with Faerie thing work anyway?"

He was looking more at ease than I'd ever seen him. I hadn't realized how uncomfortable he'd been in my world until I saw him here in his.

And perhaps he was enjoying the shoe being on the other foot because humor touched those dark, shining eyes. "I suppose I did offer to give you a history lesson sometime. But I'll do you the courtesy of the short version."

I nodded my agreement. Because it was simpler than speaking.

"Ever since some ancient goddess tore Faerie from the rest of earth for her own private sanctuary, the fae have been bound to Faerie and the land is bound to us. We were assigned to be the land's guardians, our fates rooted together and forever intertwined, and so the land protects us in kind. In practical terms, that means we possess an awful lot of magic, but most of that power stops at Faerie's borders. Which is why so few ever choose to leave. The fae-kin, like Oswell and our rock troll companion here, are less powerful, but they're also at home in both worlds."

He focused his attention on our forgetful friend now. "May I attempt to heal you again?"

"Please."

Ronan laid a hand on the troll's shoulder, and the wound on his foot knit shut. In the tunnel, it had drained Ronan to remove the bullet and offer temporary pain relief. Here, if I'd blinked, I would have missed it.

The troll shook his head and pressed his hand to his face in amazement.

"I remember…" There was a note of awe in the words. "My name is Trogar of the Stone That Shall Not Break, and I was searching for the perfect rock to use for a new guest pillow when they caught me unawares. They snapped the collar on and made me tell them everything I knew about power-amplifying artifacts, then forced me down the tunnel to guard the… Oh, it was a trap!"

"Yes. I"—Ronan's gaze flicked to me—"we found that out the hard way."

"Uh, right. Of course. But did you know they wanted to trap a fae so that they could learn everything there was to know about the iron key?"

Ronan sighed. "Yes, I've put two and two together there as well."

"Oh. Then I suppose you already know the cult is planning something really big and bad, but I'm not sure what."

Ronan and I exchanged glances. "Wait. Hale's involved with a cult? *That* we didn't know."

Aurelis withdrew something from the enchanted satchel she kept under her wing and plonked it onto the floor. A book. Except Aurelis was never rough with books. Especially old ones bound in intricately engraved leather.

"*I* knew," she muttered. "I *told* you I'd found something. There are membership records of the Order of Influence hidden within the pages of this book. It caught my attention because I could smell the wrong century ink."

Order of Influence? It sounded familiar…

Ronan magicked the book into his hands as casually as I might scratch my nose.

Anxiety stole over me as my brain forged the connections. Suddenly the control collar made sense. The Order of Influence had been founded by Colton Metcalf, the man with stupidly powerful mind-control magic who'd gained international attention for his ruthless, perverted, and large-scale use of coercion and was now in prison for it. He'd brainwashed his entire small town to dance to his every whim before ambition drove him to bigger things and he was eventually caught and locked away. But only after being responsible for dozens of deaths and untold psychological damage. That collar was probably one of his early mind-control product prototypes that had somehow escaped being seized and destroyed after his arrest.

The cult had kept a low profile since Metcalf's incarceration—or at least I hadn't seen them splashed across the news. But the fact we were dealing with an entire power-hungry faction and their pooled resources instead of a single man was not a welcome development.

As if mirroring my thoughts, Ronan had gone very tense and very still, his gaze locked on the book's pages. "Well, so much for the plan then. This changes everything."

"So much for what plan? What changes everything?" I demanded.

Ronan considered our small group. "I owe you an explanation. But first I need to update the council and my contact at the Las Vegas task force on what we've learned. Excuse me."

He walked a dozen paces away into a random patch of whiteness and pulled out his phone. A phone that still worked despite our swim, I noticed with some resentment.

Cell phones were one of the instances where the magic community had adopted human technology for their convenience. Not only to fit in, but because sometimes tech trumped magic. Communication stones, scrying, telepathy, and magic mirrors just didn't provide the same practicality.

"Can you listen in on their conversation?" I whispered to Aurelis.

Her throat vibrated in a low growl. "No. He sound-proofed his immediate vicinity."

It figured.

I pulled out my own phone to see if it had miraculously fixed itself—or if the desert heat and Ronan's magic had done the job by wicking the moisture away from its important parts.

Nope.

Ugh, couldn't anything go right today? My fascination with Faerie abruptly fizzled.

My family was stuck in a death trap. One that wasn't so readily solved as the watery grave that had almost killed me and Ronan. They were stuck in a death trap and had no way to contact me. And apparently there was an entire freaking cult behind this stupid scheme.

I stared down at the book Ronan had passed me. The relevant pages were sewn in and made of a similar enough paper that even if you'd picked up every book in the library and shaken them out, you wouldn't have found it. Not without the nose of a dragon who happened to recognize the scents of different inks through the ages.

For all the trouble that had gone into hiding it, the information itself seemed superficial. A geometric symbol I assumed was the cult's emblem was stamped at the top, followed by a list of names, dates, and sums of "initiation contributions" (some of which were eye-wateringly large).

While having a potentially complete list of members may prove useful, at first glance, it didn't tell me any more than knowing Hale was part of a cult did. So what had Ronan seen that I was missing? And what the heck should Aurelis and I try next?

I wondered idly if Ken Doll #5's name was on the list. It made sense that a cult advocating the attainment of great power would attract both those who'd won the lottery of great powers and wanted more, and those who were unsatisfied with their lots and wanted an upgrade. Like a guy whose only magic ability was communicating with an extremely narrow subset of fish, for example.

I felt Ronan's magic draw near again before I lifted my eyes from the list. Damn, he was gorgeous. And I really wanted to reach out and stroke one of those glossy black wings. But even on the remote chance my interest might be reciprocated, his home was Faerie, and I wasn't leaving Vegas for either love or feathers.

His wings shifted as if he knew what I was thinking.

He better *not* know what I was thinking. Freaking Faerie magic.

"How much do you know about the iron key?" he asked, eyes on me rather than my companions.

"Nothing really."

He inclined his head, and I tried not to take offense that he seemed to have expected my ignorance. So far he'd trusted in my competence when it counted.

"The iron key is far more powerful than the world comprehends. And we would like to keep them uncomprehending."

His eyes snared mine with an intensity that made me shut up and listen. *Really* listen.

"I cannot overstate how powerful this artifact is. The fae are unable to wield it ourselves, which is the precise reason the international supernatural community chose us to be the key's custodians. Because if it gets into the wrong hands, it will make the hundreds of thousands of supernatural deaths in Las Vegas look like child's play."

An icy chill threaded around my spine and frosted my insides. All this time I'd been so focused on the horror of the situation in Vegas, it hadn't even occurred to me to wonder what was next on the perpetrator's agenda. To consider it might only be the beginning of something worse.

Not that I'd believed Hale's "correcting the power imbalance" drivel even for a second.

But now the possibilities bloomed in my mind like harmful algae, and the implications terrified me. Not only because of what might still be coming. But because it meant that for the authorities, saving my family and the rest of the supernaturals trapped inside the anti-magic zone must become a second priority.

Hells.

"The world cannot afford for Hale—or the Order of Influence—to get their hands on the iron key," Ronan continued. "So we planned to make every appearance of cooperating by returning Hale's daughter along with a perfect imitation of the artifact. That's part of why I went to Hale's residence. To get a sense of his essence so we could tailor the imitation to him. But it's out of the question now."

"Why?"

"Because they've recruited Hatshepsut."

He said it like I should know what that meant.

"Hatshepsut?"

Ronan tapped a finger to the name on the page. "A gremlin who used to reside here. She's a master craftsmith, and there's no way in Faerie we can slip an imitation past her. She can read an object's entire history just by getting close."

"Oh."

"Indeed."

"What's plan B?"

He was starting to look worn again. "There was no plan B. Hale's daughter is the only leverage point we have, and the cult is not going to lower the force field just to get her back."

He rubbed his face.

"We don't even know where they're hiding out, but I guarantee they'll be inside another of Hale's force fields. And with all the resources of the Order behind them, not even your task force is going to be able to run down every possible hideout before people start dying."

Trogar of the Stone That Shall Not Break held up his hand like a kid in the front row. "Um, sorry to interrupt. But do you mind if I go now? Time moves slowly for a rock troll, yes, but if my memory hasn't been tampered with, five months takes the record for finding a new guest pillow. And my lady wife might be wondering where I've gotten to."

"Of course," Ronan said.

I offered Trogar my hand in a human gesture widespread enough that most supernaturals understood it. "It was lovely to meet you. Thank you for your help, and may the moon shine her gentle light on all your endeavors."

He considered for a moment, then clasped my outstretched hand in his huge one.

"Yes. Thank you for freeing me from the collar. Although if our paths ever cross again, I'd appreciate it if you'd refrain from shooting me."

His face split, scissor-blade canines shifting in an unnerving but probably kindly meant smile.

I mustered a smile in return and waited as he said goodbyes to Ronan and then Aurelis.

"Where were we?" I asked after he'd winked out of sight.

"Royally screwed, I believe," said Ronan.

"Oh."

Aurelis lashed her tail. "Unacceptable. My *hoard* is behind that force field."

"Well"—I chewed my lip—"we *do* have Hale's daughter. And it's clear from all the photos of the two of them that they're close. As much as the cult wants the iron key, Hale almost certainly wants her back."

Ronan's mouth was a tight line. "Not enough to give up his power advantage."

"Not knowingly, no."

Aurelis eyed me. "What are you thinking?"

"Madison Hale is the only tool we have. So let's use her to maximum advantage."

Aurelis waited all of two seconds, then smacked me with the flat of her wing. "You haven't explained what you're thinking."

"Oh. Sorry. Well, if Faerie releases Mr. Hale's

daughter from prison… No. We need to let her escape. If she successfully escapes, where do you think she'll run to?"

Aurelis flicked her wings irritably. "I don't know. The beach to wash the Faerie out of her hair?"

Understanding human nature was not Aurelis's strong suit.

"Somewhere she feels safe. Probably her father," Ronan supplied.

"Exactly. And if his missing, vulnerable, hunted daughter rocks up on his doorstep—or force field as the case may be—is he really going to turn her away?"

A spark of interest flared in Ronan's dark eyes. "Perhaps not."

I grinned.

Ronan did not grin back. "Even if our suppositions prove accurate, and that's a lot of ifs, the force field would only be down for twenty seconds."

"Are you telling me your contacts can't devise a way to make them count?"

"I'm telling you it's risky."

"Less risky than doing nothing."

"I take your point. But she's been trying to escape for weeks. She'll be suspicious if her next attempt suddenly works."

Aurelis was looking noticeably less annoyed now. "What if this time she has an accomplice?"

Ronan considered this. "Maybe. She'll never trust a fae or fae-kin though. We'd need a human."

I nodded in agreement. Then noticed I was the only human present.

Judging by their sudden attention, Ronan and Aurelis noticed too.

Hell's sulfurous balls. How did I get myself into these situations?

CHAPTER SEVENTEEN

Ronan's magic pushed me through the entrance of the prison. "Found her trying to sneak into Faerie without a visa. I want her held overnight so the Justice Court can do some digging into her background before we deport her."

The guard—who had silvery pearlescent skin, pale hair that drifted upward like floating seaweed despite not being underwater, and a huge, lustrous shell that started a few inches above his shoulders and tapered down his back like a natural shield—nodded. "Yes, Lord Ronan."

The fae-kin guard was supposed to be a contact of Ronan's that had agreed to two minor requests in advance. One, put me in the cell next to Madison's. Two, fail to notice the tiny tracker I had taped to my foot when he searched me.

Requests that hopefully wouldn't get him into trouble later—no matter what happened tonight.

But his face was so bland that I felt a spurt of worry this *wasn't* the guard Ronan had intended to hand me over to. I glanced at Ronan for confirmation, but his face was just as unreadable.

He left without a second glance.

Which was both necessary and not at all reassuring.

The guard led me unresisting to a small empty room and ordered me to change. I floundered with the soft stretchy forest-green fabric for a minute before working out what it was. A jumpsuit. But not the ugly orange prison kind. The runway fashion kind with a fitted short-sleeved bodice and wide flaring pant legs that would move like a dress skirt.

Trust Faerie to make prison clothes glamorous.

The guard gave me a cursory pat down, failing to notice the tracker as promised, then marched me down a cellblock hallway that was even stranger than the jumpsuit. Each "cell" was like a small but classy hotel suite, except instead of a wall dividing the "suite" from the walkway, there was a row of vertical metal bars. *Golden* metal bars, but a stark reminder that we were in a prison all the same.

"You've missed today's recreation hours," the guard drawled in a bored tone, "but last meal will be served at nineteen hundred hours."

Many of the cells were unoccupied. I caught a quick glimpse of someone slouching in an armchair with their feet on the coffee table before I was steered into the adjacent cell.

The barred door clicked shut behind me with a heavy finality, causing the welcome distraction of my own curiosity to shrivel.

I drew in a breath, trying and failing to loosen the knot of tension in my gut.

I would get out. The plan would work.

A few hours earlier, Ronan had conceded that helping Madison escape was the best option available to us, but he'd also warned the prison overseer would never agree to it. "He's a stodgy, arrogant sod who's far too proud to even *pretend* to let someone escape on his watch."

I hadn't understood the gravity of that detail until Ronan had elaborated.

"I can pull some strings to make an escape possible even without the overseer's blessing. But if we go ahead with this and something goes wrong, you could be stuck in prison for as long as a week while I convince the Justice Court and Governing Council to override the overseer and let you out. And prisoners are not allowed communication with the outside world until they've earned the privilege."

A week.

That was when the stone had formed in the pit of my stomach.

A week was ample time that should all attempts to

remove the force field fail, I would never see my family again. Not even through the stinking force field.

Because by the time I got out, they'd be dead.

I drew in another deep breath and let it out slowly. No. The plan would work. I'd make it work.

But I wished Aurelis or Ronan or anyone else was here in my place.

Step one. Make contact with Madison and convince her I was on her side. Sort of.

I looked around my prison cell and hoped that despite the luxury, she was desperate to get out. The bed was large and soft. The living area, kitchenette, and fully enclosed bathroom were elegantly yet comfortably appointed. And when you stepped a few feet away from the golden bars, some kind of glamour considerably fooled you into believing there was now a fourth wall in their place.

A modest window overlooked green grass and a distant hedge of thorns that surrounded the prison grounds but looked pretty from where I was standing. The bars on the window had a similar illusion to the ones bordering the hallway—melting away to nothing until you got close.

It was far nicer than my previous motel room, and okay, it was even nicer than my apartment. But there was no privacy. No access to the outside world. No freedom. And Ronan had explained that while each room was set up with imbued glamour that allowed the prisoner to "go anywhere" in something similar to virtual reality, prisoners never actually left their cells.

I stepped up to the bars as close to Madison's cell as I could get and rapped on the natural stone wall.

"Hey," I called. "You're Madison, right?"

A few seconds passed, and I was about to thump the wall again when the reply came.

"Who's asking?"

I conjured up the photos I'd seen of her in my mind's eye, trying to guess what kind of person she'd be most receptive to. Her social media profile had shown the same heavy eye makeup and blue-tipped hair as the photo her dad had used for his message to Las Vegas, but she'd added multiple piercings since then and an air of toughness in place of vulnerability. The sort of toughness that often masked a boatload of pain.

Her voice matched her look. The epitome of withering disinterest.

I made my own tone casual, bordering on unfriendly. I needed to pique her curiosity, not sell her in the first sentence.

"I'm Lyra. My family is stuck inside your dad's force field in Vegas."

There was another lengthy pause.

I waited.

"What do you want?"

Gotcha.

"To come to a mutually beneficial arrangement."

"I'm not interested."

"You are if you don't want to spend your next sixty years in prison. The fae are elitist jerks. There's no way they're going to give up their rusty iron relic to save a few lives. Especially the lives of other species. Their lack of any response whatsoever has made that clear enough. And that means they've got no incentive to let you out of here either."

I let that sink in.

She didn't say anything, but her lack of denial told me plenty.

"So I thought, well, if I can get you back to your dad and so reunite his family, maybe he'll content himself with that and agree to reunite mine."

"What," she scoffed, "you reckon you're some sort of jailbreak expert?"

"I've already gotten closer than anyone else, haven't I? Since the fae won't let anyone see you, I figured if I got myself tossed in here on some petty charge, we could talk. And if you don't wanna do it, then I'll be out of here tomorrow anyway. So it's up to you. But I suggest you hear me out."

She grunted. "I've been trying to escape for weeks. What makes you think you can?"

"By myself? I can't. But I've figured out how *we* can."

She chewed on that for a minute. "What'd you do?"

"Huh?" The change of subject gave me whiplash.

"To get thrown in here."

Crap. I should've prepared an answer for that. Something small enough to support the rest of my story, but big enough to get me thrown into prison... in a land I'd never seen beyond border security and now this cell. Something that would appeal to her.

"Snuck in and nicked a fae's wing feather."

I waited for her reaction. One. Two. Three. Four—

Madison snorted. "I'm impressed you got close enough."

Phew. Seemed we were bonding.

"Why'd you want the key thing anyway?" I asked.

More silence. And somehow even without seeing her, I sensed it was heavier this time.

"Do you know what my magic is?"

"Yes. I needed to come up with a way to get us out of here, so I did my research. It's like a Harry Potter invisibility cloak, right?"

"When I was five years old, I was in my room playing and Mom was with me, folding the laundry, when glass shattered downstairs. Dad was out demonstrating his services to some big shot, so there was no one else around. And Mom's magic was useless—she could bake cookies that would melt in your mouth and guarantee you sweet dreams, but that was it. So she grabbed one of Dad's golf clubs and told me to hide."

I swallowed. No longer sure I wanted to hear this story.

"I don't know why she didn't just let me conceal her too. My magic was still weak—we'd only just figured out I could hide better than most people—but it would've been enough."

That was how magic worked in human kids born since the revolution. They came into full power at puberty, but the seeds were there much earlier, usually around the time they started to walk. Sometimes it was obvious, like a baby with water magic having a little *too* much fun in the bath, but for lesser or more nuanced gifts, it could remain a mystery until middle school.

Of course, for some magics, even a trickle of power was enough to cause chaos. Baby formulas and toddler supplements *Now with natural magic-dampening effects!* had never been more popular.

Madison plowed onward through the tale I was increasingly sure I didn't want to reach the end of.

"Her motherly instincts wanted to protect me, I guess. She made me promise I'd stay hidden no matter what, then slipped outside my room and crouched by the top of the stairs with the stupid 5-iron. I didn't understand. I just knew there was something wrong with her smile."

"I'm sorry, Madison." I'd seen Mr. Hale had been widowed over a decade ago and hadn't taken the time to learn how she'd died. "You don't have to—"

"No. You ought to understand if we're going to work together."

I forced my voice to stay even. "Okay."

"It was a guy high on pixie dust who'd decided to have a little fun robbing houses. He had fire magic. When he saw Mom with the club, he freaked out and burned her alive."

Madison's voice was cool, detached, like it didn't matter. But neither of us was fooled. Even before she added, "I'll never forget the screams… or the smell."

"I'm so, so sorry."

"Sure, everyone's sorry," she said bitterly. "Anyway, I spent the next ten years or so scared out of my mind. Therapy helped, but not enough. When I turned sixteen, I was just so damn sick of being afraid all the time that I vowed I'd find a way to never feel powerless again." Her voice strengthened, ringing with conviction.

I almost felt bad now for using her to lure her dad into law enforcement's hands.

Almost.

There were ways to become empowered that didn't require putting the value of your life above everyone else's.

But it shed new light on why the well-to-do Hale family had fallen prey to the Order of Influence. Madison was focused on her own pain. But how must her father have felt, possessing a powerful defensive magic and failing to protect what mattered most?

No wonder he was messed up.

The one upside to this tragic backstory was that it must make Hale more likely to lower the force field for the daughter who needed him. How could he live with failing his family a second time?

If I could get Madison out of here that was.

"Wow. That's some story," I said after a minute.

She grunted an acknowledgment. I left the ball in

her court, sensing she'd be turned off by any eagerness on my part and that she'd prefer to feel in control of our deal. The silence between us stretched until she asked, "What's your family like?"

The stone in my stomach grew heavier. Who knew breaking out of prison together would need to be such a bonding experience?

I'd borrowed Ronan's phone and called home before coming here. Trying very hard not to think about how it might be the last time we ever spoke.

"They're the best," I said simply. I was tempted to leave it at that, but knew that wouldn't cut it.

"I'm adopted. Well, we all are. Saved from the foster system by Miles. Miles is… Well, I guess most people would describe him as a male vampire who happens to like other male vampires, but that stuff's incidental. He's the kindest, sincerest, most selfless person I know, and he has a mean sense of humor too. Although if I had to choose between starvation and eating something he cooked, it'd be a near thing."

Madison let out an amused huff, but my attention was miles away. Continents away. Recalling our last conversation.

"Milksucker," he'd greeted me affectionately, making my heart clench with that single word. "How are you holding up? I know this can't be easy for you."

In kindergarten, some kids had told me my dad was a bloodsucker. Uncomprehending, I'd gone home and asked Miles if it was true, and he'd said something that amounted to, "only if you're a milksucker." He hadn't anticipated that the next day I'd go back to school and proudly proclaim myself as a milksucker to anyone who'd listen.

Years later, he still used the pet name sometimes, particularly when he was worried I was about to run off and do something harebrained again.

Since I'd been about to do just that, I'd glossed over my response and asked, "How is everyone?"

"We're okay, darling. I let everyone stay home from school and we had a sword fight for Archer, a picnic for Sage, and a bug hunt for Blake. Blake was looking a little droopy, so I've sent him to bed early. But don't think I didn't notice you avoided answering *my* question. A little birdie told me you left the city. You're not doing anything unwise are you?"

I'd been saved from having to answer by Sage. "Is that Lyra? I wanna talk to her!"

Miles passed her the phone. "Hello! Did you hear about our picnic? A little gecko tried to drink from my cup!"

"Wow, really? That sounds fun! And what did you have to eat?"

"I heard that," Dad called. "Stop checking up on me. You survived until adulthood, didn't you?"

Sage and I both ignored him. "Daddy tried to make a chicken pasta salad, but it smelled real bad, so I accidentally knocked the pan onto the floor like you taught us, and then we got takeout salads and pizza."

"Good girl."

"I'll send you the bill," Miles threatened.

"Take me into the bathroom so Daddy can't overhear."

"Okay!"

I waited until I heard the door slam shut. He'd probably still overhear, but it would be harder for him to cut off my line of questioning. "All right, now tell me how Dad's doing?"

"He's slow without his magic. And he drank *three* bags of blood today." Her voice lowered to a whisper. "Archer says it's because a man wants to hurt us, but that can't be right… can it?"

I gripped the phone so hard it was a wonder it hadn't snapped, but I forced my tone to be bright. "Those are some excellent police reporting skills you have there, young lady. Thank you."

"Daddy's threatening to break down the door. Should I give you back to him?"

"That would probably be best," I'd agreed. "But remember I love you forever and ever." And then I'd been glad it wasn't a video call so neither she nor Dad could see me cry.

Now I blinked back tears again and realized I'd hardly started answering Madison's question.

I cleared my throat. "So um, that's Dad. Then there's Blake…"

I talked until I choked up. And when I'd finished, Madison said quietly, "I can't guarantee my father will do what you're hoping. But I promise if you get me out of here, I'll do everything I can to convince him to."

"Thank you."

"Right. Tell me how this jailbreak is going to work…"

CHAPTER EIGHTEEN

Before I could answer, the lights brightened to almost uncomfortable levels and a voice came over the speakers. "Please prepare to be searched."

"What's going on?" I hissed.

"A random search of every prisoner and cell." Madison reverted to her tone of bored disinterest. "Happens about once a week, so you lucked out."

The tracker concealed in a skin patch on my heel abruptly seemed to double in size.

No one had been willing to trust Madison to stick with me after we escaped, so that tracker was our safeguard.

What would happen if I got caught with it? Would the guards pay me extra attention, making escape far harder? Or worse, relocate me to a more secure location and make escape impossible? Even if neither of those things happened, what if Madison heard a guard questioning me about a tracker just after I'd won her trust?

I glanced surreptitiously around my cell. There were plenty of hiding places, but after years of conducting these searches, the prison guards doubtless knew them better than I did. It was probably best to leave the tracker where it was. Or flush it down the toilet. Ronan had assured me the bathrooms were unmonitored.

I deliberated for three agonizing seconds, then strode to the bathroom, shut the door behind me, and flushed the tracker down the drain.

My top priority was getting us out of here, and there were other, albeit less convenient, ways to track a person.

The risk of losing Madison's trust or screwing up the careful escape plan was too great.

But I was equally aware that if I pulled off the jailbreak only to lose Madison, we would lose the one card we'd been given in this lethal game the cult had set up for us.

It wasn't long before a guard—an ethereal sprite with lilac hair as fine as dandelion fluff and delicate translucent wings—let herself into my cell. She was about four feet tall with a face that would make a model weep, and she turned on me with a glower that forced me back a step.

"Don't even think of trying anything, new girl. I'm tougher than I look."

She proceeded to zip around my room, waving a wand—a security scanning wand rather than the kind with stars and glitter—over every inch. I put two and two together and figured it must be magicked to detect anything that didn't come standard issue with the cell.

That done, she gave me another warning glower and proceeded to pat me down, dainty hands moving swiftly and impersonally through the examination.

Her magic brushed against mine, skimming over my skin as delicately as her translucent dragonfly wings skimmed the air. It felt strange—different from anything I'd experienced before, and curiosity got the better of me.

I reached for it.

The world tilted alarmingly. Then I was somewhere else.

Some*one* else, I realized as I handed a pair of uniformed guards their evening coffee fix.

The guards smiled and thanked me, and I shoved my hands into my white coat pockets to hide their trembling. They shouldn't have thanked me. Not today.

"Are you all right, Doc?" the one on the left asked me. The kid was barely older than my son. "You don't look so hot."

"Fine," I lied. Then freed a hand to wave at the ever-present menace of the dome. "Just tired from everything going on. You know."

The guard smiled again, sympathetic this time. "Sure. It's given you a bunch of extra work. Go on in." He opened the gate, and I trod the familiar path through the security checkpoint to the medical supply room.

I unlocked the door, using a manual key since the magitech ID reader was down, and proceeded past the IV supplies I'd been using since the anti-magic field threw everything into chaos. Instead, I stopped at a rack I'd rarely drawn from throughout the decade I'd worked here.

My palms started to sweat as I loaded the alternate IV bags onto the trolley. Would anyone notice the labels were different before it was too late? What would happen to my son if they did?

He'd been snatched from student housing at Caltech and held hostage to force my hand. Even if everything went right and I followed their instructions to the letter, I couldn't be certain the kidnappers would let him go as promised.

But I had to try. Because instinct told me they'd certainly do as they promised and send him home to me in little pieces if I didn't.

The trolley rolled easily along the hospital-grade sheet tile flooring as I checked each sleeping prison inmate's data. Their vitals. Muscle tone. Brain function. Latest blood test results. When the gel that prevented pressure sores would next need changing. All that and more.

Which of the fifty-eight inmates was the kidnapper's real objective?

The notorious supernatural Serpent Strangler who'd slipped into dozens of children's bedrooms, silently cut off the blood flow to their brains through constriction with his own polymorphous body, and then eaten the evidence whole? The mind-controlling psychopath who'd made an entire town comply with his every twisted whim for years before anyone noticed—and often had unsettlingly high brain activity despite his sleep state? The lunatic who tortured his victims by using his off-the-charts healing magic to transplant limbs from multiple species to create Frankenstein levels of disfigurement?

I shook my head. It didn't matter. There were no good options. I switched out the IV bags on all of them. Then turned off the alarms that would sound an alert if any of the inmates' stats went outside acceptable parameters.

It took a few minutes longer than usual thanks to my fumbling nerves. But still under half an hour to do the unthinkable.

Moments later, I walked out of Nevada State Blackout Prison, finding the same pair of guards slumped on the ground from their sedative-laced coffees. I knelt to check their pulses. Alive. Thank heavens. But would the inmates leave them that way?

Outside, I looked up at the night sky, wishing I could see it without the dome in case it was the last time I'd gaze upon it as a free man.

But if wishes had power, I wouldn't have been forced into this reprehensible act to begin with.

I'd wait thirty minutes to give the inmates sufficient time to escape. Then I would turn myself in to the police.

My whole body jolted as if waking from one of those falling dreams. And I was Lyra again. Standing in front of the guard who was still patting me down.

"Ticklish are you? Hold still or I'll turn your limbs to wood."

My brain scrambled to make sense of what had just happened.

It had felt like I'd been "gone" for minutes. It had felt so real.

"Do you—" I swallowed.

The sprite's sharp glittering gaze speared me.

"Do you have some sort of clairvoyant or truth-seeing magic?" I asked.

Normally I gained at least some sense of what someone's magic could do as soon as I drew on it. But this time the magic had sucked me in so fast I hadn't had the chance.

She huffed, turned me around, and continued the pat down. "None of your business, new girl. I know you got caught trying to sneak into Faerie. What are you, some sort of Faerie perv?"

"No, I..." I shut my mouth. She wasn't going to tell me, and it didn't matter. If there was any chance that what I'd seen was not just some strange figment of my overstressed imagination—and somehow I knew it wasn't—I had to warn Gadson.

"I need to talk to my boss," I blurted, just as the guard finished up and reached the barred door of my cell. How could I convince her? I couldn't use Ronan's name where Madison might overhear. "As soon as possible. Please. It's important."

The sprite laughed. It pealed high and sweet like the

ring of a quarter-full wineglass. "It's just one night in prison, perv. You'll be fine."

She opened the door, sped through it, and clanged it shut.

"No, please. You don't understand. It's vital—"

The lock clicked, and the lights in my room dimmed again. I dashed after her and gripped the bars, imagining fifty-eight of the country's most vicious criminals roaming free in my beloved city. And while the LVMPD was already stretched to near breaking point in the current crisis. But the guard was already gone.

I sagged to the floor, feeling sick on a whole new level.

What if it was happening tonight? Except the vision had been so visceral, so detailed. Future telling didn't usually work like that.

What if it had already happened?

What if all those criminals were out there right now, prowling the shadowy streets so very, very close to my family's apartment?

I'd never felt the constraints of being cut off from the outside world so keenly.

But there was nothing I could do. Not now. I had to stay focused on my current task. The reason I was here cut off from the world in the first place. Otherwise, it'd all be for nothing.

Fortunately, I had a little while to compose myself before all the other cell lights dimmed and Madison and I returned to our shared wall.

When we did, she asked quietly, "Talking to this boss of yours and whatever you flushed down the toilet wasn't crucial to your escape plan, was it?"

"Nope."

The answer, as short as it was, failed to convince either of us.

CHAPTER NINETEEN

The next hours passed with excruciating slowness. I was extra on edge after the unsettling vision. If I could've enacted the escape plan sooner, I would've done it in a heartbeat. But I knew full well from having a front-row seat to all of Ronan's careful planning that without his subtle but powerful aid, we'd never make it.

My only option was to wait.

Which was excruciating.

I tried to catch some sleep while I could, drifting in and out in fitful starts.

Why break out a whole prisonful of the country's worst criminals?

In a twisted quirk of fate, my sole consolation was that while the force field and anti-magic devices were still in place, the sadistic escapees would have no more magic than anyone else. Which rendered them far from harmless but at least a whole lot less catastrophically dangerous.

Nor could they leave the city. Which was both comforting and terrifying.

Those details left me questioning whether the cult had engineered the jailbreak on top of everything else. Or if an opportunistic third party was taking advantage of the citywide chaos and the sleeping beauty's lack of magic, which had left the prisoners kept under by medical intervention alone.

Neither option was okay.

Madison woke me from stressful dreams shortly before the evening meal. To make sure I'd see the guard delivering them coming, I positioned myself against the golden bars, inside the glamour threshold that transformed those bars into a wall.

I had to play this exactly right, or our escape attempt was over before it began.

Finally he appeared. A single guard with a self-flying metal service trolley that followed him silently down the hallway.

Ronan had promised to ensure the guard delivering evening meals would be a particular gnome with metal-working magic running through his veins. I let out a breath when the gray-skinned figure coming toward me at least looked the part. Though in Faerie, that wasn't as reassuring as it might have been.

The gnome was oblivious to his part in our machinations.

He pushed a tray through the slot in the bars, and I grabbed for it like I was starving, contriving to brush his hand in the process. Ronan had misreported my magic so the guard wouldn't find the touch suspicious.

Maintaining the famished act, I hurried to the far side of my cell, clutching the tray, and sat down on the floor beneath the window. Then I sent my rapidly dwindling supply of stolen magic up the wall to slice through the bars. First on my window, then Madison's. The gnome's magic parted the metal like a knife through butter, and I topped and tailed the bars as if they were green beans.

The bars stayed where they were. Which was the plan. For now. And I dug into my meal as if I actually had an appetite.

I didn't expect it to be *good*. But it was. Turned out I was hungry after all.

I smirked, imagining the look on Dad's face when I told him even prison food was loads better than his cooking.

But my mirth soon faded, and I was back to having nothing to do except wait and hope. Hope that my weird magic-induced vision was a delusion—or at least an event far enough into the future that I could warn Gadson in time. Hope that my family was safe. Hope that the night would prevent any guards from noticing the hairline fissures in the bars. Hope that Madison would stick to her part of the bargain and not sneak out without me. And wait for the distraction

Ronan had promised would come after mandatory lights out.

I spent the intervening hours alternating between fitful sleep and lying wide awake in the dark, thinking of all the things that could go wrong. So *many* glaringly obvious things that I wondered why we'd ever gone with this plan in the first place.

What if we didn't succeed in our escape? What if we did and Madison didn't run to her father like we were counting on? What if Madison betrayed me and we needed that tracker I'd flushed?

The list went on. So many possibilities. So few of them good.

My roiling stomach suggested perhaps I shouldn't have eaten after all.

And then I heard it. The distant sounds of bells and singing and raucous laughter drifting in through my open window.

Time to go.

I couldn't hear Madison on the other side of the wall, but I couldn't exactly shout out to her either. I had to trust that she was awake and had recognized the signal. That she was making her way to the window as I was.

I switched on my bathroom light, scrunching my eyes shut to protect my night vision, and pulled the door closed. With luck, even after Ronan's urgent questions for a particular night guard were answered and the guard returned to their surveillance post, it would take them a couple of minutes to realize Madison and I weren't just in the unmonitored bathrooms.

I rushed over to the external wall and slid my window all the way open in one quick movement. The bars slipped free without a hitch. I scrambled through the gap and slotted them back into place, hoping I was buying us extra seconds rather than squandering them.

Madison was already invisible. The only reason I knew she was there in the silvery moonlight was the bars that disappeared and reappeared in her own window. Her magic didn't stop sound, but I couldn't hear a thing over the racket Ronan had arranged under a glamoured identity—paying a troupe of little noisy fae-kin to sing and dance three times around the hedge as a joke for a guard's birthday.

After a brief internal debate, I held on to the final bar as a makeshift weapon. One I hoped I wouldn't have to use. Then hunkered down against the stone wall, making myself as small a smudge in the darkness as possible. My heart was thudding in my ears, and the raucous din showed no signs of slowing, making it impossible to listen out for Madison. I could only hope she wouldn't ditch me here, leaving me stranded as a handy distraction while she made her own escape.

When she grabbed my hand as we'd agreed upon, I had to stifle a yelp. Then I was invisible too, and we slunk across the soft grass toward the prison entrance— the only gap in the living wall of thorns that surrounded the prison grounds.

We didn't dare speak even with the cover of the racket. Pairs of guards patrolled the grounds on a regular basis, and some of them would have hearing that rivaled Aurelis's.

Hence the racket.

I'd seen and experienced a lot of things in my six months as a cop. But walking in the moonlit grounds of a Faerie prison hand in hand with an invisible cult member and looking right through my own feet to the ground below was downright peculiar. Ronan had warned us to avoid the diminutive insectoid fae-kin who made their homes in grassy clearings. They were rare and tough as nails but would raise an awful ruckus if we stepped on one.

I hadn't been sure in my climate-controlled cell, but the night was balmy and perfect, with an unfamiliar sweetness hanging in the air. The grass underfoot was soft and spongy, like walking on cushioned velvet. I glanced upward between steps. I'd heard the moon was always full in Faerie, and tonight was no exception. Yet somehow the stars seemed to shine brighter against the indigo darkness of the sky, rather than becoming harder to see as they did on earth.

That was when I saw the patrol.

One of the guards was tall and gangly with alder bark skin and leafy hair in autumnal orange. A forest troll or male tree dryad perhaps. The other figure was small and slender but walked with the lithe grace of a predator. A shifter, probably feline.

The shifter tilted her head and sniffed the air.

Not good.

She was in human form, which would dull her senses a little, and the gentle breeze was blowing our scent away from her—for now. But something must have triggered her instincts. I froze, squeezing Madison's hand. And though I couldn't see her any more than I could see myself, I knew the exact moment she spotted the incoming patrol from the way her hand stiffened in mine.

What would be better? To continue on and risk making a sound or scent that would give us away? Or stay frozen in place, barely breathing, and hope they'd stroll right by us? Except at some point, that would put the shifter upwind of us.

Go then.

Heart pounding, I tugged Madison forward again. My gaze flicked between the guards and each placement of my next step. The guards were walking at a casual pace, but we had to increase our speed if we wanted to get well past them before they drew too near. Hoping Madison would put two and two together, I quickened my careful pace.

She kept up.

The shifter sniffed the air a second time, closer now. Her eyes reflected the moonlight, and I saw them shift to the grass near our feet.

Soft grass. Flattening beneath our weight with every step. The movement visible to a cat even in the darkness.

I squeezed Madison's hand again, trying to prepare her, and tightened my grip on the bar. Our invisibility would give us a slight edge. But I couldn't fight one-handed and I was unarmed except for the bar. There was no way I could take on both guards and win.

The shifter murmured something to her companion, then raised her voice. "We know you're there. Surrender and we'll return you safely to your cells. Run and we will detain you using whatever force necessary."

Madison wrenched her hand from mine, leaving me with maybe thirty seconds of invisibility. The grass must have betrayed her movement because the shifter's eyes darted across the ground and sprang forward, her body morphing in mid-air to that of a sphinx. The dryad or troll charged after her.

I rushed to intercept the shifter, dread unfurling in my gut at what I was about to do. What I'd *have* to do to take her down.

Shifters' rapid ability to heal was legendary, and that combined with their strength and speed made them nearly impossible to restrain while they were still conscious. Normal LVMPD protocol was a full voltage Taser, a heavy dose of tranquilizer, and a pair of magitech cuffs.

I had none of those things.

Which meant my only option was to injure her so badly her body's healing capacity would be temporarily overloaded.

Since she was a shifter, that meant breaking her

spine, causing serious internal hemorrhaging, or delivering a blow to her head that would kill anyone else. Misjudge the blow and it could kill a shifter too.

All because she was doing her job.

I wasn't a stranger to violence, but any other time I'd inflicted bodily harm, I'd been doing it to protect someone. This was my first experience on the other side, and I didn't like it one bit.

Either Madison's magic was already fading or the shifter sensed me through some other means, because she swerved to meet me just as I slammed the metal bar down with all my strength.

I'd been aiming for her back, but the bar glanced off the side of her skull. Bone cracked and caved in, and the sleek, muscular body of the sphinx crumpled to the grass.

Please don't be dead.

Feeling sick, I swerved to see the second guard's horror and outrage directed right at me. I was no longer invisible.

I braced myself against my own horror and the imminent attack.

But it never came.

Burgundy sap-like blood gushed down the dryad-troll's knobbly chest as an invisible weapon opened up his throat.

He fell forward, legs collapsing beneath him as he reached for the gaping wound like his hands alone could stop the blood.

But neither trolls nor dryads had shifters' powers of healing.

"What are you waiting for? Let's go!" Madison hissed.

But I was cold and hot and frozen, rooted to the ground in shock, and time seemed to flow sluggishly around me.

There was nothing sluggish about the blood spilling into the grass.

My head pounded, and the raucous laughter and music that continued unabated felt like some surreal and obnoxious joke.

"I can't," I choked out. "He'll die without immediate help."

"So?" Madison oozed teenage contempt. "It's just a tree thing." When I didn't move, she added, "Our families are more important!"

I shook my head like it could shake off the magnitude of this decision—the very real risk of never seeing my family again—and sank to the grass between the shifter and dryad-troll's bodies.

Madison's voice rose in fear or disbelief. "Get up! Come now, or I'll leave without you!"

I reached for the shifter, relieved to feel her magic pressing against my palm, to see the way her skull was already reshaping itself. She would live.

I tugged on that healing magic—the only magic I *could* siphon from a shifter—and reached for the dryad-troll too, pushing the healing power into his woody flesh and toward the wound at his neck that was still pumping out blood.

It closed. Slowly. So, so slowly.

Lucky shifter healing magic worked autonomously because I had zero medical expertise.

I poured an extra few seconds of magic into him, aware he could still die and hoping it would somehow help with all the blood he'd already lost.

He took a big shuddering breath. His first in a while, I realized. And relief flooded through me, quickly overwhelmed by fear. I had to get out of here.

Heart in my throat, I snatched the bar I'd dropped and shoved myself up onto unsteady legs. "Madison?"

I wasn't surprised when she didn't answer.

Our plan had been to walk right past the distracted guards at the gate, and Madison had likely done exactly that. But without her magic, I'd have to find another way out.

If I didn't, I'd be stuck here. Maybe indefinitely. Because after aiding Madison's escape and very almost murdering two of the prison guards, not even Ronan would be able to get me released anytime soon. If at all.

Keeping low, I sprinted for the hedge of thorns, heedless now of any possible tiny ground dwellers. There could only be seconds before the alarm was raised and all hell broke loose.

Up close, the living blockade was a chaotic forest of tangled stems that stretched ten feet deep and over twice my height, wicked thorns glinting like crystal in the moonlight. A perfect amalgamation of beauty and intimidation. I eyed the army of slender needles and swallowed.

But I'd run out of options the moment I'd stayed behind.

This was my only way out.

The nearest woody stem yielded grudgingly beneath my fingers, the thorns slicing into my skin and taking their share of blood as payment. I pushed another one aside with the bar I still clutched and eased into the space they'd vacated. Despite my care, wickedly sharp thorns stabbed me in a dozen places through my jumpsuit.

Ouch.

But I didn't stop, wresting myself out of one set of thorns straight into another. Skin and fabric tore alike. But the wounds were superficial compared to what we'd done to the guards.

The hair on my neck prickled as I imagined the shifter stirring behind me. Felt her fierce gaze lock onto my back. Anticipated the vengeful claws ripping into my flesh.

I worked faster, using the bar to shove more branches out of my way and repeatedly stabbing myself on their bloodthirsty spines.

Better than a shifter's claws.

Better than never seeing my family again.

I was halfway through when I discovered the trap for what it was.

The stems that had yielded so grudgingly out of my path came alive with motion. I ducked one grasping stem, which suddenly resembled a barbed tentacle more than any plant. But others struck and found their marks. Snaking around my arms, waist, and legs and pinning me in place with the thorns they buried in my flesh. I cried out in pain, adrenaline and instinct shouting at me to run, to fight, to flee.

But I couldn't fight. To so much as twitch would be excruciating. And each irregular, shallow breath earned fresh lances of fiery pain from the embedded needles.

The hedge had won.

I tried to calm my ragged breathing, but the black hole of despair swallowed me. I'd failed. Failed my family. Failed Ronan and Aurelis. Failed the supernaturals of Las Vegas. And the consequences of that were so unbearable I couldn't even think of them.

An alarm began wailing.

And the black hole of despair spat me out again. Because that was when I felt something. Something besides the pain and fear and failure.

The faint brush of the plant's magic.

I'd never sensed magic from anything except other sapient beings, but I supposed this Faerie plant *was* sapient.

The magic was alien, metallic for some reason, and hungry.

Bracing myself for who knew what, I drew on it.

Nothing happened. No flood of power nudged me

toward a newfound ability. The strange magic filled me but gave me nothing.

Except...

The hedge's grip loosened. The sharp thorns skewering me in place withdrew, and the stems returned to their dormant, waiting state. As if, with the plant's magic flowing through me, it no longer recognized me as separate from itself. As prey or threat or captive.

Barely daring to breathe, I reached out and brushed the nearest stem, drawing more magic from it. The movement caused fiery twinges of protest throughout my bleeding body, but it was nothing compared to when the thorns were still embedded. And no branches snaked to re-ensnare me.

Running footsteps thudded past from the prison side of the hedge, barely audible over the wailing alarm.

And then I was through to the other side, stumbling toward the gateway Ronan had pointed out on my way in. Had that really been mere hours ago?

I dove into the hole that looked like a giant prairie dog burrow—the grabby hands and mind-combing far less bothersome this time compared to my torn and bloody flesh—and tumbled out into an alleyway in Pahrump.

Ronan released his concealment glamour and strode toward me. "What happened? Why are you covered in blood? And where's Madison?"

CHAPTER TWENTY

"Where's Aurelis?" I countered.

I searched the lightening sky, hoping to catch a glimpse of her. In part to give me a moment to collect myself, in part to conceal the rush of relief I felt at seeing Ronan, but mostly because I was really, really hoping my dragon partner was tailing Madison.

Ronan had arranged for the gateway to spit us out in a quiet alley in Pahrump. A central location large enough to ensure Madison and I would be able to access a car and any other resources she deemed necessary, then drive in just about any direction. We'd wanted things to move along as quickly as possible between her escape and her ending up at her father's hideout.

Unfortunately, that also meant that if Madison had gotten away from us, it would make her very hard to track down.

Aurelis was supposed to be watching this alley while

Ronan was busy distracting the guard on surveillance duty and I was busy escaping. Just in case something went wrong. Like it had.

Regardless of whether Madison's magic worked on dragons—something that depended on a power's strength and whether it worked directly on others; i.e., influencing the minds of onlookers, versus passively; i.e., turning Madison literally invisible—Aurelis should still be able to smell and hear her coming through the gateway. Or so we'd figured. *Should* being the operative word.

"I don't know," Ronan said. "I only just arrived myself. Why are you covered in blood?"

"Forget about the blood. I had to flush the tracker, and Madison ought to have come through here minutes ahead of me. We have to find her."

Which was true. But it was also true that even with all the lacerations, the worst of the blood wasn't mine, and I wasn't ready to rehash what had happened. What I'd done. What I'd come so close to doing...

One thing was for sure, I'd never be welcome in Faerie again.

"Forget about the blood?" Ronan repeated. "Your clothing's torn to shreds, and you look like you're a victim in some B-grade horror film."

"I've looked worse," I assured him, patting my pockets for a phone that wasn't there. "You should've seen me covered in extraterrestrial walrus gunk." I belatedly remembered my phone didn't work anyway.

"Now give me your phone so I can call Aurelis. Please."

Mutely, he handed it over along with one of his magitech earbuds. Then he won my adoration forever by handing me the coffee he'd been drinking too.

"What?" Aurelis answered, loading an impressive amount of irritation into that single word.

I took a swig of the not-quite-hot heavenly liquid. "Do you have eyes on— I mean, do you know where Madison is?"

Aurelis huffed. "I *did* about three minutes ago. Until the little snot caught sight of me and ran into a shopping mall with a dozen exits."

"And now?"

"Do you know how hard it is to track a human by scent alone? I'm not a bloodhound. Why didn't you plant the tracker?"

I shut my eyes. Took a deep breath. "Okay. She's probably stealing a car as we speak. Can you get to the shopping center's parking lot?"

"I don't know. Can you stop asking stupid questions? I'm here, but I've lost her scent and there's more than one parking area. She could well be gone already."

I leaned against the dirty brick wall and resisted thudding my head against it. Mostly because I didn't want to risk spilling the coffee. "Right. Well, there are only a few highways out of Pahrump. You can fly along one and search for her while Ronan and I acquire fast cars and try the other routes."

"Or I can hack into traffic and security footage and find her that way."

"You can?"

The familiar sound of beating wings made me raise my eyes to the roofline. Aurelis tucked her wings at the last possible moment and landed neatly on the street. She gave me a once-over.

"I know, I know," I said, trying to stave off whatever cutting comment she had for me and speed things along. "My clothing's ripped to shreds, I'm covered in blood, and I probably have hedge in my hair. Now care to explain this hacking ability of yours I've never heard about?"

"Actually, I was going to say I'm glad you're okay."

Oh. "Really?"

"No. But even ripped to shreds, that jumpsuit is way more stylish than what you normally wear."

"I'm normally wearing my uniform," I protested, envious all over again that I had to wear neck-to-ankle khaki while she got away with a dragon-sized badge over her chest.

She bared her teeth in the dragon equivalent of a smirk and slipped two items out of the physics-defying bag that I'd privately dubbed as her *Mary Poppins* satchel.

One of them was a large and weird-looking keyboard, perfectly spaced for her talons. The other was a tablet computer.

"Why have I never seen these before?"

"Because we have an almost adequate IT department, and you already whine enough about doing the reports."

I opened my mouth and shut it again. Then took another swig of coffee. Now was not the time to argue the point. "Fine. What can we do to help?"

"Look through this traffic cam footage on each highway out of here for Madison or a car apparently driving itself that shouldn't be. I'll find out if there have been any reports of a stolen vehicle around that shopping center yet."

I nodded and started scanning the footage Aurelis shouldn't have had access to. Of course, there was a small chance Madison could've acquired a self-driving model that would confuse things, but since they were expensive, they also came with a bunch of biometric security that ought to keep her out.

Ronan came to watch over my shoulder. His presence at my back was warm. As warm as the radiator my sister needed in her New York apartment. I supposed I hadn't been this close to him other than when we were both sopping wet. Maybe fae ran hotter than humans. Except the warmth spread through me, pooling in my torso and spanning outward. Dammit, he was undeniably attractive and he'd sacrificed his coffee to me, but that was no reason for my body to decide—

Oh. He was *healing* me. The deepest lacerations and puncture wounds around my wrists and abdomen gave up the sharpness of their bites and partially knitted closed. The myriad of stinging scratches remained. But it was far more than I would've expected, considering how limited Ronan's magic was out here. And how important this mission was to the fae.

"Thank you," I murmured.

Something on the screen snatched my attention back.

"There!" She had a hood pulled deep over her head, but it was unmistakably Madison. "She's heading north along Route 160 in a blue pre-rev Ford F-150."

"Good." Aurelis yanked the tablet out of my hands. "Let's go."

Except I didn't have transport organized. Because I was supposed to be with Madison.

"Um, how would you feel about...?"

My dragon partner launched herself into the air without me.

I suppose that answered that then.

Ronan was swinging his leg over a Ducati motorcycle he'd had parked in the alley. His mouth compressed a fraction before offering, "You can ride with me."

I hesitated for half a second, then scooted onto the back and got a face full of invisible feathers. I sneezed.

Yeah, that was probably why he'd chosen a motorcycle over a car. And maybe why he hadn't looked thrilled about the prospect of riding double.

"My feathers are dust-free and nonallergenic," he informed me stiffly.

"Sure, but stick a feather high enough up someone's nose, and they'll sneeze no matter how clean it is."

"How clean it *was*," Ronan muttered, tossing me his helmet and bringing the engine to growling, purring life.

We peeled out onto the street, and I had no choice but to slide my hands past the silky soft feathers and around his taut, muscular abdomen.

Yeah. Woe was me.

CHAPTER TWENTY-ONE

Ronan's smell—a clean, woody scent of ancient, untouched forest with delicious undertones of something like caramelized butter—was distracting. Even traveling sixty-five miles per hour, the appealing aroma infiltrated its way past the helmet's protective visor to tease my nose. And that combined with the ridges of muscle beneath my hands and the soft feathers brushing against my bare arms and sheltering me from the thrashing wind was having unwanted effects on my body.

Okay, not *entirely* unwanted. But there was a time and a place and a partner, and this wasn't any of those.

The trajectories of our lives were such that as soon as this was over, however it was over, our paths were unlikely to cross again. And we had far more important things to be doing than sharing a few delicious yet fleeting moments.

Ronan's voice came through my loaned earbud. "The task force has been busy looking into every name on that list Aurelis found and cross-checking it with their own records to identify potential hideouts for Hale and whoever's with him. There are over a hundred possibilities spread across the four states surrounding Las Vegas. But as soon as Madison gives us a clear direction, they can start narrowing them down and make sure the incursion team is set up on-site before she arrives."

Yeah. That was the sort of stuff I was supposed to be thinking about. Because—

I swore. "I almost forgot. I need to call my boss."

Ronan slipped his phone into one of my hands, and I mumbled my thanks through a mouth that had just gone dry.

Having disentangled myself from the snare of arousal, my brain now noticed that the asphalt was vanishing beneath us at speeds that made me distinctly uncomfortable so close to my unprotected skin. Plus we were zipping past cars and trucks that loomed large and dangerous beside the insubstantial mass of our bike as we hurtled down the highway, trying to catch up to Madison.

I chewed the inside of my cheek, then reluctantly withdrew one of the arms securing me to Ronan so I could dial. Which only reinforced the discovery that I felt far more secure on dragonback than this mindless two-wheeled speed contraption.

To be fair, far more people died from motorcycle

accidents than flying on dragons. So my nerves were perfectly rational, right?

I eyed the phone. This was going to be a fun conversation.

Would Ronan listen in via the second earbud? It was a moot point anyway. It's hard to get much privacy on the back of a motorcycle when your companion has supernatural hearing. Besides, with Aurelis for a partner, a vampire as my father, and an assortment of adoptive siblings, I was used to having my conversations overheard.

This one was just likely to be more unpleasant than most.

I toyed briefly with dialing 911 to avoid having to give Gadson the bad news myself, but I worried my weird and unverifiable information wouldn't make it to him in time in the current upheaval. I knew a handful of numbers by heart thanks to all the instances my phone had been in the shop for cracked screens or specialized cleaning after exposure to a variety of strange and nasty fluids. And my captain's was one of them.

After realizing who'd called him, Gadson sounded less grateful for that stroke of luck than I was.

"What is it this time? If you've been poking around without authorization, I'm going to extend your suspension indefinitely."

I made an abrupt decision not to explain *where* I'd learned this information.

"It's a long story, but I had this magic-induced

vision. You need to find the doctor responsible for the prisoners at Nevada State Blackout Prison. He's being blackmailed into—"

"Dr. Trajkovski? Yes, he turned himself in to the precinct hours ago. *After* releasing fifty-eight highly dangerous criminals into the already chaotic streets. I'm about to be dragged to a damn press conference about it."

"Oh."

"Yes. Oh. So unless you have any *timely* information to give me, I'd better get back to the thankless task of putting out fires while everyone complains about how I'm doing it—and you kick back and enjoy *not involving yourself.* Do I make myself clear, Officer?"

I suppressed half a dozen responses and went with, "Yes, sir."

He sighed. "We could really have used Aurelis right now."

Like it was *my* fault she'd decided to poke her nose into the sewers that night. Admittedly, I was grateful she had. For the most part.

"Um, yes, sir," I repeated. "Best of luck, Captain. I think you're doing a fine job." And then I shut off the call before I got myself into any more trouble.

I was glad to pass the phone back to Ronan and hold on with both arms again. As if the motorcycle wasn't dangerous enough on its own, my head was spinning. The vision I'd seen was *real.*

Had already happened, in fact.

I'd sort of assumed it wasn't just a vivid hallucination, but having its accuracy confirmed made me feel like a heavy stone gargoyle had come to roost on my chest.

I consoled myself that at least the escaped inmates didn't have access to the powers they'd been locked up in that particular maximum-security prison for.

Except if what we were in the middle of attempting with Madison actually worked, they'd get their magic back at the same time everyone else did.

I swallowed hard, trying *not* to imagine what those felons might do with their unexpected and limited freedom—what unspeakable horrors their victims might be made to suffer—before law enforcement managed to re-apprehend them.

A phone call came through the loaned earbud, and Ronan answered, allowing me to listen in too.

Aurelis. "I have eyes on Madison. She's still in the F-150 and just turned onto Route 95 heading northwest. How far behind are you slowpokes?"

"We'll catch up in a few minutes," Ronan said confidently, and the motorcycle revved beneath us with a fresh surge of speed.

I may or may not have tightened my grip.

"You might want to glamour Lyra's prison jumpsuit before you do," Aurelis pointed out.

Ronan grunted acknowledgment. And just like that, I was dressed in a black leather jacket and tight gunmetal-colored jeans. Except I could still feel the wind rushing over my skin and the wide legs of my torn prison jumpsuit billowing out behind us.

It was freaking disconcerting. Worse than being invisible. Probably because not being able to see myself was sort of akin to moving around in the dark. You couldn't see, but your other senses told you what was going on. Whereas Faerie glamour meant my eyes and the rest of my senses were sending conflicting messages —and my brain was glitching trying to make sense of it.

I snapped my eyes back to the road ahead. The leather jacket had looked so *real*. The subtle grainy texture catching every angle of light and shadow, the material shifting and creasing in all the right places around my frame and the whipping wind.

Maybe it was my line of work, but my brain spun off ideas for all the crimes you could commit with magic like that. So many types of fraud it made my head implode. And this was just one of the capabilities Ronan wielded without apparent effort.

The fae already possessed the kind of power the Order of Influence was willing to kill hundreds of thousands for. Had it done them any good, I wondered?

We overtook another massive truck, its malodorous cargo of chickens forcing Ronan to give it an extra-wide berth. After that, I appreciated his clean, woodsy, yummy scent anew but this time for different reasons.

Then the stolen vehicle we'd been pursuing came at last into view.

Relief washed over me, followed quickly by a stomach-swirling combination of hope and fear. We'd found her. The plan was back on track.

What if it didn't work?

What if it did?

Ronan settled into position a few cars behind Madison. And as mile after mile of patchy asphalt and desert terrain was swallowed under the motorcycle's wheels, my tense anticipation was slowly edged out by boredom.

Depending on where Hale had holed up, this might be a very long ride. And I had nothing to occupy myself with other than trying not to fall off the bike. Well, that and trying not to fantasize about the man I was holding on to.

A yawn overtook me, and I realized the first of those objectives might be harder than I'd thought. The sleep I'd snatched in my hotel room and the jail cell since all this had begun had not been enough.

"You promised me a history lesson. I'm calling it in."

"I already gave it to you."

"Not the personal version."

"I never promised you the personal version."

"You never specified either way. That's a good place to start, actually. Are the fae really bound to keep their word?"

Ronan sighed. I could feel it in his abdomen and the slight shift in his wings.

"Not in the way you mean. Only by honor. But to be without honor in our culture is to be without money in yours. Except politics and principles make poor bedfellows, and like so many once good things, over the centuries we retained the trappings of what it meant to be honorable but lost the spirit of it."

"Is that why folklore says you're magically bound by your word but will trick us if you can?"

"Yes. It was an unintentional fiction at first, but a useful one. And soon it became a game to those who ventured from Faerie or had contact with the outside world. A game that's now played in much the same way *within* Faerie."

I was pretty sure I didn't imagine the bitterness in that statement.

"Tell me about Faerie. What's it like, really?"

"I love it," he stated simply. Except there was nothing simple about the myriad of emotions underlying those words. The way he said it made my stomach twist with pity instead of the positive feelings the statement should've evoked. "I love it, and I wouldn't wish it on anyone."

I hesitated. "Care to elaborate?"

"No."

Well, ask a stupid question…

"I refuse to have this as a one-way conversation," Ronan said. "Tell me about the blood."

I shut my eyes, even though he couldn't see them. Even though my eyelids did nothing to block out the images that question conjured.

And then I told him.

"Thank you for saving the guard," he said when I was done. "That was honorable of you. The true meaning."

I swallowed. Saw again the shifter's broken skull. The dryad-troll's blood spilling into the grass under the light of that too-bright moon.

I didn't feel honorable. I felt dirty. Ashamed. I grasped for a change of subject.

"Do you have a large werewolf population? Or do you get many applying for residency?"

"Not really, no. Why?"

"The moon's always full in Faerie," I quoted lightly.

There was an awkward silence.

And then it was my turn to sigh. "My first serious relationship was the classic story of the werewolf next door. I liked him. He liked me. We dated for a few years. And I thought we'd wind up married until he ran off to NASA so he could get closer to the moon."

"Ah." I could hear amusement in Ronan's voice. "The moon only *appears* full in Faerie. But you know the moon thing is a myth, right? It was just safer for them to shift at night, and then they were most often glimpsed under the light of a full moon."

I shrugged. "I know. It's just more fun to tell it my way." I could almost *feel* Ronan laughing at me. "What about you?" I asked.

"Have I ever dated a werewolf? Or have I ever run off to NASA to get closer to the moon?"

I snickered in appreciation. "Both. Neither. I don't know. What was it like growing up in Faerie? Who were your neighbors?"

"Alas, I wasn't allowed to play with the kids next door. But I did have an imaginary friend for many years. You remind me of her actually." He shut up abruptly. Was that a blush shading the edge of his unhelmeted cheek?

Aurelis phoned again. "Have one of you updated the task force on Madison's continued direction? Also, Madison's car has just been reported stolen. I'm going to land for a minute and delete the report. We don't want some helpful cop to apprehend her prematurely." She waited a beat. "*If*, that is, you two think you can manage not to lose her a second time?"

It was several hours and many miles later that Ronan's task force contact confirmed they'd completed searching our narrowed-down list of hideout possibilities.

They'd located Hale with a small group of other cult members on a cattle ranch not far north of our current location.

I was exhausted, my shoulders were aching—either from clinging to Ronan for so long or the unceasing tension of the past forty hours—and my teeth felt as furry as an arctic fox shifter's wintry backside.

But anticipation thrummed through me at the news.

At the crazy wonderful thought that if this worked, I might be able to hug my family again in just a few short hours.

Never mind the brutal and powerful criminals who'd suddenly have their magic back. I couldn't think about that now. Not when hundreds of thousands of lives might depend on the events of the next half an hour.

Ronan told the task force we'd meet the others there ahead of Madison, and the bike put on a fresh burst of speed. At some point along the journey, I'd become inured to the flesh-shredding asphalt whizzing beneath my toes and the incongruity of my glamoured clothes. Bully for me.

Aurelis continued to track Madison from high above in the stolen vehicle's blind spot. The dragon was plenty fast enough to peel off at the last minute and beat her to the action.

We overtook the F-150, and ten minutes later, Ronan slowed and turned the bike off-road, following the task force's directions over the mostly barren farm-land so we could avoid being spotted coming up the long, winding driveway. Even so, Ronan was using glamour to hide the dust we kicked up.

The motorcycle rattled so hard my skin itched from the jiggling, and I envisaged my poor brain being cata-pulted around my skull like Jell-O on a bouncy castle. It was a relief to reach the impromptu command station that had been set up behind a small ridge overlooking the cult's location.

I unpeeled myself from the bike, and we joined the incursion team behind the large glamoured barrier being maintained by another fae.

He and Ronan exchanged nods while I looked around.

We were a good distance from the sprawling ranch house and the gravel driveway Madison should be arriving on any minute now. But large screens showed multiple views of the force field surrounding the rather nice home, along with several shots of the driveway.

A compact, capable-looking woman in tactical gear strode over to clasp Ronan's hand. "Representative Nightwing, thank you for your cooperation. I'm Acting Commander Quinton. Would you like a run-through of the incursion strategy?"

"Please."

"And, Officer Ridley, I believe we have you to thank for aiding in Miss Hale's convenient escape?"

I shifted uncomfortably, wondering if it was better she *didn't* know my name so that tidbit didn't get back to Gadson. "It was a joint effort," I mumbled.

"Excellent." She clapped her hands together, already dismissing me.

"As you can see, we have remote video and audio surveillance covering as much of the grounds as possible. It's not perfect because we've had to resurrect pre-rev technology given the magic-resistant properties of the force field. But at least using old tech ought to reduce our risk of being detected by the Order of Influence before we're ready." She strode to another section of the site, assuming we'd follow. "We did check, by the way, and as we suspected, anti-magic devices don't work out here, so there goes the simplest solution."

She patted the pointed nose of a strange-looking transport thing. A second one sat beside it. They had the aerodynamic noses of a bullet train and small fin-like wings, but each one was no larger than an SUV. "Unlike our surveillance equipment, the magitechnology in this beauty is brand-new. The XZ33 hover shuttles will make sure that should the force field come down, our specialized incursion team will reach the ranch house in ten seconds flat."

Ronan looked through the small windows to where a dozen people and thrice as many weapons were seated in uncomfortably cramped quarters.

"I believed I would be part of the incursion group."

Quinton's smile faltered before flicking back to full wattage. "Sorry, but our people are trained to work as a cohesive team, and there's limited room in the shuttles. You're welcome to stand with me and watch everything on the audio and visual feeds."

"I understand," Ronan said. And only the rigidity of his wings suggested he was anything less than pleased.

I didn't feel great about having everything yanked out of our hands either, but no one asked me.

Aurelis swooped down and landed behind the glamoured barrier, instantly making the busy, orderly command station feel smaller.

"Madison's just turning up the driveway," she reported.

It was go time.

CHAPTER TWENTY-TWO

Aurelis seemed no more pleased to be relegated to spectator duty than Ronan and I were, but there wasn't time for argument. A cloud of dust coming up the driveway heralded Madison's imminent arrival.

Someone channeled the audio through a speaker so everyone could hear as Madison, not bothering to use her magic, exited the stolen vehicle and approached her father's force field.

"Who the hell just rocked up?" someone inside the ranch house demanded.

It was jarring to realize that despite the hours we'd spent sharing a wall, our family histories, a prison break, and one of the most unsettling nights of my life, this was the best chance I'd had to study her.

She was thinner than the photos I'd seen from before her imprisonment, and she looked pale and exhausted. Dark half circles underlined her eyes, and her ponytail was scuffed from the car's headrest. At some point in the shopping mall, she'd traded her prison clothes for a baggy hoodie and ill-fitting leggings. Despite all that, I thought I saw barely contained excitement in her step as she drew closer to her father and expected refuge. I found myself unwillingly moved by it. Like watching footage of soldiers returning home to their families after months on tour... Except with far less honor in Madison's case.

She walked toward the ranch house, looking small and fragile on the screen despite the tough-girl aura she liked to project, and banged on the transparent surface of the force field. Bright orange sparks of light radiated from where she struck, the same way the one in Las Vegas had done under my probing fingers a couple of nights prior. Geez, it felt like a lifetime ago.

"Dad? Can you hear me? It's Madison. I got out!"

"She's probably a fae in disguise," someone inside the house warned. Out of sight but not out of audio pickup. "Don't you dare let down the force field."

"But what if it *is* her?"

"No one escapes from Faerie prison," said the same skeptic.

"Other people have underestimated Madison too. You can stay inside where it's safe while I go out and talk to her. I'll know my own daughter up close."

That's right. Jason Hale was the only person who could pass through the solid walls of his force fields. Hope danced in my chest. Maybe we could use that.

Maybe we wouldn't even need him to decide to lower it to let Madison in so long as he ventured outside. Just for a moment. Just to clasp his daughter's hand or give her a hug or—

"And risk having a sniper take you out?" the second speaker hissed. "That's even worse."

"I'll stay inside the force field until we know for sure," Hale growled. "But I'm going to talk to my daughter."

His tone brooked no argument, but the other guy gave him one anyway.

"Even if it's her, this could be some kind of setup. Send her away to wait at a hotel. We're too close to victory to risk everything now. This isn't the time to forget our higher aims."

Two sets of footsteps suggested Hale was striding toward his daughter and the other guy was hurrying after him.

"She's been in prison for weeks after an impossible mission *you* assigned her!" Madison's dad sounded like he was forcing the words out past gritted teeth. "I'm not sending her away. I failed to protect my family once. So help me if I ever fail again."

"Fine." The other man snarled. "I'll get Wyatt for backup then. But don't you dare go out there or bring down the force field without consulting us. All our futures are at stake here."

Hale came out the front of the house and strode across the porch and dirt to meet Madison. He was still clean-shaven, but he'd ditched the suit jacket today, and his light brown hair was disheveled like he'd been raking his fingers through it.

"Hi, honey," he said with a tight smile. "We just need to check you are who you say you are. You understand, right?"

On the screen, I saw Madison's shoulders slump. "Yeah, yeah."

It was probably not the joyous reunion she'd been imagining through her long weeks in Faerie prison.

"Tell me something only you would know." He lowered his voice to a bare whisper. "And if this is some kind of setup, scratch your nose or something."

A second man stepped out onto the porch. He was small and slight and walked with his hands buried deep in his pockets like he rarely used them.

"That's Wyatt Bradshaw, a powerful telekinetic," one of the guys manning the surveillance equipment supplied.

Madison glanced at the newcomer but focused on her dad, chewing her lip in consideration. "Remember when I was—"

The telekinetic studied Madison, who choked off midsentence as the drawstring of her hoodie wrapped itself around her throat.

"Madison?" Hale asked in concern.

Her hands flew to the cord beginning to dig into her flesh, wide eyes fixing on the man standing behind her father.

Hale whirled. "What the hell are you doing?" he shouted.

The telekinetic didn't reply. His attention was on Madison, and a nasty expression of ill-concealed satisfaction suggested he was enjoying the power trip.

Madison's face shaded an unhealthy red, and she began thrashing and clawing at her neck with the uncontrolled terror of violent oxygen starvation.

"He's going to kill her," I murmured in disbelief. "Aurelis, we have to stop this."

Acting Commander Quinton made an abortive gesture. "No. This could be good for us. Stand down."

Jason Hale launched himself at the other cult member. But Hale's magic was defensive, and he wasn't used to fighting physical battles. The telekinetic used a fresh surge of power to shove Hale against the porch rail and pin him there without releasing his stranglehold on Madison.

What was Bradshaw doing? Did he think Hale wouldn't risk lowering the force field if his daughter was already beyond saving? It was a huge gamble to take.

Madison continued to fight. A blood vessel had burst in one of her eyes, and her own fingernails had gouged bloody scratches in her neck in her futile wrestle with the drawstring.

Commander Quinton's face was unmoved as she watched.

I remembered Madison recounting the horror of her mother's death. All the years she'd lived in fear. How many times must she have relived those moments? And now she was dying by someone else's magic, so close to her father, so close to the place she thought she'd find sanctuary.

Madison staggered and fell forward into her father's force field. Her thrashing was growing weaker. Weaker but no less desperate.

It took about four minutes of continued strangulation for brain death. How many had it been? One? Two? And how many seconds would it take for us to reach her? To rescue her from an assailant we couldn't touch?

"Aurelis, please," I breathed.

Her tail wrapped around my waist faster than the thorny stems of the vicious prison hedge and deposited me on her shoulders. Then we were launching into the air, obliterating the task force's cover. And setting metaphorical fire to the innumerable hours and resources that had been sunk into this operation.

"You sure know how to piss off your superiors," Aurelis observed cheerily.

"So do you."

"Sure, but I don't need and love this job. You do. Plus this was your idea, not mine."

There was no time to respond because Aurelis was already swooping toward Madison.

"What's the plan here?" she asked.

"Grab her and carry her out of range?"

I prayed that Bradshaw's range was short. Brain damage could occur well before death.

Aurelis huffed. "Why am I lugging your insignificant but irritating weight along then?"

But she adjusted her trajectory to snatch Madison up in her talons, just as the girl went limp.

I was expecting a telekinetic assault and was ready to draw on Aurelis's magic resistance, if I could. But instead, Wyatt Bradshaw crowed in triumph. "I was right!"

Then Aurelis was gaining altitude and arcing around, her wings beating hard to return her human cargo to the doubtlessly pissed task force and the medic that must be standing by.

"Is she alive?" I asked anxiously.

"How should I know? My talons aren't designed for taking someone's pulse."

We landed seconds later, and as I leaped off Aurelis to check on Madison, I heard the audio feed still carrying to everyone in the group.

"You bastard!" Hale was snarling. "You tried to kill my daughter!"

"Actually," the other man purred, "I stopped you from making a monumental mistake. This was a setup. As I just demonstrated."

Madison was limp and unmoving, her complexion pallid now except for the bright red ligature marks and bloody scratches around her throat. I fumbled for a pulse.

Her father's voice rang out on the speaker. "You conceited ass. I don't give a damn *what* your reasons were. I might just lower the force field and let them take you!"

Madison had a heartbeat. Alive then.

Someone squatted next to me, and since they had a medical field kit with them, I made room.

"Oh, settle down," Bradshaw said. "I wouldn't have let her die. Just bring her near enough to it to force a fae to give up their glamour or else flush out anyone hanging around as backup."

I didn't believe him. Looking up from Madison's inert form, it seemed Hale didn't believe him either. He was still fighting against the telekinetic pressure holding him against the porch and looked ready to strangle Bradshaw the old-fashioned way.

"Besides, if we get the iron key, we could have brought her back to life. True resurrection. Not just a necromancer's reanimation."

Hale stopped struggling, and we all listened to his ragged breathing. "Really? It's that powerful?"

"Why do you think we're going to such lengths to get it? And now—"

Commander Quinton shut off the speaker with a gesture. "Monitor the feeds and report to me immediately if there's anything I need to know."

Then she rounded on me, her voice counterintuitively soft.

"Officer Ridley, wasn't it? And Officer Aurelis?"

As with most of the perps I dealt with, Quinton aimed the bulk of her displeasure my way instead of at the formidable dragon beside me. But in this case, it was probably warranted. While Aurelis had done the actual saving, she wouldn't have bothered if it wasn't for me.

"You just squandered hundreds of thousands of taxpayer dollars and jeopardized the lives of every super-natural in Las Vegas to rescue one criminal who may not have even *needed* saving."

I stood my ground, full of righteous anger that she'd been prepared to let a minor die in front of her. "My duty is to serve and *protect*."

"Your duty," she echoed with an underlying snarl, "is to uphold the law and follow orders! If someone is about to shoot you, do you let them do it for their protection? Because that girl is prepared to murder thousands of strangers to get what she wants."

I licked my lips and said nothing.

It was true. She was. But how different might things have been if we'd managed to protect her mother thir-teen years ago?

Quinton shook her head in disgust.

"You destroyed this operation and disobeyed a direct order. I'll see your career ruined over this."

CHAPTER TWENTY-THREE

The task force personnel cleared out in record time, taking a still unconscious Madison with them. The medic assured me quietly out of Quinton's earshot that he'd get her the care she needed. Only the surveillance equipment and a few people to man it remained in place.

Ronan rubbed his face as the last vehicle drove away.

"That's it then. I guess this is where we part ways."

He didn't sound nearly as pleased about that as I might've expected. At some point during the failed incursion, he'd let go of the glamour that hid his wings, and I was embarrassed to realize I'd missed them.

Yet if wings were capable of wilting, his were doing a bang-up job of it.

"I'm sorry, Lyra, Aurelis. The Faerie Governing Council will not trade the iron key for the supernatural population of Las Vegas. It would be like giving the enemy a nuke to neutralize a hand grenade."

I recalled what he'd told me about how powerful the artifact was. Powerful and dangerous enough that I'd realized then saving the supernaturals of Las Vegas could only be a second priority. But now, facing that reality in earnest, I couldn't accept it.

"What do you mean?" I demanded. "This can't be it. You can't just walk away. The fae might be the only ones that can stop this—"

"I'm sorry," he said again. And the genuine sorrow in that apology, the resolute finality of it, stole the air from my lungs.

It began to sink in that we might have saved Madison's life, but I'd failed to save the hundreds of thousands trapped in the anti-magic zone.

Failed to save my family.

Failed.

Grief and guilt and despair threatened to drown me even as I stood in the middle of the desert.

The question escaped before I could think better of it. "Do you think the commander is right? Did I make the wrong call saving Madison?"

Ronan's expression softened. "You did it out of a desire to protect. That's an honorable goal. But rightness is rarely measured in absolutes." He paused. "Which means only you can answer for yourself whether what you did was right."

He shrugged, his wings echoing the motion of his

shoulders. "If you hadn't intervened, the telekinetic may or may not have killed Madison. And Hale might've dropped the force field in retaliation, or self-preservation could've won out. You'll never know. All you can do is examine your heart and see if you can live with the decision you made. But if the answer keeps you up at night, don't forget to question whether the alternative would've let you sleep any easier. Sometimes there is no decision available that will leave you unburdened."

His wisdom sat heavily—uncomfortable yet comforting at the same time.

"You sound like you're speaking from experience."

He turned away. "Perhaps." He walked over to the motorcycle and unlocked the seat. "It escaped my mind earlier, but while you were in prison, I took the liberty of getting you a new phone and having a technician transfer everything over. Since yours drowned in a trap set for me. I have the rest of your things here too."

He pressed the pile of clothes, my gun, and his gift into my hands.

"Thank you." I hoped he understood I meant for more than just the phone. "How... how did you get so wise so young? And, uh, how old are you anyway?" With the fae, it was impossible to tell.

"I'm twenty-eight. And the answer is trial and error." He grimaced. "Lots and *lots* of error."

Huh. I couldn't say it had worked for me.

"Farewell, Lyra." He gave the dragon another courtly bow. "Aurelis."

Then he walked away, leaving the motorcycle for those of us who couldn't find a Faerie gateway home.

I tried not to stare after him, more stung than I should've been that I'd likely never see him again, and hyperaware that there were far, far bigger tragedies playing out right now. Even so, I breathed in his lingering scent before it drifted away on the breeze.

In spite of everything, his kindness had left me slightly bolstered. I turned over the new phone, surprised (and a little disturbed) when it unlocked at my fingerprint, only to see a news alert in the list of notifications.

First Supernatural Dies As Las Vegas Hostage Situation Stretches On

CHAPTER TWENTY-FOUR

One of the surveillance guys who'd remained behind was giving us dirty looks.

Aurelis stretched herself to maximum height and flared her wings. "Ingrates. I prefer to be heralded as a hero after going to the trouble of saving someone's life. And they wouldn't have even had the *hope* of infiltrating the force field if it wasn't for us."

The man of the dirty looks adjusted something on the surveillance equipment. "It's not *just* that today's operation failed. You've made things worse. Now the Order of Influence members *know* we know where they are. So there's no chance of them growing complacent and giving us an opening. And right now they're figuring out a way to ensure Hale can't take down the force field without the other members' cooperation."

Aurelis bristled, but I touched her shoulder. "Come

on, hero. I need to find somewhere to crash, and I'd appreciate your company."

She eyed me. "I'm not sleeping in any crappy motel *you* can afford."

Which only served to remind me I was suspended. And probably fired too after Gadson heard about this debacle. Especially after he'd explicitly ordered me to stay away from this case.

My body ached with exhaustion, my sleep-deprived brain felt like four-day-old mashed potatoes, and my heart was a leaden weight in my chest. The hope and purpose and adrenaline that had been fueling me until now were gone, leaving only fear and a sick feeling in the pit of my stomach.

How many more would die before this was done?

How long did my family have left?

And if I hadn't saved Madison, would this nightmare have all been over now?

I didn't know. But Miles's voice was so clear in my head that he could've been right there beside me. "Go to bed, milksucker. You can't fix the whole world in a day."

It was advice he'd repeated to me often over the years. And it usually helped. So I walked over to the bike Ronan had left me, bumped my way back to the road, then rode onward to the nearest motel.

Despite Aurelis's earlier words, she accompanied me, flying high above until I pulled into the dirt patch that passed for a parking lot at the No-Frills Motel. She landed long enough to give the ugly brown building with small windows and neon signage a once-over, then professed she'd prefer to sleep on a bed of boxthorns and left me there.

I got myself a room and scrubbed the blood and grime off my skin with the weak spray I could coax out of the showerhead. Fatigue made the job arduous, but I couldn't sleep covered in the prison guard's blood. My own wasn't much more desirable.

By the time I got out, it was all I could do to stumble to the bed.

Despite not knowing whether saving Madison had been right or wrong, despite the supernatural who'd died today of magic depletion, despite everything I loved being in jeopardy, as soon as I fell onto the lumpy mattress, oblivion took mere moments to smother me.

There was more bad news waiting for me when I woke. Four more supernaturals had died. All of them elderly or vulnerable in some other way. But it didn't make their loss any less tragic. And I knew the momentum would only build from here.

Breakfast, which was actually at dinnertime at the No-Frills Motel, was worse than the lumpy mattress. A toasted BLT sandwich that was simultaneously burned and frozen in the middle.

I mustn't have slept long enough because the terrible food brought a lump to my throat. And not because my

ISLA FROST

body was trying to block access to my stomach—but
rather that it reminded me of my dad's cooking.

I missed him.

And I didn't know what to do. Return to Las Vegas
and spend every remaining minute with my family?
Even if all those minutes were through a force field or a
screen? Or keep fighting when it was clear no one else
believed I should? When there was a risk I'd make everything worse? Again.

I swallowed the last charred and frozen bite of my
sandwich and video-called Dad. Not because I'd come to
any kind of decision, but because I desperately wanted
to see his face.

Probably because he was the one I'd always turned to
when I was feeling down.

His beloved visage appeared on my screen. And the
deep affection I saw there filled me with comfort and
warmth and simultaneously twisted the knife of grief so
painfully that for a moment I couldn't breathe.

Would it always hurt this much?

"You're looking pale," I admonished. "When did you
last drink?"

Vampires' skin tone turned pallid and bloodless
when they hadn't had sustenance for a while. Sort of like
an anemic person. And since people mostly saw them
just before they fed... Well, that was where the whole
undead theory had spawned from.

"The city's in chaos, sweetie. I can wait a bit longer
for a resupply."

I pursed my lips, remembering Sage telling me he'd drunk more than usual. How long ago had that been? Was he really low in stock now—or was he being evasive in an attempt to conceal just how badly the magic depletion was affecting him? Neither was good. Now more than ever he needed to keep his strength up—

"You worry too much." He gave me a pointed look. "It's not what I would've chosen for you."

This was why I didn't want to tell any of you yet, was the subtext. And while I hated the deceit, I had come to understand his reasoning. Against my better judgment, I was grieving his loss while he was still here. Still had years yet to live. In what world did that make sense?

And yet… if I hadn't found out, he would've shouldered the terrible weight of that secret in isolation for every one of those years.

Of course, after what I'd done earlier today by rescuing Madison, *years* might be optimistic.

"Have you opened your present yet?" I asked abruptly.

Even if he never got the chance to use the gift, I was going to snatch this opportunity to at least convey the sentiment I'd intended.

This opportunity might be the only one I got.

"No," he said. "I thought I'd wait for you—"

"Open it now."

"I promised the kids I'd let them help."

"I'll wrap something else up for you they can help with. I'd like you to open it now… Just us."

Looking concerned, he did as I asked.

"What is this, Lyra?" His eyes went wide at the large mud-colored gemstone, and then his expression turned pained. "It's too much."

"It's not nearly enough." The words wrenched out of me with so much conviction that Miles must've sensed this was a fight he couldn't win.

The object in his hand was called a sentiment stone, and they were ludicrously expensive because they apparently required phoenix ashes as one of the key ingredients.

I'd snagged this one cheap because it had come out a muddy color and the crafter claimed Miles had once done her a kindness and she'd like to repay it. Even so, it had set me back most of my savings.

Sentiment stones were aptly named. They recorded all the intangible sensations of a moment in time, then allowed the stone's owner to re-experience those sensations in perfect clarity.

Photos and videos were lovely keepsakes, but they didn't capture everything. The very essence of joy, love, laughter, connection, belonging. The feeling of being someone else's world.

The feeling of family.

I knew Miles had spent most of his decades without that. I didn't want him to ever be without it again.

Yet no matter how much I railed against the disease eating away at his brain, his memories, his very identity, I couldn't stop it from happening.

I could at least give him this.

I swallowed the lump in my throat. At least I'd *thought* I'd be able to give him this. Now there was the very real possibility that the end would come far sooner.

"You can tell people it's for when you outlive us," I explained after I regained the ability to speak.

The downside to being a vampire parent of mixed species is that you were likely to outlive your kids.

Of course, we both knew Miles wouldn't. But sentiment stones were commonly gifted to someone who was losing their loved one. A mother dying of cancer might give one to her child. A terminally ill husband might give one to his partner. It was the gift of experiencing the fullness of their love, even when they were no longer around.

In Miles's case, this common usage offered a convenient explanation to everyone who didn't know about the disease intent on erasing all that he was.

The real reason was more complex.

I met my father's blue gaze, patient and attentive, waiting to hear me out. Hell, he'd always been so patient with us. Had always been ready to listen and never made us feel like our concerns were petty or trivial. Even if they were. It had been a heady experience as a small child to have that patient attentiveness fixed on you, secure in the knowledge that you would be heard, understood, supported.

"I got it for you because…"

Great. I was already choking up. But I knew Dad would wait patiently for me to finish.

"Because I want you to know… right up until the end… no matter what else you forget"—my voice broke, and it took longer this time before I could continue—"that you are adored and loved and part of a whole. That in a world of cruelty and division, you found love and belonging." I swiped at the tears and swallowed past my increasingly restricted throat. "No. You didn't just *find* love and belonging. You carved it out for yourself. And you carved it out for me. And my siblings."

I was crying openly now. But I wasn't embarrassed about it. This man had witnessed more of my tears than anyone else and never once been judgmental.

It was so unfair. He'd graced the world for hundreds of years and been valued for so very few of them. Why couldn't we have shared more of that time?

Miles had gone even paler. Looking like I'd knocked the wind out of him. And he had tears running down his cheeks too.

After so much time on earth, it took an awful lot for him to cry.

"Oh, honey. It's been a privilege to see you grow up, to watch you develop into a person I'm so very proud of. By getting to share in who you are, you've given me far more than I've ever given you."

By the time we said goodbye, I was so emotionally wrung out that I felt like crawling back into the lumpy motel bed and having another nap. But I was grateful we'd had the chance to share our hearts so openly one more time.

The nap would have to wait. I still had a decision to make.

I called Aurelis. "Want to join me for a meal?"

The BLT I'd eaten earlier was sitting funny in my stomach, but I'd learned it was better to entice Aurelis with something appealing rather than just asking for her attention. And perhaps we could find a place that served better food.

Aurelis made a contented noise. "No, thanks. I just had beef."

Suspicion trickled into my mind. "*Fresh* beef?"

"Sure. I figured anyone prepared to let a homicidal cult hole up on their ranch deserves to lose a cow or two."

I sighed but didn't argue. Sometimes you had to pick your battles. "Want to join me anyway? I'm trying to decide whether to give up and go home or not."

Well, not *home.* My family was my home. And if the fae didn't hand over the iron key to save the supernaturals of Vegas—something Ronan had made clear they wouldn't do—then soon I wouldn't have a home to go back to.

I choked up again.

Despite that threat, or perhaps because of it, all I wanted was to be close to them. As close to them as possible anyway. And if that meant on opposite sides of the dome, it was still better than being out here in the middle of nowhere, futilely throwing myself at the impossible.

"You're thinking about *giving up*?" Aurelis's voice was incredulous. "I thought you were too hardheaded to let an idiot like that commander get to you. It's one of the few traits I admire about you. What about my hoard? What about your family? Are you really going to stake their futures on the pretentious, overbearing numbskulls on the task force?"

The razor edge to her questions made me glad we were having this conversation over the phone.

"If you're so convinced the task force is useless, why don't *you* come up with a new strategy?"

"Because. If there's one thing you're *occasionally* better at than me aside from using a can opener and getting yourself into giant steaming messes, it's coming up with harebrained schemes. Sometimes they even work. Besides, you might be the only person on the planet who could take down the Las Vegas force field without Hale doing it directly."

That didn't do me any good unless I could convince Hale to let me close enough to touch him. But still...

"Was that a compliment?"

"Tell anyone and I'll burn your apartment down."

"What are you, the big bad wolf?"

"A wolf is no match for a dragon."

I snorted. But her words had reignited a spark of hope. "Thanks, Aurelis."

"I just want you to stop moping and make yourself useful. I only care about my hoard."

"Naturally."

She hung up, and my grin faded quickly.

The thing, with my brain functioning again after a good night's rest, I *did* have a harebrained scheme. A probably suicidal scheme. But it was the best chance I could conceive of for saving the people of Las Vegas.

The problem was, to pull it off I'd need the support of the Faerie Governing Council and the cooperation of the task force.

Neither was likely to give it to me.

But there was one person I could think of who might at least hear me out…

CHAPTER TWENTY-FIVE

I had to talk to Ronan.

But how was I supposed to get in touch with him? It wasn't like I could hunt down a gateway, rock up at Faerie border security, and demand to speak to Lord Ronan Nightwing. I'd get tossed back into prison faster than I could spit out his title. Or be overcome by gateway nausea halfway through saying his name and throw up my BLT on the nice white floor.

If only we'd exchanged numbers. Unless…

I scrolled through the contacts on the phone he'd gifted me. There. He'd added in his details. The discovery warmed me in a way I didn't want to examine too closely. No doubt he'd done it for purely practical reasons. The same way he'd sought out our help in the first place.

He was probably about to regret that.

I dialed the number.

"Lyra?" he answered.

"I have an idea. But neither your Faerie Council nor the task force is going to like it."

To my surprise, cautious hope colored his reply, and he only hesitated for a moment. "They don't have to *like* it if it's viable. Let's meet in person. Where are you?"

There was something vaguely absurd about sitting across from Ronan in the No-Frills Motel. Even with his wings hidden, he looked out of place. He sat too far forward on the crappy plastic chair, stirring but not drinking the stale, lukewarm coffee on the table in front of him.

Despite the absurdity, my foolish heart was all too pleased to see him.

He was here. He believed in me enough, cared enough, to leave Faerie and hear me out. It was more than I could say for anyone else I'd worked with. Excepting Aurelis of course.

Ronan listened as I outlined the plan, his jaw set, not offering so much as a breath of feedback. When I was done, he said, "You're right. They're not going to like it."

My hopes sank. Ronan was my one chance. If I couldn't convince him—

"Neither do I," he added. "But I don't like three hundred thousand supernaturals dying in Las Vegas either."

He swiped a hand across his face, and I realized how tired he looked. Like he hadn't slept at all. Which was saying something given he'd just come from Faerie. His words from the day before echoed back to me. *Sometimes there is no decision available that will leave you unburdened.*

His weary eyes met mine. "You need to understand what you're asking. But it might not change the outcome. And I'd have to put you under a geas to explain more."

"You mean like a magically enforced nondisclosure agreement?"

"Yes."

I wished Aurelis was here so she could warn me if this was a terrible idea. But Ronan had trusted me enough to show up here. The least I could do was return that trust. Up to a point. "Fine. Do it."

He stretched his hand toward me. "Are you sure?"

No. "Yes."

The air around us took on an odd, stilted quality. Like we were audibly cut off from the mostly deserted dining area and the rest of the world. I could no longer hear the clank of cutlery from what passed for the kitchen or the shrunken man in the corner, slurping his beer. Then Ronan brushed my lips with his thumb. Fire scourged my mouth and throat, and my vocal cords locked in rigid agony. The pain was gone before I could do more than flinch.

"What do you know about the origin of the supernatural peoples?"

Still reeling from the brief but intense pain, I shook my head.

"No one is old enough to know for sure of course, but the most ancient supernatural lore from different species all around the globe holds echoes of the same narrative. Supernaturals were created as playthings of ancient gods. Unlike humankind who were allowed free will and the ability to rule over one another, the supernaturals acted on the will of the gods, with little leftover for themselves. They were forced to commit terrible atrocities on the gods' behalf, acting upon their desire for entertainment or glory or whatever was popular that century. And it was during this period that so many of humankind's mythologies warning of the evils of supernatural beings were formed."

I could feel myself frowning. Ronan was a good speaker, and it was an interesting tale. But what the hell did this have to do with potentially allowing thousands to die in modern-day Vegas?

I forced myself to listen. Wait. Trust that Ronan had a reason for going this far back in the murky realms of largely forgotten history.

"However, time crawled on and the gods' hold on the world began to weaken. It was then the supernaturals united against them to win their freedom. They gathered every relic, every god-touched item of power, everything they could get their hands or paws or claws on, and poured their combined magic into a single artifact."

He paused, and I didn't like where this was leading.

"The iron key. Though it doubtless had a different name back then."

Nope. I didn't like it at all.

"They used the artifact to irreversibly purge the gods from the earth and attain freedom."

I'd grown up in a world and family where magic and supernatural beings were almost as ordinary as electricity. But there was still a sense of newness, a sense of change, a sense of wonder to those things. In part because every book, web page, song, TV show, building, and so many other things in existence up until twenty-three years ago so clearly illustrated what life had been like before the revolution.

Yet somehow Ronan's tale of god-touched artifacts and forgotten deities and a united fight for freedom felt like no more than make-believe to me. How could this ancient fable-like artifact have anything to do with the real and urgent disaster waiting to devastate my beloved home and city?

"The supernaturals had agreed to destroy the artifact after the deed was done. Because they wanted to remove their too-powerful tyrants, not replace them. But the key proved immune to destruction. It turned out that anything its power had been used for, like its own forging, was irreversible. Or at least, its power would not act against anything it had wrought, which amounted to nearly the same thing. So the guardianship was given over to the fae. For within Faerie, few might challenge us. And the artifact was fused with iron to render it unusable by our kind."

His eyes met mine, then flicked back to his untouched coffee. "We have been guarding it ever since."

There was an odd combination of something like reverence and resentment in that last statement.

I opened my mouth, then shut it again without coming up with anything to say.

"The iron key has been used only one other time in all of history. Wielded, as it was the first time, by a largely unified supernatural community across the world. Our forbearers used it to buy their freedom from the gods, and thousands of years later, twenty-three years ago, we used it to buy our freedom a second time. To gift humankind with magic so that we could at last come out of hiding."

I shook my head as what Ronan was telling me finally snapped into cold hard reality.

I wished I could give the knowledge back.

The Faerie Council was right to keep the iron key secure no matter what the cult threatened.

No matter the cost of that security.

The *horrendous*, unfathomable cost.

Ronan's analogy about handing the cult a nuke to stop a hand grenade was *understating* it. The reality was closer to giving a terrorist group every nuke in existence and leaving the world defenseless.

Did Hale and his buddies understand just how

powerful the iron key was? Or was it merely the first powerful artifact they found mention of and managed to track down?

As Ronan had warned me, it didn't matter. Because the outcome was the same.

My plan was too risky. Ronan was right to deny—

"I will take it to the council," he said. "Push them to at least workshop the idea from every angle and see if we can shore up the risk to a point of viability." I had the distinct impression he'd prefer to have every one of his teeth chiseled out without anesthetic by an especially impatient tooth fairy. "I'll be in touch."

I was so gobsmacked that I forgot how bad the coffee was and took a sip.

Ronan was already halfway out the door when I spat it back into my cup.

CHAPTER TWENTY-SIX

Everyone converged back at the cattle ranch, and this time no one was trying to hide. We stood around the force field in plain sight. Hopefully *not* giving the cult members reason to back out on the agreed terms.

But why would they? As far as they knew, they'd be getting everything they wanted. And the only thing they had to worry about was one measly girl.

That'd be me.

I had far more to worry about. Seven cult members. All with powerful magic ranging from telekinesis to emotional manipulation and who knew what weapons. And if I screwed this up and yet somehow survived, there were plenty of people on the *outside* of the force field who'd happily murder me.

Commander Quinton was making no effort to disguise her sneer.

I turned away and focused on the one person that

wholeheartedly supported my going through with the plan. "Got any more pep talks for me?" I asked Aurelis.

"Try not to die. I'd hate to have to break in a new police partner."

"I love you too. It's been a wild ride."

Smoke wafted from her nostrils, and I winced. "You did *not* just use the word *ride*."

Well. Now there was no one wholeheartedly supporting me.

"Sorry."

Ronan was nearby too, his glorious wings once more on full display. But every line of his athletic form was stiff with tension. And if I'd thought he'd looked weary the last time I saw him, now he looked like he'd spent every intervening hour in his own personal hell. He was frowning at the heavily enchanted strongbox he was clutching. The one that held the all-powerful iron key.

The *real* iron key. Nothing else would get past the gremlin Hatshepsut.

Ronan had stuck his neck out by championing this plan to the Faerie Council, and I wondered if he was already regretting it.

"Are you okay?" I asked quietly.

His dark gaze met mine, deep and intense and perhaps a little haunted.

"What's the point of protecting the world from this artifact for thousands of years if in doing so we turn our backs on one of the greatest threats in modern history? Can it be right to guard against the risk of a *potential* atrocity, a far greater atrocity, yes, but one that might never come about, in exchange for allowing the very certain death of three hundred thousand lives?"

"I don't know." My voice was small. Would I have still saved Madison if I'd fully understood and had time to consider the consequences? I didn't know that either.

He grimaced. "Despite what I told the council, neither do I."

"If it helps, a wise man once told me that rightness is rarely measured in absolutes."

"Oh?" Amusement flashed across his striking features. "That's not very practical advice for making decisions with. You ought to point that out to Mr. Wisdom the next time you see him."

Despite everything, I laughed. "Well, whenever I'm overthinking something, my dad likes to remind me the world has survived a surprisingly colossal number of poor decisions so far."

One dark brow lifted. "Comforting."

"Sometimes I thought so. Sometimes I wanted to beat him over the head with a pillow."

That won me a smile. A brief smile, but I'd take it. Then his attention returned to the strongbox.

The fae had put clever safeguards in place—some of which we'd been sure to detail to the cult members to stop them from killing me and snatching the prize. Namely that the fae-magicked strongbox could only be opened by me. And I had to be alive to do it.

But those safeguards were not fail-safe. It would take

time, days or even weeks, but eventually the protections would break. They could not hold strong forever outside of Faerie.

Which meant killing me was not out of the question. Merely inconvenient.

I drew in a deep breath and released it slowly. Even if they planned to kill me, I should be able to save the people of Las Vegas before that happened. Which would buy everyone else time they didn't currently possess to find a new way past this force field. That would have to be enough.

My roiling stomach informed me I was not nearly so calm about the prospect of dying as I wanted to pretend.

But surely the cult would try it the easy way first? To keep me alive and persuade me to unlock the strongbox?

Rather than murdering me the instant I passed through the force field.

My plan relied on it. Relied on them feeling so unthreatened by a single unarmed girl without any magic of her own that they couldn't resist seizing the chance for immediate gratification.

The question was, what *would* they try? What counterplans of their own had they made?

Neither side expected the other to play nice. We'd negotiated and agreed on terms, but we both expected the other group to cheat, double-cross, deceive, and do any and everything possible to gain the upper hand.

I scanned my own side. There was one additional person here today who hadn't been present on our first failed attempt to infiltrate the ranch house. She was well-dressed and slender with a serene face, dreamy eyes, and long, tumbling dark hair. Weirdly appropriate for a sleeping beauty. The Disney version anyway.

On the other side of the force field, seven figures were gathered on the porch, saying very little. According to the surveillance team's observations, everyone was accounted for, but they'd warned me the old magicless technology wasn't infallible—and the cult members had been well aware they were under surveillance. I stared at the seven of them unabashedly, linking their flesh-and-blood faces with the pictures and magic information I'd memorized.

I didn't know whether to be encouraged or disconcerted that Hatshepsut was there, sporting a dark red gemstone in one pointed, green-hued ear.

Since my rescue of Madison had revealed our hand, the gremlin had apparently used her special brand of craftsmith magic to secure the force field around the ranch house. Now, instead of being held up by Hale's will alone and therefore revocable by his will alone, some or all of the power keeping the force field erect had been channeled into a bloodstone. Which meant Hale would need the bloodstone holder's cooperation to lower the force field.

A Faerie consultant said *without* that cooperation, the only way to get the force field down would be to acquire and destroy the bloodstone.

Easy, right?

It might be if the ruby-red gemstone in Hatshepsut's ear was the one I needed.

So was it carelessness, arrogance, or sly cunning that had her wearing the jewel that looked an awful lot like a bloodstone as if it were a piece of jewelry?

Or maybe as soon as she'd confirmed the iron key's identity and scanned me for weapons, she'd hotfoot it to a more secure location.

Because I was going inside. That was the agreement we'd negotiated. I was the good guys' guarantee that the Order of Influence would uphold its end of the bargain by removing the force field around Las Vegas. Because as soon as Hale shared his magic with me to get me and the iron key through the wall, I could dissolve *that* force field myself. And in return, I would deliver the iron key into the cult's hands.

Sort of.

Oh, and Madison would be released from the secure government facility where she was being held. But no one except her father cared about that.

At some invisible signal, Hale stepped up to the force field, his hands glowing with cold orange light.

Ronan in turn strapped the strongbox to my torso, his movements strained and precise. When he was done, his haunted eyes met mine again, and this time I thought some of the concern in them might be for me.

My top two priorities were to take down the Las Vegas dome and prevent the iron key from remaining in the cult's hands. My own survival was a distant third. So he was probably right to be concerned.

I was trying not to dwell on it. All the risks I would be taking today. All the lives that were at stake. To hold the weight of them in my mind would paralyze me.

Perhaps that was why, with his stupidly appealing scent all around me, his wings shielding me from the people I was about to fight, and the worry written across his normally composed face, my thoughts shifted to how I should've kissed Ronan while I'd had the chance.

Hale's voice yanked my attention away. "We're ready for you."

I gave Ronan a short, quick nod and then strode over to hug Indah, the flown-in sleeping beauty from Denver, as if she were my best friend. Her mission-critical magic flooded into me. But given the circumstances, I would've preferred to hug Aurelis.

Or possibly Ronan. Riding for hours with my chest pressed against his feathers and my arms wrapped around his abdomen had apparently left a lasting impression on my libido.

Instead, I stepped up to the force field in front of Hale and his glowing hands.

Hatshepsut had come up beside him, and she leveled a suspicious glare at me.

I knew that behind me everyone else was stepping back. Leaving me physically isolated.

The gremlin nodded. "She's clear of any metal, gems, or stones except for the iron key."

We'd taken care to ensure I wasn't carrying anything that might set off her radar. Every passing second before I got inside counted.

Hale stretched his arm through the thick force field. I could see some of my own tension mirrored in him. This was the first test.

Ronan had suggested there was a slim chance I'd be able to use Hale's magic to take down the Las Vegas dome before I was all the way through this one. In which case I could try to get out before ever entering the lion's den.

He'd also warned the cult might attempt to snatch the iron key from my person without ever allowing me inside. Which was why the strongbox was physically attached to my torso. And why there were plenty on my side ready to intervene if they tried anything.

With one arm clamped over the world's most powerful artifact, I raised the other and pressed my palm against Hale's. His skin barely breached the protective surface of his force field, but his magic pushed against my palm. I allowed it to flow through me.

The power was complex and unfamiliar, but I could immediately sense that *this* force field was different from the others. I ignored it, stretching my awareness toward Vegas. *There.*

Hale's fingers locked around mine, and telekinetic magic yanked me through the wall.

I stumbled as I emerged on the other side of the force field. The *inside*.

The strongbox containing the iron key was swiftly wrenched from my grasp as the pyromancer burned away the straps and the telekinetic snatched it out of reach. Someone growled at Hale to "Search her." But my mind was on the more immediate matter of using the dregs of my borrowed sleeping beauty magic to shove every one of the seven cult members into slumber.

They swayed and dropped. But sleeping beauty magic required continual maintenance, and I'd had so little left to begin with that I had seconds at best.

I lunged to meet Indah, who was running toward me, and used Hale's remaining magic to shove my hand through the force field to touch hers. Juggling two unfamiliar magics at once was not something I'd had much experience with—I usually had enough trouble finding *one* person willing to let me draw from them—and my palms were already clammy with sweat.

But there was no room for self-doubt.

I pushed more sleeping magic at the restless cultists and dashed back to Hale.

Ignoring the blood drumming in my ears and every instinct screaming I was in lethal danger, I grasped his disconcertingly soft fingers. Then reached again for the distant but immense force field smothering Las Vegas.

There.

I brushed my awareness over it, making sure I had the entirety of its essence firm in my mind, then let

Hale's magic guide me in altering the solid impenetrable walls into harmless nothingness.

My ears popped like I'd just undergone a dramatic change in altitude, and then it was gone. The dome that had caused so much pain and chaos and terror, the trap that had taken some and threatened so many more lives, ceased to exist.

Relief threatened to overwhelm me. But there was no time for weakness. And there was certainly no time for celebration.

"Dome is down," I shouted.

Back in Vegas, teams were standing by in the sewers to deactivate the anti-magic devices. Experts estimated it would take ten to fifteen minutes before magic was restored throughout the city.

I shoved to my feet and sent up a brief prayer no one would die in the interim. And a second prayer that the LVMPD might have caught the remaining half dozen escapees who had still been at large this morning.

Outside the force field, a cheer went up. But the slumbering cultists were stirring again as my sleeping beauty magic ran dry.

I staggered back to Indah for a refill, then scanned the porch for the strongbox. "Anyone know where the iron key ended up?"

"Inside the house," she said. "Beyond that, we couldn't see."

I cursed. If it'd still been within reach, I might've grabbed it and escaped. With Las Vegas freed, the cult members could stay stuck inside the ranch house and rot for all I cared.

Well, no. I'd prefer to see them in prison, but I'd settle for being alive to hug my father again.

Unfortunately, a dose of Indah's magic wouldn't buy me enough time to search the frustratingly large house, draw from Hale again, and get out before everyone woke up.

So instead, I launched myself at Hatshepsut who was sprawled halfway up the porch steps. More specifically, I launched myself at the blood-red gemstone in her ear. I pried it off, drawing in her magic on autopilot and flinching when she let out a gravelly snore. The red stone had magical properties. I could feel it through Hatshepsut's ill-fitting power. So I stomped on it as hard as I could.

It didn't break. Dammit. They were supposed to be weaker than normal gemstones.

Glancing around for a brick or something, I spotted the brawny figure of the strength amplifier snoring his head off a few paces away. I rushed for him, drew in his magic, and crushed the bloodstone between my fingers.

But the force field didn't go down.

The Faerie expert had warned me that Hatshepsut could've shored it up in a number of different ways. And bringing the force field down could be a matter of just destroying the bloodstone—or *bloodstones*—or else require both the release of the stored power in the stones *and* the application of Hale's magic.

Feeling like a ping-pong ball—a highly endangered ping-pong ball—I scrambled back to Hale and reached for the force field surrounding the ranch house again. But it was still remote, detached somehow. Swearing, I returned to Hatshepsut and used her power to search for other magic-imbued items.

One crazy glowing thing must have been the iron key somewhere inside the house. But there were four additional small gems scattered about—at least one of which was *also* somewhere inside the house. The other bloodstones were probably held by other cult members, but no one else had theirs on display like Hatshepsut.

I'd never manage to find them all in forty-second increments.

Once more, the cultists began to stir.

"Change of plan," I shouted as I sprinted for Indah again. "I need anti-magic handcuffs. Now."

I thrust my hand through the force field and received several pairs of them. Indah touched my arm to allow me to draw her magic simultaneously. Then her eyes went wide.

I flung her magic behind me at the cult members. A gun went off, painfully loud in the quiet dome. I whirled, wondering if I'd been shot and just hadn't registered it yet. Then saw the gun a few inches from the strength amplifier's motionless hand. Where he'd dropped it. When I'd pushed him into sleep. Moments before he'd been about to shoot me in the back.

Shakily, I scooped up the gun and hurried to

neutralize the most dangerous cult members first. The telekinetic and then the pyromancer, I decided.

My heart was racing a million miles an hour, every moment bringing me closer to the one where something would go irretrievably wrong. But I grabbed Wyatt Bradshaw's bony wrist and used his telekinesis to drag every other cult member into a neat, orderly row along the porch railing. Everyone except Hale, who I shoved a short distance to lie at Indah's feet. Then I slapped the cuffs on Bradshaw, looping the chain around the post so he couldn't go anywhere.

With the cuffs on, his magic was as inaccessible to me as it was to him. But when he slumped back onto the ground, a red gemstone tumbled out onto the dirt.

I snatched it up and shoved it into my pocket, then stood. Swayed. I'd never used this much borrowed magic in quick succession before. Or maybe it was the potent combination of action and adrenaline, relief, and terror.

The unwelcome thought that Hatshepsut's craft-smith magic might be able to subvert the handcuffs if it wasn't neutralized led me to slap the next set of cuffs on her. The third pair I used to secure the pyromancer, and then I pushed myself toward Indah.

Movement flashed in my peripheral vision. The *wrong* side of my peripheral vision.

I spun just in time to see a figure coming out of the ranch house. Then a glowing chain of magic lashed toward me and something cold and heavy wrapped around my calf.

Before I could even look down, the thing around my leg yanked hard, and I was being dragged across the dirt. I cried out as the chain links bit into my flesh, then forgot about my calf and tried to protect my head from smashing against the porch steps.

I slid to a stop at my assailant's feet.

A cold, handsome face stared down at me. A face that hadn't been in my study materials.

An *eighth* cult member.

Looked like the surveillance guy had been right. The old equipment they were using was far from infallible.

CHAPTER TWENTY-SEVEN

I flung myself toward the cult member I knew nothing about, trying to make contact with the skin at his ankle. But at a flick of his wrist, the magical tether around my calf jerked me out of reach.

Although the new guy's hand held one end of the glowing links, the chain moved to do his bidding like a separate entity. Far more versatile—and dangerous—than any normal version.

He smirked down at me. "You've pissed off the wrong group of people, little girl. I'll enjoy watching you learn your lesson."

But I was only half listening. My eyes caught on the strongbox he'd slung around his neck like an absurd necklace—and the ruby-red gem dangling beside it. A replica of the one I'd found on Hatshepsut.

Perhaps I wouldn't have to go searching through the house after all.

"Come closer and say that," I sneered, trying to draw magic from the chain the way I'd done with the prison hedge.

It didn't work. But then I hadn't really expected it to.

My captor smiled. "Now why would I go and do a stupid thing like that?"

Behind me, the other cult members were waking up —with various degrees of grogginess and cursing. Not good. My margin to act was rapidly diminishing. But if I could just snatch the iron key and tag Hale on my way out, I might still live through this.

I shrugged with feigned carelessness. "Worth a shot." The movement of my shoulders disguised my reach for the gun I'd confiscated earlier and stashed in my waistband.

It wasn't there.

Probably dislodged when the chain mage had skidded me across the dirt on my ass.

One of the waking cultists raised their voice in complaint. "What the hell took you so long that the bitch managed to cuff me?"

I recognized the whine. The telekinetic who'd tried to kill Madison.

"Get me out of these now!" he hissed.

My captor didn't look particularly moved by the demand. "Where's the key for the cuffs?" he asked me, jerking the chain for emphasis.

"Outside."

"Figured as much." His gaze flicked to Bradshaw. "You'll have to wait until we—"

In that moment of inattention, I yanked my tethered leg back as hard as I could, causing him to stumble half a step toward me. It was enough. I kicked out with my other leg and landed my boot in his crotch.

The chain around my calf slackened while its operator doubled over in agony.

I shoved it off over my foot and lunged for the iron key. My damaged leg protested the movement, but my fingers brushed the strongbox.

Then someone grabbed me from behind. The strength amplifier. I could tell because the crushing grip was threatening to snap my ribs, but I concentrated on drawing in his magic.

"Don't let her touch your skin," the chain mage growled.

Too late. I stomped on my attacker's instep with his own bone-shattering strength. He howled, and I whirled to connect my elbow with his face, except the blasted chain bit into my leg and yanked me to the decking again. I tore at the chain with the strength mage's fading magic. It snapped, and its wielder cursed like it hurt. But before I could take advantage of my momentary freedom, darkness clouded my vision. Either I was dying from a wound I hadn't noticed yet, or the shadow caller had joined the fight.

I stopped dead, unable to see a damn thing. Outnumbered and outmaneuvered. Then the cold links of the chain snaked around my arms and torso and dragged me backward until I slammed into something hard.

The shadows dissipated, leaving me squinting at the now too-bright daylight. I was inside. Sitting up, I noticed belatedly. The chain that was pressing into my chest making it hard to breathe also bound me to a heavy wooden chair. I had a brief impression of a stone fireplace, thick carpet, grand, heavily laden bookshelves, high ceilings with exposed honey-colored beams, and a decor of comforting earthy tones.

I was far from comforted.

Five cult members surrounded me. Everyone I hadn't managed to handcuff. And though two were smiling, none of them looked friendly.

A wave of fear hit me, so powerful it made bile rise in my throat. I was going to die. No. I was going to be brutalized and shamed, I was going to fail, was going to let down the entire world, and *then* I was going to die. My heart thudded painfully in my chest, and every injury I'd sustained in the past minutes throbbed with new intensity. But the fear… the fear was the worst.

I whimpered.

One of the men's smiles widened.

The empath projector who could mess with other people's emotions, I realized through another wave of gut-churning dread.

"Stop it," I hissed. If I threw up from the fear, I hoped I could aim it at his shoes.

Lewd enjoyment was written all over his face. "That's an appetizer of what's to come," he promised.

His evident pleasure made it worse, even as he allowed the unnatural fear to fade.

The chain mage stood to my right, still holding one end of the chain. He removed the strongbox from his neck and dangled it in front of me. The others watched and waited. Apparently, he was in charge now that I'd taken out the telekinetic.

Who the hell was this guy? And how had we missed his existence?

Hale had only been the figurehead of the scheme. The diversion. He was standing a little farther back than the other four. Like he was subconsciously trying to distance himself. Like perhaps he'd never imagined things would go so far.

The chain mage thrust the iron key closer to my nose. Closer, but not close enough for me to make contact with his hand with the small leeway my bindings permitted.

"Open the strongbox, *now*. And perhaps I'll convince the others to go easy on you."

Judging by the glint in his eye and the fact I'd kicked him in the groin, I doubted it. I could still hear the telekinetic cursing outside. And the strength amplifier I'd hobbled—and the empath I'd done nothing whatsoever to—were looking at me with sinister promise.

Going easy on me was the last thing on their minds.

Anxiety filled me, and I thought it might be my own this time.

I tried not to let it show. "I'd prefer to die than let the iron key fall into your hands."

The strength mage selected a book from a nearby shelf and slapped me with it so hard it left my ear ringing. Something wet trickled down my jaw. He probably hadn't even used his magic.

"Don't give her a concussion just yet," the chain mage chided. "We want her reasoning faculties intact for a little longer."

He returned his attention to me. "So you're prepared to die, are you? How admirable." His sneer undermined the compliment. "After witnessing you rush in to play hero to Hale's daughter, we thought you might say that."

His lack of concern made me tense in anticipation.

"The question is..." He waved forward the shadow caller who was fiddling with a laptop.

With a flicker of annoyance at her colleague's high-handed need for showmanship, she turned the screen around and thrust it at my face.

"...will you let your family die too?"

Horror engulfed me. And this time it was entirely my own.

They had my family.

This cult—which had been willing to slaughter thousands to satisfy its thirst for power—*had my family.*

A scream of outrage lodged halfway up my throat.

This *couldn't* happen. This wasn't part of the deal. I'd entered this den of homicidal assholes to *save* my family.

But on the laptop screen was a live video feed showing my beloved father and younger siblings held hostage by two men I wished I'd never had cause to lay eyes on.

I recognized the room. The cozy living area in my family's apartment where we'd shared so many happy memories.

Blake and Archer were on the floor, bound at their wrists and ankles, their expressions angry and frightened. Miles was slumped horizontally across the three-seater couch and looked so ill he might not have had the strength to sit up even if it wasn't for the ropes binding him. And Sage was in the corner a short distance from her brothers, curled into as tight a ball as she could make herself, so small and helpless in the face of her captors they hadn't even bothered to bind her. Although a purpling bruise on her cheek suggested they'd bothered to *hit* her.

Hells, it hurt so much to look at her. To look at what I'd caused to happen. She didn't deserve this. Didn't deserve any of this…

I wrenched my mind off the road to despair and focused on the good parts. They appeared to be largely unharmed. And the bindings meant they weren't being mind-controlled.

Yet.

How many minutes had it been since I'd managed to

get the force field down? My brain scrabbled to work it out.

"Lyra Ridley, meet Colton Metcalf," the chain mage said like we were at some schmoozy networking event, "the founder of our beloved Order of Influence, now freed from his inconvenient imprisonment."

Yes. Metcalf. The psychopath who, as an adolescent, had famously tortured his parents and childhood best friend for no other purpose but his own gratification.

In the same room as my family.

I glared at him with a hatred I hadn't known I possessed. There was no doubt now whether the prison break had been part of the cult's scheme all along. Or why he was one of the last escapees the LVMPD hadn't managed to track down.

"And I believe you're already acquainted with Hendrix."

Hendrix, aka Ken Doll #5. The man I'd faced down in the tunnel.

His action-figure physique was even more apparent in the context of my family home. He loomed over my incapacitated father and siblings, his bulging muscles seeming like overkill. But his presence paled in comparison to Metcalf.

Metcalf leaned forward and smiled, showing off too many teeth. He was not a physically intimidating man, his frame was scrawny, and years in a sleeping chamber without sun had left his skin pasty white. But the power of his mind, the ability to compel others to do anything he wanted, up to and including taking their own life, was legendary, and the flat calculation in his eyes left me cold.

"Ah, Lyra," he said. "Thank you for organizing the deactivation of the anti-magic devices around the city and distracting so many of the government's special operatives while I complete my escape."

My gut twisted again. *No.* They couldn't have foreseen this. They hadn't needed me to bring down the force field or the anti-magic field.

But they *had* needed me to convince the fae to hand over the iron key before that happened.

My stomach wound tighter. *No. No. No.* I'd been so naive to think I could change things for the better. Instead, I'd messed everything up. And my family was about to pay the ultimate price for it.

"If you survive the next few minutes, I look forward to exploring your mind with the iron key at my disposal," the bastard added.

Then he stood, and my heart all but froze in my chest for what must be coming. But he merely nodded at Ken Doll. "You know what to do."

He strolled out of the screen, and judging by the familiar creak of the door, out of the apartment too.

My first instinct was relief. Then Ken Doll #5 unsheathed a knife from his utility belt.

Another onslaught of emotion punched through me. So intense it felt like my bones might crack under the weight of it. My family was going to die. They were going to be tortured, and then they were going to die. And it was going to happen right in front of me. Because of me. Even though I was over two hundred miles away. Even though I'd been trying to save them. They were going to die.

Beneath the gibbering terror, I was dimly aware of the empath smiling beside me, but I couldn't tear my gaze away from the screen.

Miles's eyes had shuttered, the magic starvation and his degenerative disease doing the cult's work for them. And my brothers were staring at the knife held by Ken Doll as he made a show of inspecting its wicked edge. But Sage's dark brown eyes were fixed on me, shining with a heart-wrenching combination of terror and trust. So I tried very hard not to whimper again.

"Open the strongbox," the chain mage demanded evenly.

The threat didn't need to be stated to break me.

Empath magic pushed me toward hysteria. I wanted to shriek and wail and throw myself to the floor and bawl like a child. I wanted to thrash and claw at my captors, at my clothes, at my face and hair. I wanted to run and run and scream and scream and find some sort of absolution in the numb emptiness of exhaustion. Only the chains and Sage's expectant gaze stopped me.

Tears poured down my cheeks, and my constrained hands dug fingernails deep into my thighs.

This time I couldn't stop the whimper.

Because I *couldn't* unlock the strongbox. Physically could not.

That had been one of the cards I'd been holding up my sleeve. Sure we'd *told* the cult I was the only one it would open for to make them think twice about killing me. But the only way the fae would let the iron key out of Faerie was on the condition no one but Ronan could unlock its protective case.

Which meant I couldn't be forced into betraying the world no matter what the cult did to me. And my sacrifice would buy the good guys extra days, maybe weeks, to figure out an alternate way to take down the Order of Influence and retrieve the iron key.

It had been a sacrifice I'd been sort of okay with for the sake of saving hundreds of thousands of lives.

But I was *not* okay with sacrificing the lives of my family too. What sort of abomination would it be to steal Sage's gentle soul from the world? To snuff out Archer's energetic enthusiasm? Or Blake's earnest, sensitive intelligence? And Miles was far too needed as a beacon of hope and peace and sanctuary in this broken and divided earth.

The problem was, the choice was out of my hands.

I'd traded it up willingly, having no clue as to the true cost of that exchange.

"Go ahead and open it," the empath crooned. "It's

only a matter of time until we break into it ourselves. So save us a few days' effort, and we'll save your family's lives."

My pain-filled hysteria cracked and fell away like broken glass. And in its place, I found myself eager—so, so eager to please.

The combination of that eagerness and the relief from the barrage of terror was almost indecent.

Ken Doll #5 towered over Miles's inert form, bare blade at the ready. But I couldn't even summon the undesirable emotions I knew I should be feeling. *Must* be feeling on some level.

Sage's frozen gaze was still on me.

Run, I wanted to tell her. *Don't just sit there.* But if I let my lips part, I was worried I might moan in pleasure instead. So I tried to convey the message with my eyes and angled my head ever so slightly toward the door.

Ken Doll's attention flicked toward the camera. Then he grabbed a handful of my father's thick red hair and wrenched his head back to expose his throat for the waiting blade.

"Last chance," the chain mage warned.

That was when my little sister leaped to her feet, used the couch as a launching pad, and headbutted Ken Doll #5 in the skull with a sharp, satisfying crack.

CHAPTER TWENTY-EIGHT

Ken Doll #5 toppled.

Sage, with her skull and horns designed for impact, was unhurt.

Blake and Archer whooped and began calling for her to grab the knife and cut them free from the rope that bound them.

And inspired by my terrifyingly courageous little sister, I launched myself, chair and all, at the man holding my own bindings.

He was too shocked by what he'd just witnessed to react quickly enough. My face collided with his torso, catching his bare arm as I fell. And then I was free of the chain and repurposing it to bring the chair down on his head.

The chair cracked. He went down and stayed down. And I used the opportunity to siphon more of his power while I was still on the floor.

A wave of desperate fear battered against me, followed by hopeless despair so deep it felt like falling to the core of the earth. But either I was already wrung dry from the excessive emotional rollercoaster, or it wasn't enough to stop me.

I flung the chain at the shadow caller's legs—deeming her the next biggest threat—and yanked them out from under her. The laptop she'd been holding smashed to the floor.

Once again my vision blackened. But this time I didn't need to see. I pulled the chain and its captive toward me, much as the chain mage had first done to me, then reached down blindly until I found flesh.

On my left where I'd last seen the empath, I thought I heard a gun safety click off. The shadow mage punched me in the face, and hot blood gushed down my chin.

But I'd already taken what I needed to clear my vision and blacken the empath's and strength amplifier's. I didn't know where Hale had gone.

I used the last bit of chain magic to fling the shadow caller into the wall. Then flung myself at the blinded strength mage.

He heard me coming and swung, but I ducked under his arm and stomped on his already injured foot. He cursed. Loudly. And a gun went off. The empath shooting blind. I shielded myself behind the strength mage's bulk, brushed the back of his neck, and used his magic to deliver an excruciating blow to the kidney. I kicked him forward to stumble into the empath just as the shadows covering both their faces dissipated.

Neither were as incapacitated as I'd prefer. But at least the empath had dropped the gun. I backed away, holding my hands up like I was thinking of surrendering. Until my ankle reached the chain mage's outflung arm.

The strength amplifier picked up the nearest object —a heavy wooden desk—while the empath scrabbled to retrieve the gun and leveled it at my torso.

I dove to the floor behind a couch and sent a chain spinning through the air toward them. It hit the strength mage's thick neck and pivoted around to catch the empath's too. Then I tightened it. Fast.

Their heads smashed together with a crack that resembled Sage's headbutt.

A smile flickered across my lips.

Panting and shaking and bleeding and smiling, I scanned the room for the iron key.

It wasn't there.

Which was when I realized what Hale had done. He'd snatched up the strongbox, run to the adjacent dining area, and raised a personal force field. Effectively locking both the iron key and himself out of reach.

Which meant I couldn't get out.

Couldn't retrieve the artifact.

Couldn't get help.

Couldn't find safety.

Unless…

Some of the fallen cult members were groaning, and I didn't know how long they'd stay down. But if I could find and smash the last four bloodstones, the force field around the ranch house might fall even without access to Hale's magic. And then the task force could take care of the rest. With his allies defeated and no way to open the strongbox on his own, Hale couldn't hold out forever.

I already had one gem in my pocket from the telekinetic, and I knew the chain mage possessed a second. Could I find the other two?

I eased myself out from behind the couch. No one shot me. So I wrenched the red stone from the chain mage's neck and relieved him of any weapons he might try to murder me with later. Then I staggered forward and retrieved the gun from the empath's limp grasp, aiming it at the strength amplifier as I leaned over to draw on his power. The two bloodstones I'd collected fractured beneath my fingers.

Two left to find.

Swaying on my feet, I used some of the strength mage's magic just to keep myself going and patted him and the empath down, careful to keep the gun trained on them, just in case. I found one gem in the empath's back jeans pocket and destroyed it.

One more to go.

I was so, so weary now. My head hurt, my leg hurt, my back hurt, my chest hurt. Everything hurt. My nose was still trickling blood from the shadow caller's well-aimed blow. And who knew what damage I might've done to myself by using my magic so heavily. But the thought of what the cult would do to me and the hope of seeing my family again spurred me on.

I stumbled over to the shadow caller, cursing myself for flinging her so far, and praying I would find the last bloodstone on her unconscious form. Too weak to squat, I dropped onto the soft carpet beside her and searched the usual places. Pockets. Ears. Neck. Hands.

Nothing.

It must be on someone else.

Fighting back tears at the insurmountable task still ahead of me, I forced my legs beneath me once more. Then belatedly noticed her strappy sandals had a red gem in the center of each foot. Except one was a slightly different hue and size than the other.

My fingers closed around the darker gem just as an all-too-familiar chain bit into my calves and yanked my legs back out from under me. I slammed to the floor, breaking the fall painfully with my forearms, then twisted to see what was coming as I was dragged across the carpet. The chain mage had eased himself into a sitting position while I'd been otherwise preoccupied.

I sent shadows leaping at his face to blind him and aimed the gun I'd commandeered with my left hand. My right was still clutching the all-important final bloodstone.

I shot him. I'd been aiming for his heart but hit him in the stomach.

I really *was* tired.

He screamed. The chain released me. But only after pitching me almost into his lap. I kicked off him, trying to get away, to clip his stomach wound, to free up my arm to shoot again, anything. But I was too late. The chain smashed the gun out of my hand, breaking several of my fingers with the force.

I cried out, and the chain mage grinned through his own pain. How he'd managed to disarm me while blinded, I had no idea. But the shadow dissipated as I lost concentration, and then the chain was around my neck, tightening fast.

Panic made me claw at my throat like Madison before my training kicked in. Lower my chin. Hunch my shoulders. Protect my windpipe. But it only helped fractionally. The end result would be the same.

The man I'd kicked in the balls, shot in the stomach, and whose little show I'd well and truly ruined, watched my distress with vengeful pleasure. His eyes latched on mine.

I held his gaze. Hoping he wouldn't notice as I fumbled to push off one of my sparkly trainers.

My vision blurred.

Something in my neck cracked.

If I passed out, I would never wake up again. The feral glint in the chain mage's eyes was a promise of death.

The shoe came off. I focused on the sock. Thank heavens I was wearing ankle socks. The magical chain had me pinned in place, and there was no way I'd be able to reach him with my broken hand. But I scraped the sock off. And then stretched my leg out slowly, carefully. The tip of my toe just managed to brush his ankle.

My darkening vision made his face seem to blur into the bookshelf behind him, and his magic felt heavy and clumsy in my grasp.

Before I was dragged into unconsciousness, I threw up a chain like an emergency flare and brought the heavy bookshelf down on us both.

CHAPTER TWENTY-NINE

I woke up in a hospital bed.

With a copper dragon squeezed into the small space where a second bed would normally sit.

"Aurelis?" I rasped. Then immediately wished I hadn't when the word caused my throat to burn in protest.

"Ah. You're finally awake." She surveyed my damaged body with a critical eye. "This is why you should never go into battle without me. Humans are just so breakable."

"What happened?"

I had so many other questions. Where was my family? Where was the iron key? Was everyone okay? Were all the cult members in custody? How was I alive?

But the pain of squeezing the first three words past my traumatized throat convinced me to shut up.

Aurelis huffed. "That's what I wanted to ask you. But

your neck's as black and blue as an NYPD uniform, so I suppose I'll go first."

She used a talon to press the button that raised me into a sitting position, her movements careful and precise in the too-small space.

"There's a juice box for you on the side table by the way. The doctor said you should drink it."

I found the promised juice box with a handy straw already in it, along with a small assortment of cards and flowers. I reached for it, relieved to discover that while my whole body was stiff and aching and my ribs hurt like I'd been galloped over by a herd of unicorns, nothing else was as painful as my neck. Including the splints and heavy bandaging on my left hand.

Aurelis gave me the rundown while I sipped on my juice. She'd seen me yanked into the ranch house and then had no idea what was happening until the force field flickered out. She told me this in an offended tone —like it had been *my* idea to take the party inside.

At that point, the task force rushed in and apprehended the cult members, and Aurelis had found me unconscious under the bookcase, alongside the chain mage's lifeless body.

I'd killed him.

I tried to process that. During my six months on the police force, I hadn't actually killed anyone before. It felt sort of unreal somehow. And yet maybe it was the drugs I was on, but I couldn't quite bring myself to care.

Aurelis went on to say that several of the other cult

members were being treated for head trauma and the odd broken bone, and the rest were already locked up. With all his allies neutralized, it hadn't taken long for Hale to surrender himself and the iron key. He'd negotiated a visit with his daughter in exchange.

My family was okay. Miles had been taken to the hospital and was recovering well now the magic was back. Ken Doll #5, aka Hendrix, was also in custody after being taken down and trussed up by my younger siblings. But Metcalf, the psychopath with mind-control powers, was still at large.

My family was okay. I closed my eyes for a moment and let that sink in. Then frowned.

How was it that *I* was okay too?

"I don't understand why the force field came down," I admitted. And then, since the juice seemed to be helping a little, added, "The chain mage attacked me just before I could destroy the last bloodstone."

"We found red fragments on the floor next to you. We assumed you'd broken it. But maybe the bookcase crushed it along with you and the bastard who strangled you."

I'd gotten lucky then. Though I didn't entirely *feel* lucky right now with more aches and pains than I could currently catalog.

I sucked down more juice. "Not that I'm not glad for your company. But why are you squished in here with me instead of cozying up with your hoard? Is your hoard okay?"

She snorted. "I'm *here* because my hoard—despite most of it being both nonsentient and composed of fragile paper—is better at looking after itself than you are."

"Oh. Well, thanks."

"I didn't get you flowers or cards or anything dumb like that. But I've graciously brought my limited-edition hardback of *The Hitchhiker's Guide to the Galaxy* for you to read while you're finishing up your suspension."

My eyebrows shot up. Even that hurt.

"I'm still suspended? But I saved the freaking city!"

Aurelis flicked her wings in a shrug and looked irritated when they brushed the walls. "Afraid so. Here, one of these cards is from Gadson."

She used her magic to flick one of the envelopes over to me, apparently deciding moving in the cramped space was more trouble than it was worth.

The card had a picture of a penguin on it with a thermometer stuck in its beak, and I suspected Gadson hadn't picked it out himself. Though come to think of it, I wasn't sure what type of card he *would* have selected. One that said *GET WELL SOON* followed by a checklist of recommended protocols for an efficient recovery maybe.

Officer Ridley,
You're still suspended. But I've ordered payroll to reinstate
your pay. I suggest you use the remaining days to rest and
spend time with your family. And if you can possibly

299

manage to stay out of trouble for the duration, I'll let you
come back to work.
Captain Gadson

I grimaced and slumped back against the pillow.

Aurelis eyeballed my dejected form. "I know you haven't seen yourself in the mirror yet, but trust me. Even though the healing mages have mostly mended your broken fingers, broken ribs, broken nose, and the fractures and most significant damage to your neck, you look like you're going to need that extra recovery time."

I grunted in reluctant acknowledgment.

My dragon partner looked amused. "Anyway, since you're okay and completely useless at satiating my curiosity, I'm going home to catch up on some reading. When you've tired of the repetitive drivel in your get-well-soon cards, I recommend you do the same."

She extracted herself from the space with great care, having to lower her head and clamp her wings to her sides to fit through the doorway. Ten seconds later, I heard her growl at someone down the hall.

Imagining some poor nurse having the misfortune of getting between Aurelis and her books, I scrunched my face in sympathy. Then reached for the stack of cards.

Before I could go through them, I learned who Aurelis had really been growling at.

Ronan knocked at my open door and stepped inside.

Maybe it was the painkillers, but he looked even better than I remembered.

He came over to my bedside and perched awkwardly on the visitor chair that hadn't been designed with wings in mind.

"Thank you for protecting the iron key," he murmured, eyes scrutinizing my current state.

I flinched, remembering the agony of knowing I couldn't open the strongbox even to stop the cult from killing my family right in front of me. Then flinched a second time at the awareness things might have turned out very differently if I could have.

His intent gaze sharpened at my reaction, lingering on the apparently impressive bruises on my neck. "I was told you would be healed."

"I have been." Allegedly. "The remaining stuff is superficial." I swallowed and forced my uninjured fingers to unclench. "And you of all people know I didn't have a choice."

He dipped his head.

"Even so, you could have saved yourself. Left it in their hands. And no one else could've pulled off what you did. Your magic is powerful. Peculiar, but powerful."

I'd never thought of my magic as an asset before. I'd been bullied throughout my school years for having no real magic of my own. *Lyra the leech* was one of the nicer names they'd dubbed me with. And it usually felt like more of a liability than strength in my professional life.

I certainly hadn't *felt* powerful, scrambling madly

about the ranch house trying not to die. Yet I had taken on eight powerful cult members and *won*.

Saved the city. Saved the iron key. And my sister had saved our family.

An unexpected warmth spread through my chest. Before I could finish processing that, Ronan spoke again.

"I told your police captain as much, by the way. Acting Commander Quinton's report glossed over your involvement in two uncharitable sentences, so I thought he should know the truth of it."

"Oh." Was that why my pay had been reinstated? "Thanks."

Ronan shrugged off my gratitude. "I've also started the process of trying to have the charges dropped against you in case you ever want to visit Faerie in the future." A grimace flickered across his face. "That task will be far more difficult. I believe your captain is fond of you. The prison overseer is not."

I lifted a shoulder with a nonchalance I didn't feel. "It wouldn't be the first time I've pissed off a superior."

But I was uncomfortable remembering how close Madison and I had come to killing the two prison guards. Unlike the chain mage, they'd just been doing their jobs.

And a small voice in the back of my mind was wondering if *Ronan* was fond of me. At all. Even a little bit.

Because this might be the last time I ever saw him.

And I'd come to like this man who assumed competence, who was quick to listen and slow to give advice, who gave my ideas and fears the same grave consideration he directed to everything else. His roots were as deep as Faerie's and just as inaccessible. Yet he'd allowed me a glimpse once or twice. And what I'd seen was someone honorable, insightful, and perhaps braver than I could truly comprehend in convincing the council to risk everything to save the people of Vegas.

Unaware of the turn my thoughts had taken, Ronan pressed on. His dark eyes serious, compelling, his scent more than a little intoxicating.

"Although not everyone on the Faerie Governing Council will admit it, we owe you a debt. If you ever need the kind of assistance only a fae can provide, I'll do my best to aid you."

Even on the painkillers, I was *pretty* sure he didn't mean assisting me in exploring my sexual fantasies involving a pair of deep soulful eyes, inviting lips, perfect abs, and soft black wings.

I cleared my throat and hoped I wasn't blushing. "Thank you. But you're the one who convinced the council and task force to go along with the plan. Who's repaying you?"

He canted his head, like I was a puzzle he couldn't quite figure out. "You're not at all like I expected," he said.

"What did you expect?"

"Well, most of my experience with humankind before now came from telenovelas."

My eyebrows shot up. "Telenovelas? Like the Spanish soap operas?"

"My favorite childhood tutor and bodyguard loved them and used to watch them with me all the time when I was growing up. And I don't have anything to do with the holidaying tourists, so…" He quirked a brow.

I chuckled. "Ah, well as far as I know, I'm not pregnant with my sister's husband's child, nor in a coma, nor do I have a long-lost evil twin, or a strapping but mysterious romantic interest who is almost definitely hiding something from me." I wriggled my own eyebrows and added in a stage whisper, "But I can't guarantee it."

Ronan smirked. "My favorite character was the one later revealed to be a robot slave on a secret mission for the rich but cruel baron. You aren't, by chance, an android are you?"

"Afraid not. Sorry to disappoint."

His smile was wry. "You haven't disappointed. Merely disconcerted. If you'd shrieked and fainted in the trap Hale set for me, I'd be dead."

"Hang on a minute. If you thought humans were like the characters in telenovelas, how come you thought I'd be competent enough to help?"

"I saw you take down the drones, remember? Besides, anyone who'd managed to befriend a dragon had to be special."

Maybe it was the drugs, but I blurted, "You think I'm special?"

"Yes," he said simply.

He rose to his feet with his usual grace. "Take care, Lyra." Then he slipped out of my room and was gone.

Probably forever.

Before I could feel too melancholy about that, Miles appeared in my doorway. Unlike my other visitors, he was wearing a hospital gown that matched my own.

He walked up to me—well, shuffled really by vampire standards—and his beaming face and greeting of "Hello milksucker" made my heart brim over with love and gladness and an echo of remembered fear.

We hugged. Gingerly.

Which was when I realized how little I hurt compared to when I'd first woken up. Either the IV in my arm had given me additional pain relief, or Ronan had subtly healed me. Again.

Miles stepped back, and I drank in the sight of him. Here. In the flesh. With no barrier between us.

"You're looking better," I observed with satisfaction.

My father shot me a half-mocking, half-mournful look. "I wish I could tell you the same."

I crossed my arms as best as I could between the IV and the splints. "Don't think you can change the subject that easily. *You* should've gone to hospital ages ago," I chided him.

"And leave the kids alone when the whole city had gone crazy? I don't think so." He paused. "Though I have to admit they rescued me rather than the other way around… It gives new meaning to the custom some species have of producing offspring so they'll look after you when you're old."

I narrowed my eyes and pretended to consider this. "You're already old."

"My point exactly."

We both laughed. I stopped abruptly when it caused shooting pain over several ribs. But couldn't help the grin from spreading across my face. "You should've seen Sage fell that six-foot-tall bruiser. It was beautiful to behold."

Miles grinned too. "Oh yes. Blake and Archer have been singing her praises to the moon and back. I'm so proud I'm thinking of sticking the X-ray of his skull fracture on the fridge or something."

I snickered. Carefully. "I know you drink blood and all, but I would never have described you as bloodthirsty until today."

He clutched his chest. "Oof. And I thought I'd raised you better than to kick a man when he was down."

I sobered. "Actually, you taught us to kick a man whenever and however necessary to protect ourselves. Thank you for that."

We talked and laughed and caught up—even though doing so made my throat progressively more painful again—until a nurse came in and shooed Miles away so we could both have our final checkups before being discharged.

An hour and a half later, we left the hospital together and caught a cab. Fifteen minutes after that, we were finally home.

We took the elevator rather than the stairs and limped and shuffled our way to Miles's apartment where our neighbor Mrs. Zucker was watching my siblings.

Archer must have smelled us coming because the door flung open before we could reach it. And then we were enveloped by a jumping, shouting whirlwind of small hands and soft kisses.

Including one courageous half-faun girl with the gentlest of hearts and hardest of heads that I was incredibly proud of.

I knelt down to tell her so. To tell her how her courage had saved me too.

And realized that maybe being suspended for a while longer wasn't such a bad thing after all.

EPILOGUE

My family was safe. Las Vegas was back to being a holiday destination for gambling and debauchery. My bruises had faded to a pale yellowy-green reminiscent of goblin skin. And I only had two days left of paid suspension.

Aurelis had *not* agreed to carry anyone else in the interim. She also hadn't let me forget that I owed her a scale spa voucher for carrying me when I was covered in walrus monster slime. And she wanted her limited-edition hardback of *The Hitchhiker's Guide to the Galaxy* back.

I opted to find these things comforting, proof that everything was going back to normal.

The cult founder Metcalf remained at large, but seemed to be lying low for the meanwhile. I was trying not to wonder about his future plans, hoping that more qualified people than me would put a stop to them.

Tonight, for the first time in weeks, I was taking my recovering body out for a jog on the streets of my deeply flawed but beloved city.

I'd missed this.

My cheap, sparkly trainers pounded the pavement in a satisfying rhythm as I passed the mostly darkened shop fronts. It was a warm pleasant evening and late enough that the sidewalks were quiet.

Except for some drunkards peeing on the traffic lights up ahead.

I turned down a side street to avoid having to deal with them. It was one of those narrow utility laneways made primarily to keep the commercial dumpsters off the main thoroughfares, and I immediately regretted my decision. The aroma of fresh urine would've been preferable.

I dodged around a dislodged drain cover and clamped down a twinge of unease. Not every skewed manhole or storm drain was the beginning of an evil master plan. And I was off duty. No, *suspended*, dammit. I fixed my eyes on the end of the laneway and put on an extra burst of speed.

Something clanked behind me, and then I heard the slap of footsteps.

I whirled, wishing I had my Taser with me. And suddenly found a glowing chain in my hand.

I gawked at it. Then at Stewie and Zeus who'd stepped out of the shadows. Then back at the chain.

"Sheesh, guys, you almost gave me a heart attack."

But it wasn't the fright that was responsible for my elevated heart rate anymore.

This wasn't possible. I'd never retained anyone's magic for more than a minute before. Certainly never for *days*.

But the chain was undeniably there. In my hand. Glowing eerily the way I remembered.

I lowered it to my side and willed it to dissipate.

Just when I was starting to like the power I'd been lumped with, it went and pulled the rug out from under me. Except I'd never heard of anyone's magic *changing*. People got better at utilizing their gifts, sure, but the mechanics of that power were a done deal.

Surreptitiously, I tried to make one of the shadows move.

Nada.

I swallowed hard. I'd never killed anyone with their own magic before either.

Stewie was waiting patiently for me to pull myself together. Or rather, he was watching me with an odd look of contemplation on his rugged face.

Then he gave me a nod.

"Heard you saved the city, boss. I always knew you were good people."

I let out a long, slow exhalation and brought myself back to the present moment.

"Couldn't have done it without you, Stewie."

He shrugged it off, but I thought I saw his lips twitch in a smile.

Which made me smile too, despite my unease and the barrage of questions I didn't have answers to.

"I was thinking I could go for a hamburger," I said. Even though it was after ten and I'd already eaten. "Would you and Zeus like to join me?"

Stewie hitched up his rucksack. "That'd be nice, boss. But Zeus only eats at the classier joints. He doesn't like them preservatives."

I hid a grin and knelt down to scratch the scruffy little black dog. "Sure," I said. "Can't blame him for that."

With my paycheck reinstated, I was more than happy to spring for the biggest, juiciest burgers available at this time of night.

The three of us headed back to the main thorough-fare, walking in comfortable silence.

Until Stewie murmured, so soft I barely heard him, "I always wondered if your magic was one of them that had been artificially tampered with, boss. If it were me, I wouldn't let word get around that you're one of the lost experiments."

I stopped and stared, unsettled and unsure whether this was one of his paranoia-induced conspiracy theories, or he knew something I didn't. But his blue eyes were calm and steady as they gazed into mine.

Despite the warm night and the layer of sweat I'd worked up from my jog, a shiver rolled down my spine.

He reached out and patted my shoulder. "Don't worry, boss. Your secret's safe with me."

WANT A SNEAK PEEK OF WHAT
RONAN'S UP TO IN FAERIE?

SPOILER ALERT: SOMETIMES EVEN WISE,
WINGED MEN DO FOOLISH THINGS.

READY FOR THE NEXT PART OF
LYRA'S STORY?

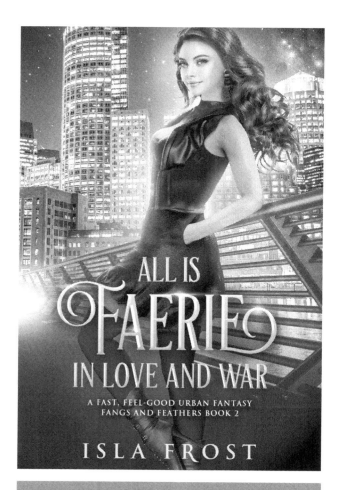

ABOUT THE AUTHOR

Isla Frost is the pen name of a bestselling mystery author whose first love has always been fantasy. She loves to write about strong heroines in fast-paced stories full of danger, magic, and adventure that leave you feeling warm and satisfied.

She also loves apple pie.

For updates and sneaky discounts on new releases plus occasional bonus content, sign up at www.islafrost.com

ALSO BY ISLA FROST

Fangs and Feathers Trilogy

Dragons Are a Girl's Best Friend

All Is Faerie in Love and War

Vampires Will Be Vampires

Firstborn Academy Trilogy

Shadow Trials

Shadow Witch

Shadow Reaper

Made in the USA
Monee, IL
05 April 2023

31416701R00189